LOVING
Camilla

J. Lynn Bailey

For my mother, with love.

Prologue

"What do you mean, it isn't there?" Nathan pulls his cigarette from his mouth. "Dig fucking deeper." He takes one hurried last puff and tosses the cigarette into the moist soil that sits underneath the canopy of redwood trees.

The kid digs deeper.

Nathan watches closely, eyeing the eighteen-year-old they hired about a month prior. "Kid's not going to make it, Mikey," Nathan says to his business partner and friend.

"Too soft. But let him dig. Let him finish the job, Nathan," Mikey says in a slight Italian accent.

Nathan and Mikey watch as the young kid sweats, digs, and pants.

"You got a tractor or something? Something that can move the dirt quicker?"

Nathan and Mikey exchange looks and then laugh at the stupidity of the boy.

Hard work has somehow missed an entire generation, Nathan thinks to himself as he pulls out his gun and takes aim at the naive stripling.

The kid looks at Nathan and immediately stumbles back, dropping the shovel and holding his hands up. "Look, I-I just came here for a summer job, trim work—that's it, man."

The quiver in his voice is powerful, and Nathan has always liked that. The fear he creates with a gun. The power.

"The kid's seen too much," Nathan says to Mikey.

"Let him dig." Mikey's tone is firmer with his old friend. Mikey walks to the boy, picks up the shovel, and gently puts it in the boy's hand. "Dig."

Shaking, the boy takes the shovel and begins to dig again until the shovel hits something hard several minutes later.

"See, nothing to worry about," Mikey says. "Retrieve the box in the ground, please."

Mikey has always been the softer one, the kinder one, Nathan thinks.

The boy reaches into the hole and takes out the box.

"He could be good, Nathan. Strong like an ox." Mikey speaks of the boy.

"Open the box," Nathan commands.

With a few unlocked levers and pulls, it opens.

But this isn't going to end well.

No.

Not at all.

Inside the box, Nathan's money is gone. All two million dollars.

Fueled with rage, Nathan aims the gun at the boy and shoots. The boy falls backward, holding his middle as his life leaves his body before he hits the ground.

I

Camilla

Perhaps it is the sun's fault. The summer, the sun, the moon, the stars, and all that. The entire solar system maybe, for throwing me off course into a different life, certainly not the life I expected.

Through my kitchen window, I watch Calder build the fence. The sun's morning light makes its way over the mountain of redwood trees, igniting the Eel River in soft rays of orange and yellow hues. I consider how his muscles contract and shift under his white T-shirt, drenched in hard work, and it makes me wonder if Calder will ever settle down with a woman. One that makes his heart beat the way it should when one is in love, like Joe did for me.

Anyway, my property ends just west of Fortuna.

I have a ranch.

I have land.

I have a roof over my head.

My son is cared for and loved and fed.

But I'm still a widow. Nothing will ever change that. There are still pieces of the lost eighteen-year-old that just needed a soft pillow and space to breathe.

Nothing will ever change the fact that I fell in love and married a man ten years my senior. He rescued me when I needed it most.

And everyone has their secrets. Everyone. If someone tells you they don't, they're lying. Like how I ended up in Humboldt County from Salinas, California. I couldn't face what I'd done every day. It stared back at me, taunting me, so I left.

The ground was hard from insufficient rain, and the blood thickened and pooled as it sat and then absorbed into the dirt before we could get the body in the ground.
My sister dug the hole with the tractor.
Sam (my friend) and I moved the body.
And my mother stood there, shocked.

When I heard from a hired hand, Phillip, one of the men on our farm, that there was fast money up in Humboldt County for trim work, I took it. I left against my mother's wishes and all of her rosary beads. I knew I had to get the hell out of Salinas as quickly as possible, so I got into my car and drove north to Humboldt County, where, according to Phillip, one could never be found.

Working in the mountains of Humboldt County for an illegal marijuana grow, I was able to disappear and make money, and I suppose I would've stayed if it wasn't for the handsome cowboy who showed up in his old Ford one day. He sat there on the tailgate of his truck, picked his nails with his pocketknife, and from underneath his cowboy hat, he said hello in a tone that slithered over my way, against the earth so smoothly that it scared me.

I didn't plan on falling in love. I planned to take the money I'd earned and leave and get on the right track. The track didn't involve seeds, soil, and seasons. It didn't involve backbreaking work and long days and the hot sun.

What Joe was doing in Southern Humboldt that day we met, I had no idea, but I also knew I'd never be the same.

It was a romance slowly built on hellos, stolen glances in smoke-filled rooms, and quiet feelings that somehow felt bigger than we were.

But that was when the whole mess got started.

I saw things I shouldn't have.

I did things I shouldn't have.

Made choices I'd rather bury away and never remember.

"Mom, I'm running out to feed the goats," Malik says from the doorway to the kitchen, bringing me to the present moment.

He looks like his father in my opinion, though, many says he looks like me. Amber eyes, long jawline, and dimples. Maybe he has my temper, but he has his father's deep, methodical ways. Malik has had to grow up quicker than most boys.

I walk to him and pull his long, skinny twelve-year-old frame into my arms. I take in his scent and quietly pray that God continues to watch over him.

"Mom, you can let go now."

He squirms and smiles, and I laugh and let go.

"I love you, Mal."

"Love you too." He turns to leave and then stops, turns back around. "Calder said he could work on some pitching with me after my homework and chores are done. Is that all right?"

Sports are not something I'm fond of. Sports will not get you an education. It will not give you the grades you need to succeed in college. My number one rule is school and academics, and Malik knows this.

Silently, he mimics praying, just to be funny.

"That's fine. But chores must be done first."

"I know; I know." And he runs out the back door.

"Hello?" I hear Calder's voice.

"In the kitchen," I say and use my hands to smooth over my dark brown hair.

"Hey." His cowboy hat is between his fingers. His white T-shirt clings to his torso, and I try not to notice. "I told Malik I'd help him with some pitching stuff. Would that be all right?" Calder asks, his dark blue eyes staring back at me.

"That's fine."

Calder nods, leaning against the counter, and crosses his arms over his chest.

"Here." I motion him to the stove. "Please, make yourself a plate and come sit down."

"Thank you, Camilla, but I'd best be getting home."

"That's not the agreement. I said I'd let you help me around here and that I'd pay you in food."

Calder laughs a slow, throaty laugh.

"Please, Calder. Just some bacon and eggs. Lord knows we have too many eggs with Joan and Jett laying all the time. Even after the farmers market last week, I had to give some away."

"All right." Calder sits down at the table, setting his cowboy hat on the back of the chair.

We eat in silence, and I wrestle with the fact that the only way I can pay Calder is through his stomach.

"Thank you," I whisper into the silence, "for your help."

Calder sets his fork down, swallows what's in his mouth, puts his elbows on the table, and says, "It's no bother, Camilla."

I nod, knowing he'd say those words, just as he does every time I bring this up. "But for your help with Malik too. I'm grateful you teach him what men should be teaching their boys. For teaching him how to mend fences and break horses and play baseball."

"He's a great kid, Mil."

And when he says Mil, short for Camilla, it makes my stomach twist into a ball of knots, just like it always does.

Calder reaches for my hand.

In all the years he's been with me, after Joe died several years ago, there was one single hug where Calder and I clung on too tightly and too long, and it made for several weeks of silence between us.

So, when he reaches for my hand, I hold back, not ready for the guilt that will settle in my bones when he leaves. Not ready for the unresolve, the feelings that will dance inside my heart and fill my head with unwanted thoughts.

That's when Malik waltzes through the door.

The moment disappears among the scent of cooked bacon and the sunlight that pours in through the window above the sink.

"Saw Mabe Muldoon drive by, and she said she has some yard work she'd like done this weekend, if that's all right, Mom?" Malik drops into the chair next to Calder and grabs a biscuit, bringing it to his lips. His eyes dance between us. "Did I miss something?"

"Nope," I say. "Sounds good."

Calder stands and takes his plate to the sink, loads it in the dishwasher, and grabs his hat from the back of the chair. "Ready, buddy?"

"Yep. I'll grab my bat and glove on the way out."

If there's one thing that Malik loves most in this world, it's baseball. He's a pitcher, and if I'm being honest, he's a great one at that, according to several coaches he's had in the past. The body, however, will eventually wear out, and it will not be able to operate at the same level forever. He'll need an education, and no one can take that away from him.

The front door shuts, and I walk to the sink and start the morning dishes.

Just when I'm about to turn on the water, the phone rings.

I wipe my hands off with the towel. "Hello?"

"Where's the fucking money?" a deep, dark voice barks across the line.

"E-excuse me?"

"Where's the money?!"

"Who is this?"

"Don't play dumb with me. Where's the money? 3284 Waddington Road. That's your address, right?"

Then, *click*.

7

The hair on my neck rises. I gently place the phone back on the receiver.

Calder pokes his head in through the back door. "Hey, can I—" But he pauses mid-sentence. "Camilla? Are you all right? What's wrong?" He steps into the doorway, his height filling the frame of the door.

"Nothing." I walk back to the sink and again start the dishes, my body vibrating from the exchange of words with the unknown caller.

I feel his eyes on my back and pray he'll just leave it alone.

"Okay, well, I'm just going to take Malik into town and grab a few more baseballs at the Mercantile." I hear the uneasiness in his tone.

"Sounds good." I smile, staring down at the soap that's pooling from the fallen bottle.

The phone rings again.

I close my eyes and push the fear down.

"Hello? Crane residence." Calder answers this time.

Silence.

Then, "Yeah, she's right here."

2

Calder

I give Camilla one last look before I leave with Malik. Something about the look she gave me when the phone rang wasn't right at all.

"Catch!" Malik says as he throws a baseball my way and I catch it. We hop in my truck.

Williams, one of our black tri Aussies from the ranch—my favorite one—hops in with Malik.

I've always known Malik to have a gentle spirit, but there's just something extra special about this kid and dogs. Malik seems to fall right into the pack.

"Have you talked to my mom about it yet?" Malik asks, his arm around Williams.

"Not yet, bud. I will though; don't worry. A kid needs a dog. I'll talk to her." I ruffle his hair with my hand. "How'd you finish the school year?"

"Straight *A*s. You know my mom. Won't let me get anything less."

"She expects the best from you, Mal. You're a smart kid. College is a necessity nowadays."

"What college did you go to?"

"I didn't."

"Laurel and Daryl didn't make you go?"

I shrug. *Tough questions from a twelve-year-old boy.* I was offered a few baseball scholarships and then, "I was stupid, threw out my arm. And that was that."

"That's when you stopped pitching?"

"I did. I guess I just sorta lost the love of the game I couldn't play anymore."

"Did you want to go to college?"

"I suppose, maybe. But my passion, aside from baseball, was the ranch. I wanted my ranch one day and knew I'd have to put the work in to get there."

We pull up to the Borges Atwood Little League Field at the end of town, just past the Fireman's Pavilion, grab our gear, and head to the dugout.

Williams's favorite drill is hitting. He gets to chase all the balls that we hit to the outfield. But he'll have to wait, and he knows it because he lies down in the grassy patch just off the dugout.

When Malik takes the mound, I bend to catch for him. I wonder if Camilla knows how talented he is at the game of baseball. The knowledge, his form, the movements, the patience, and the strategy to play the game come naturally to him.

After warming up his arm, Malik says, "Hey, Cal!" He throws his slider, and it pops when the ball hits my glove. "You ever think about coaching Little League?"

I laugh. "No." I throw him the ball back.

"Why not?" He walks back to the pitcher's mound.

I sit back down and wait for the ball.

"I think you'd be a good coach." He's quiet for a minute, then says, "I think kids would learn a lot from you."

"It's not the kids I'm worried about. It's the parents."

Malik starts his windup and throws a nasty curve. "Kids need good coaches." He smiles. "To hell with the parents."

I throw the ball back, grinning. "I'll think about it."

I notice Williams has moved to the middle of the outfield, waiting for the ball, so I throw it out there, and he chases after it.

After a few hours, we grab our gear, and I take Malik home.

Camilla isn't in the kitchen when we get to the house, so I walk out back and see her in her garden. I watch her.

Dark wisps of her hair fall down her back, and her hips move in such a way that suggests she has no idea I'm standing here. Her sundress moves as she sways, as if she's at peace out here in her garden. As if her husband didn't die and she wasn't left to raise their son alone. As if she didn't have a ranch to worry about, bills to pay, and fences to mend. She's strong, a lot like my mom, independent, with a take-no-shit attitude. I know she makes ends meet with her farmers market sales through September and does quilting for customers in the wintertime, but she never takes time for herself.

Malik and her—that's all it's been since Joe died several years back.

And I've also never seen the fear on her face that I saw earlier in the kitchen, and that's why I'm out here.

Camilla turns and pulls one of her earbuds out. "I didn't know you were there."

"Didn't want to scare you."

She approaches the fence that I rest my forearms on.

"Who called earlier?" I ask, cutting to the chase.

A wrinkle forms at her brow line. "No one."

I nod, knowing she's not telling the full truth. I know she can take care of what's hers, and it's her business, so I figure she'll work it out.

"Anyway, listen, Malik's birthday is coming up, and I was hoping to gift him one of Williams's pups. Mom bred him as a stud, and the pups are coming soon. We get the pick of the litter."

Camilla leans on the fence, our elbows just inches apart, and I notice the glimmer of her skin in the sun's light. "Cal, you can't keep giving Malik things. He needs to work for them."

"What? I don't give him a lot."

Her mouth falls open. "You bought him a brand-new baseball glove, a bat, a bucket of balls, and two tickets to the San Francisco Giants game."

When she says it like that, then, yes, but I plead my case. "Mil, that's been within a year. It's not like—"

Camilla stops me by raising her hand. "He needs to work for things. How is he going to appreciate what he has if it's all given to him? Now, I'd be open to a puppy only if he pays half with money that he earns from his paper route. And as his birthday gift, you can pay the other half."

"But it will be given to us. Stud fee."

Camilla turns and slowly walks away and calls behind her, "Donate the money then."

I drop my head and smile at the ground. *Stubborn as much as she is independent.* "Deal."

Camilla nods with her back to me.

I think twice about asking her if she wants to come with us.

Me. Camilla. Malik. Not as a family—that's not what I'm trying to do—but maybe as three souls just trying to find their way through life.

And if I'm being honest with myself, Camilla has always been it for me. But I'd never let her know that. The reason I'd never let her know that is, I'm scared to death it will give her a reason to push me away. I'd rather just be in their lives even if that means I can't make love to her. Even if I can't be the one to hold her at night. Have her whisper her fears, her sorrows, her dreams into the night as we lie there, naked, covered in each other. The truth is, I don't want to ruin what we do have. So, I'll take our friendship and hold it sacred and never allow anything to destroy it. It's just too risky. Besides, I know Joe was the love of her life. Some things you just can't make right, no matter how bad you want to.

Camilla and Malik will always come first.

I turn and walk away from the fence, gather up Williams, and we head back to my ranch.

Driving down Waddington Road, I feel Williams stare at the side of my face.

"What?"

He tilts his head, as if he understands what I just said. He lets out a low growl.

I roll my eyes. "Look, you know how it is. I can't just tell her how I feel."

Williams barks and stares at me again, then turns to stare out the window, as if he's too annoyed to discuss it any further.

I reach over and give him a pet. "Buddy, life is hard."

Still, he stares out the window, unaffected by the excuses.

Isn't that what they are—excuses?

I turn into the ranch driveway as Jones, Whitley, and Brooks run out to greet us.

Williams jumps, and all four dogs jump and nip and bark as they take off running toward the barn.

Daryl, my dad, comes out of the house with his phone. "I can't figure out how the hell to pull up my email."

"You got an email address?" I ask.

Dad walks over and hands me his phone, and then he leans on my truck bed with his hands. "Mom said if I didn't learn to check my email, she was going to stop making her apple pie. She even programmed it in there for me, but hell if I can find it."

Laughing, I lean over and touch the white envelope. "That is your email."

Dad slides his glasses over his nose and tips his head up to use his bifocals. "Well, I'll be damned," he says as his email loads.

"Why does she want you to learn to check email?"

"Says she can't do it all."

"She has a point."

"She said, 'If I die tomorrow, how will you pay the bills?' I told her I'd figure it out. She said that if I can't figure out the internet, then I can't pay bills."

"Email or the internet?"

Dad shrugs again. "Both, I guess."

The dogs come running back up.

"I'll feed these guys and then head up to Lost Barn and close it up."

Dad nods, scrolling through his emails. "Sounds good, son."

I start to walk toward the barn to saddle a horse, and Dad says, "How's that girlfriend of yours who never comes around?" He winks.

"She's not my girlfriend."

"Could have fooled me. Beginning to think you're ashamed of your family."

I stop. Turn to look at my father. "That's not it at all. Just don't want to mix business with pleasure."

"Have you asked her to come over?"

I keep walking and ignore his question because I haven't ever asked if Camilla and Malik want to come over for dinner, or Thanksgiving, or Christmas, or anything. It would only blur the lines that Camilla has laid out.

My phone starts to ring from my pocket.

"Hey."

"Hey," she says breathlessly.

"What is it? Are you all right?"

"Can-can you come over? There's something I need to show you." Her voice breaks, and I know something is wrong.

"I'll be right there."

3

Camilla

A heifer lies in the front yard, killed by two gunshots. "When I got back from town, she was barely alive. I- I had to shoot her again, so she'd no longer suffer."

"Where's Malik?" Calder asks.

"He's with Dunn Anderson at his house in town." Dunn Anderson is Malik's best friend.

"The heifer was right here when you got back?" Calder asks.

"Making awful noises. So, I got my handgun from inside and shot her again." My insides are shaking.

"Which is your shot?"

I point to the bullet hole at her heart. *Shoot to kill*, is what Joe always taught me.

Calder examines the wounds on the animal. "Could be a pistol or a rifle. Did the Belottis or the Lockharts hear anything?"

It's now that Lance Belotti pulls in the long driveway, gets out of the truck, and walks toward us, scratching his head. "Well, that maybe explains the black SUV speeding down

Waddington like a bat outta hell." Lance adjusts his hat. "What the hell happened?"

"Black SUV?" I clarify.

"Yes, ma'am. Driving like he was late for heaven or somethin'."

"Where's Malik?" Lance asks.

"At the Andersons'," Calder answers for me.

My ears are still ringing from the gunshot that I had to take, and I debate whether to tell Calder about the phone call earlier. The two could be unrelated, but I sure as hell don't see anyone in Dillon Creek mean enough to shoot a perfectly healthy heifer.

"I'll go get my tractor, so we can move her," Lance says.

When Lance walks back to his truck, Calder turns to me. "Mil, you were scared earlier when the phone rang. Why?"

"It's nothing. It's my business, and I'll take care of it."

But something shifts in Calder's eyes. Maybe it's fear or distrust, or something more, but he closes his eyes and says, "Dammit, Mil. There's a dead heifer and a black SUV, and you tell me that you can take care of it?"

I will not involve Calder. "Yes. I will handle it."

"Do you know what even needs to be handled?"

"I'll make some calls."

"Did … did you piss someone off?" Cal of all people knows that I'm not one to piss people off.

"What, you think I sold bad strawberries at the farmers market or something? I don't know." *I don't know about the dead heifer and the black SUV. I know about the money, and I'll take care of it.*

Now, he sees my fear because I feel it radiating from my skin, disguised under sweat. Like a dog with a bone, he won't let go until he gets answers. I know it's for my own good, but he wouldn't like the answer I would give him because I won't give him one. It's my secret to keep.

We stand off, staring at each other.

Lance comes down the driveway with the tractor, and I walk to the side gate and open it up to the back pasture, so we can bury the heifer.

It's well into the evening after we get the heifer underground and clean up the mess, and Calder and I are in the kitchen.

"Wine?" I ask.

"I shouldn't."

"Suit yourself." I pour myself a glass and take a sip, thinking.

I look at Calder, who's leaning against the sink, his feet crossed, his arms crossed, staring down at the hardwood floor.

Cautiously, I start. "When Joe died, I was worried that I wouldn't be able to make it out here. Be independent, much less run a ranch. But I did. I began to rely on solely myself. One day, amid my grief, I watched my baby begin to walk—one baby step at a time—and I knew that I had to do what I had to do to support us, keep this ranch alive. I'd do everything in my power to protect my son at all costs." I take another sip of wine. "I received a call earlier, right before you walked in. The person on the other end of the line said Joe owed him money."

"What money?" Calder turns toward me.

I shrug. "Joe doesn't owe the man money." Which is the truth.

"And you're sure it was a man?"

"Yes."

I don't like to talk about my time on the grow outfit that I worked on before moving to Dillon Creek. It's something I'd rather keep private.

It's a small town and people talk, I'm well aware. I noticed when women in town looked at me funny. *Joe Crane with a young woman on his arm, ten years his junior. Mail-order bride,* they assumed.

17

Assumptions. Accusations. Though I never took them personally.

But after Joe died, the people of Dillon Creek surrounded Malik and me with love, meals, phone calls, and sugar. Gave me so much quilt work that I almost struggled to keep up around the ranch.

Calder is still staring down at his feet, biting his lower lip. Sharply, he looks at me. "You called me, Camilla. You called me because you were scared and you needed help. Sometimes"—he sighs—"I wish that you'd drop the tough act and just let someone in." He walks to the kitchen table, pours wine into a glass, takes it down in one mouthful, and leaves the kitchen.

"Where are you going?" I try not to allow his words to settle in my bones.

"To sleep in my truck. There's no way in hell I'm leaving you here by yourself."

"You don't have to sleep in your truck, you know," I call after him, but he's out the front door before he can hear me.

Having Calder here in my house, when the lights are off and it's just the two of us and summer greets us with the scent of leftover sunshine and the wine, it's probably better that he sleeps in his truck.

I don't want to wake up tomorrow with regret on my hands.

I shove off the table, put both wineglasses in the sink, cork the bottle, and put it in the cupboard above the sink. Walking to the linen closet to get a blanket for Calder, I hear my phone chirp, signifying an incoming text message.

It's Malik, saying good night.

After there was a miscommunication about where he was going after baseball practice one day, I decided to get him a phone. Not that I was scared about his safety in Dillon Creek. That wasn't it at all. It is my past that haunts me. Decisions I made. I worked for people whose sole purpose in life was greed, money, and secrets, and things tended to get tricky. And while I have my own secrets, I know it's just a matter of time before everything breaks wide open.

I respond to his text.

Me: Good night, son. I love you. Sleep well, and I'll pick you up in the morning.

Shoving my phone in my back pocket, I retrieve a few blankets and a pillow from the linen closet and walk them out to Calder, who's got his feet propped up on the frame of the open passenger window.

"They don't make trucks for tall people." I hand him the blankets and pillow through the window.

"Thank you."

"You don't have to sleep out here, Cal. You can sleep in Malik's room or on the couch."

"Fine right here, Mil. Thank you."

I know he's annoyed. But some things are better left untold.

I turn to leave but stop. Turn back. "I didn't thank you for coming over at my request." I look back at Calder.

The Marlboro Man is whom Cal reminds me of. Though he's not as thin—and I like this about Calder. Along with his broad chest from hard days on the ranch. Big hands. His long, lean, tan face from tending cattle, fixing fences, and many days in a row spent helping me.

I try to push these thoughts aside because a warmth spreads throughout my entire body and makes my body feel things I shouldn't—things that I haven't felt in a long time, things that I only feel when Calder is around and the moon is right in the sky and the stars have said their hellos. I haven't allowed myself to feel anything toward Calder because my want, my need, isn't—and shouldn't be—my focus. Where my head needs to be is on helping my son become a good man, an educated man. Get him off the ranch and a good start in life.

"Thank you."

"Good night, Mil," he whispers, and I feel his words float through the space between us, reaching my heart.

"Night."

A clanking outside makes me jump. My eyes open, and I listen.

It's quiet.

Then the clanking again.

I hold my breath and listen.

Clanking once again.

I jump out of bed, but not before I get my handgun from my nightstand, load it, and quietly tiptoe out of my bedroom.

My breathing is measured, calculated. My heart is slamming against my chest. I reach the living room and scan it, my gun still aimed at the floor.

A shadow emerges through the side slider off the living room. His face is still in the shadows. He's quiet when he pushes it open. Stealthy.

"Freeze!" I yell and point my gun at the figure.

The man looks up, and when I realize it's Calder, I lower my weapon.

"Calder," I say breathlessly, scared out of my goddamn mind.

"Goat got caught in the fence. He was trying to get the bucket." Calder holds up the bucket.

When he emerges into the light, his naked chest is what I stare at.

"Do you always sleep with your shirt off?"

"Do you always sleep in just a T-shirt?" Calder smiles and looks away. "Anyway, Bill's all right. Put him back out to pasture," he says before stealing one last glance at my bare thighs. He goes out the way he came.

My body screams at me to stop him, to tell him to sleep on the couch or in my bed. When he turns, I see the muscles in his back contract, and I know it's tension and not some god-awful dance that the male species does to win over a female he wants to mate with.

I know because I feel the same tension, the same stress, and we both wear it well.

"Good night," he says and slips out the slider.

"Night." I walk back to my bedroom, click the safety back on, unload my gun, and peek out my window, barely pulling back the sheer curtains just in time to see Calder try to get comfortable in his truck. I watch as his hands cover his face, as if he's made a mistake or a terrible judgment call.

I climb back into bed and quietly pretend the sheets are Calder's hands, caressing my hot skin and addressing the ache between my legs with slow touches.

Having Calder here to help us around the ranch, doing odd jobs, has always affected me. I've always been able to push the feelings aside, but it's getting harder and harder. There are too many things, issues, that come along with an Atwood man— or maybe issues that I've dragged along with me.

What would people think if a widow and single mother took Calder off the market?

A single woman without baggage would surely be a better fit for him.

Women throw themselves at Calder, and he doesn't take notice, as if their breasts in his face don't faze him. Like their expensive perfume doesn't make him want them. Perhaps it's all an act. Maybe this is what he does in front of me as a sign of respect—or something more. But what I've learned about the Atwoods is, they're real, honest men with good heads on their shoulders. Gentlemen. And what you see is what you get.

Maybe one day, when the time is right, when Malik is raised and off at college, things could work. But there will always be Joe. A man I fell in love with. A man who will always have a piece of my heart, no matter how long he's been gone. I see him in our son with certain looks he gives, certain gestures. No, Joe is alive and well in Malik, and I'm grateful for that.

But this thing—with the phone call and the dead cow and the SUV—I'm sure it will blow over. Maybe it's some kid playing a practical joke. Killing someone's livelihood though is a bit more sinister than a practical joke. But maybe it's not a joke. No matter what, I won't come clean over what I did, what I took, not even over Joe's dead body. No, I'll hide it for as long as I can. They'll have to kill me before I breathe a word to anyone.

Besides, some secrets stay with us for a lifetime, and that's exactly what I plan to do even if it means giving up everything I own to keep the secret safe.

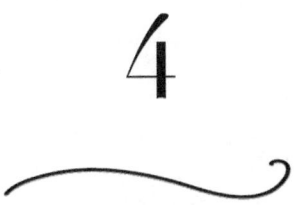

4

Calder

I rub my face with my hands, trying to gain clarity. I hate what Camilla can do to me. Her small hips in that little white T-shirt. Her bare legs in the moon's light. Her chest against the fabric of her top.

I had to get the hell out of there, afraid I'd do something I'd regret.

Pushing thoughts of her, of us, from my head, I try to piece together the connection, if there is one, between the call that Camilla received, the dead heifer, and the black SUV. I make a mental note to run down to the Dillon Creek Police Department to see if they have any information on a black SUV. Besides, Denton, a police officer, owes me a favor. Not that I've ever collected on a favor—it's just not my style—but this time, I need to.

Camilla's always been private about where she was before she made it to Dillon Creek. Sure, she's opened up about her family. A younger sister, a mom, and a dad who owned a farm down in Salinas. But everything after that gets a little fuzzy, less detailed, spotty, I guess. Mysterious maybe. Why did she leave?

But the one thing I've always trusted is the look in Camilla's eyes when she speaks. I don't think that woman could ever tell a lie. Hell, I don't think she could do it, even to save her soul. To protect her son, to protect others—yeah, I could see that. She's a woman of her word, and that is what makes me want to put the pieces together. It's like she's not running, but staying under the radar. I'll get to the bottom of it.

I'm willing to go all in for Camilla Crane.

I meander inside Camilla's place in search of coffee. She's sitting at the table, thankfully with more clothes on than last night, gently holding the newspaper between her fingers.

"Mornin'." I walk to the coffeepot and fill up a mug and sit down across from her.

"The cover of the *Dillon Creek Echo* has an interesting cover story," Camilla says and sips her coffee. Slides the newspaper in my direction.

On the cover is a picture of the dead cow in her front yard with a headline that reads:

HEIFER DIES FROM GUNSHOT WOUNDS AT
CRANE PLACE

"Did you expect that Michael wouldn't cover the story?"
She shrugs. "Where'd they get the photo?"
"Beats me."
"Belotti?"
"No, he wouldn't have done that."
"Michael?"
"Possible." I pull the newspaper closer, but under the photo, it says in small print, *Photo Belongs to the Dillon Creek Echo.* "It's a small town, Mil, so I'm not sure what you expected."

"I guess I expected to keep my private business private."

I laugh out loud. "Well, you know as well as I do that nothing is private in Dillon Creek. You've just never been in the limelight before."

Camilla traces the whimsical design on her coffee mug with her finger.

"Listen," I say before I take a big swig of coffee, "I'm going to run down to the police department and see what I can drum up on a black SUV."

"No, Calder. As I said, I've got this. I'll make a few calls. I'm not letting you get involved. And, quite honestly, I shouldn't have called you in the first place."

My jaw grows tight at her comment. I stare back at her.

She closes her eyes. "That's not how I meant it, Calder. Listen, I had a life after I left Salinas and before I came to Dillon Creek. That's it. I will not let you get involved because you are a good man."

"Like it or not, Camilla, I'm involved. And I got involved the moment I saw the look on your face after that call in the kitchen. You didn't have to tell me what was wrong—I saw it on your face. So, yeah, I am involved because I choose to be involved. Now, whether you want to tell me what happened in that period of your life, that's up to you, and whether it has anything to do with what's going on with the heifer and the phone call, I don't know, but I will certainly get to the bottom of it. Nobody—absolutely nobody—messes with the people I care about."

"I did tell you about the phone call. The man said Joe owed him money. He doesn't. End of discussion. Have I ever given you a reason not to trust me?"

"No."

"Then, stop."

"I'm still going down to the PD to check about black SUVs."

She sighs. "Fine, suit yourself. There's breakfast in the oven for you, and I'm going to pick up Malik at the Andersons'. I'll be back in fifteen minutes."

With a nod, I stand and take the eggs, sausage, and biscuits from the oven.

Before she walks out of the kitchen, she turns to me and says, "There are some secrets that people take to the grave, no matter the consequences. And maybe that's because they're protecting the people they care about."

"I'll take my chances, Mil."

She turns on her heel and leaves.

Tenacious.

I shake my head and make a call instead. "Denton, it's Calder."

"Hey, man. What's up?"

"I need a favor."

"Name it."

"I need to see if there were any calls on a black SUV in town within the last week or so. Speeding, running Stop signs, whatever."

I hear Denton typing. "Let's see ..."

I take a bite of eggs.

"Yeah. Got a hit. Looks like, yesterday, a call was made about a black SUV speeding on Waddington."

"Was the stop made?"

"No, we never caught up to the driver."

"Okay. If you get any more calls about the black SUV, let me know?"

"Sure. This about the dead heifer at the Crane residence?"

"Maybe. I'm not sure yet."

"I'll make a call to the Humboldt County sheriff's office and the highway patrol and see if they've had any incidents with black SUVs recently."

"Appreciate it."

"I'll get back to you as soon as I can."

"Thanks." I hit End on my phone, finish breakfast, and do my dishes before Malik and Camilla return.

I'm behind on my work at our ranch, and Dad will take notice.

"Was that Camilla's place they found the dead heifer on?" Casey asks as we saddle the horses.

"Yeah."

"The article made it sound a bit like a mystery."

"Yeah. Camilla had to shoot it again. Guess whoever had shot it left it to suffer."

Casey doesn't respond for a minute. "Who the hell does that?"

I shake my head. "Don't know, but whoever shot it either needs to work on their aim or did it to prove a point."

"Prove what point?"

"I don't know yet."

"Who does Camilla know that would do that?"

"I don't know."

"You think it's someone threatening her?"

I tighten the saddle on the horse. "Lance Belotti said he saw a black SUV speeding away."

Casey stops. "That dumb asshole almost made me drive off the road too. Sped past me at about eighty miles an hour."

I stop what I'm doing and listen.

"Nearly took off the whole left side of my truck. If I hadn't swerved out of the way, that asshole would have hit me head-on."

"What kind of SUV would you say it was?"

"A Tahoe. A new one because it had the silver plating above the word *Tahoe*. Made sure I at least got a description in my rearview mirror. Dickhead."

"License plate?"

"No plates that I noticed."

"Shit."

Casey and I finish saddling up the horses just as Dad meets us at the fence on his horse. The three of us head out to a lower section of the property and move the cattle up to the Lost Barn area, so they can graze on the property up there.

I survey our land from here and figure out what needs to be cut back this summer to make hay.

"Going to cut the lower-right side of the property for hay," I say to Dad and Casey.

"You heard from Cash and Scarlet yet?" Dad asks, switching subjects, trusting I'll get done what I say I'm going to get done.

"Yeah, got a text from him yesterday," I say. "Somewhere on the East Coast. Coming back this way in September."

Dad and Cash haven't always seen eye to eye. But I can tell Dad has been missing him since he and Scar left for their honeymoon. Cash might think he's always been the black sheep. I think that's because Dad loves him the most. Dad was just too let down every time Cash disappointed him.

We make our way back down the hill, but Dad stops and holds up his hand.

"What?" Casey whispers.

There's movement right against the tree line.

"Damn mountain lions have been bad this year." Dad pulls his gun from his saddlebag, loads it, and we slowly crawl toward the tree line on our horses.

"No point in scaring him. We've got to kill him. Took down a steer just last week," Casey says.

But it's too far for Dad to make the shot. The mountain lion will disappear into the trees before we get anywhere near it.

Dad fires a round into the air, and the cat moves so quickly that we can barely make it out. He looks back at us. "The lions are closing in."

5

Camilla

Standing in the large barn just off the house, I look down at my harvest for this week's farmers market. Strawberries, blueberries, raspberries, blackberries, tomatoes—heirloom, grape, and cherry—apples, cucumbers, and green onion are all ready to go for Thursday.

"Mom?"

"Hmm?"

I hear Malik's footsteps behind me, and it reminds me of when he was a much younger boy with the same heavy footfalls. *Some things never change.*

He sets a crate full of potatoes next to the harvest. "If I get all my chores done, can I go uptown with Dunn to see a movie?"

I eye him with curiosity. "What movie?"

"*The Goonies*. It's Rewind Night."

"I can give you five bucks, but the rest you'll need to take from your allowance. It's tight this month."

"It's tight every month," Malik says under his breath, rolling his eyes, and turns to go back outside.

"I'm sorry, Malik, but we aren't made of money." My tone is sharp, and my stare is hard. I will not raise an entitled child. "Malik Crane. Stop right there."

He drops his head and turns back to me.

"What's gotten into you?"

He shrugs.

"Look at me."

Malik looks up.

"What is going on with you, son? This isn't the way you act."

Malik shrugs again. "We don't have any extra money for anything, Mom. It's always tight. You're always working. How are we going to pay for college if you can't even pay for a movie?"

"It's not that we can't afford a movie. It's that there are more important things to pay for than a silly movie, Malik. Once you get older, you'll understand."

He rolls his eyes and walks away.

"Be home by eight!" I call behind him, going back to my inventory.

Malik doesn't remember the good times when his father was alive. He doesn't remember when the ranch made good money on its cattle, when I didn't have to work, when the Christmas tree was loaded with gifts that we didn't need.

I sigh and sit down on a crate, pushing the loose strands of hair behind my ears. We make enough to get by. Besides, Malik needs to see what hard work looks like. Sure, we don't vacation in Hawaii or Tahiti, and we don't spend Christmases in Aspen, but my son will sure as hell know that he grew up in a clean home, and that his mother loves him with all she has.

My thoughts are interrupted when I hear the gate open. Wyatt—the only ranch hand we have left, the only one we can afford—is here to take a few heads of cattle to sell at the auction yard.

I pull myself up from the crate and walk outside into the sun's light just as Wyatt is saddling his horse.

"Hey, Mrs. Crane."

"Wyatt. Good morning. Thanks for doing this."

"It's no bother. Besides, I'm taking a few of my own. What are a few more? And it's numbers 2750 and 2780, right?"

"Yes."

Our cattle are identified by the brand they wear on the hindquarters and the tags they wear on their ears. Unfortunately, if it's tight for the month, if I can't make ends meet, I sell a few heads of cattle just to get by. And I've had to do that a lot lately. Coming off winter is hard. The quilting is busy, but between keeping the cattle from dying with winter conditions and my obsolete fruit and vegetable harvest during the winter months, it gets extra-extra tight.

Leaning on the fence, I watch Wyatt fish out 2750 first. I can tell because there are two big brown spots on his side that look like two people kissing.

Joe taught me a lot about cattle.

Don't get attached.

Don't pet them.

Don't look at their long, full eyelashes because it makes them humanlike.

He knew the trick for me was not to fall in love with the animals. I had been raised on a farm where dogs and barn cats ran amok. We had goats—for milk only. We hadn't had animals we raised for harvest.

The thing of it is, people need to eat and sad things happen.

After cows are sent to the auction yard, it's usually for meat. But I do like number 2750. I like his markings. I like how he's always running behind the herd. I like how he watches me while I'm in the garden, planting or mixing up the soil.

"Wyatt!" I call to him.

He looks up.

I shake my head. "Scratch 2750 and take 2781 instead. Sorry about that."

Wyatt nods and pulls the rope from number 2750's head, and he takes off in search of 2781.

I head back to the barn to pick through the fruit for the farmers market.

Just as I'm moving the last of the eggs, I hear Calder's truck pull up and look at my watch. *He's not supposed to be here today.* Quickly, I pull my hair back and retie it up again, pulling a few strands down to make it look like I'm still put together after a day's work.

"Hey." He leans in the doorway, his hands shoved in his pockets.

"Oh, hey," I say, trying to act casual.

"Have a minute?"

"Sure." I rest my hands on my hips. "What's up?"

"Denton down at the PD is checking with the sheriff's office and the highway patrol to see if there's been anything to do with a black SUV. Casey though confirmed it's a new Tahoe. Said it ran him off the road about the same time Lance might have seen the vehicle."

My stomach grows queasy. There's no way the two are connected. I mean, maybe, but one thing's for sure: I shouldn't have called Calder, and now, I'm kicking myself.

You shouldn't have involved him. Now, he won't let go.

My eyes find Calder's, and for a moment, I think I see doubt.

"Mil, whoever called you is behind this."

"How do you know?"

"Just say it's a hunch."

I know I need to tell Calder what I know and what I did, but until I know for sure who's behind this, I just need to keep quiet.

I change the subject. "Wyatt's heading to the auction yard."

"Thought he was taking 2750 with him?" Calder asks, looking back toward the pasture, where Wyatt is.

"Decided on 2781 instead."

Calder looks back at me, and the corners of his mouth turn upward. "You like 2750."

"I do not."

"You're breaking the rules, Mil. Joe said not to fall in love."

And with these three simple words that Calder has put between us, we freeze. Stand motionless and try our best not to acknowledge that what was just said was anything deeper than cows and numbers.

I can tell Calder wants to clarify by the way he runs his hand through his hair and looks away.

Joe said not to fall in love with the cows, but somehow, I think, with what Calder just said, maybe the universe is telling *us* something different. Maybe we're not supposed to fall in love, or maybe we are. But I think both roads are difficult, and there's no way to get out of this one.

6

Calder

"You said what?" Casey asks, and then his head falls back as he laughs.

"I don't know why I even opened up to you in the first place." I walk away from Casey. "And for the record, I didn't mean it as it sounded."

"You told the woman you love not to fall in love." He laughs.

"It was about cows!"

My phone rings, and I retrieve it from my pocket. Casey walks outside.

I answer the call. "Hello?"

"Cal, got a hit on the description you gave me," Denton says. "California Highway Patrol finally caught up to him, going about ninety-five miles an hour on the freeway. Several people called it in. You know, that's what I love about our community, Humboldt—we all look out for each other."

"Denton, what's the information you have for me?"

"Oh, right. So, the Tahoe is registered to a Cannon Watson out of Tennessee."

I reach over the kitchen counter for a piece of paper and a pen and jot down the information. "Thanks, D."

"And don't worry; he got a ticket for speeding and no license plate. Pretty hefty fine these days."

Just then, Dad walks into the house and motions for me to follow him.

I nod and say to Denton, "Is there anything else?"

"No, no, I think that's it for now. However, I'll try to dig deeper with the tools I have."

"Thanks, D."

"No problem."

I hang up and follow Dad outside to the fence that overlooks the pasture.

"Mountain lion got another one of our heifers," Dad says as Casey joins us. "Found it this morning. You two take care of it."

While Casey saddles up the horses, I walk out to the heifer. Its stomach was eaten away. Its flesh chewed and swallowed. The blood trail is dark, almost black, and leads to pieces of the flesh that trace back to the trees. Looks like the lion felt vulnerable out here in the open, so he tried to drag his prey— or what was left of it—to a place he felt safer.

Casey rides up, another horse in tow, and I hop on.

"Grab your gun?"

He nods, and we follow the blood trail to the trees. It stops just at the edge of the forest that goes uphill at a slight incline.

I motion for Casey to follow with my hand.

As the horses move slowly, we hear the breaking of sticks and leaves under their hooves.

We stop. We wait and listen.

A growl.

Then, nothing, except silence.

A low growl starts again, and I feel it in my chest.

I look at my brother, and he's quietly pulling his gun from his saddlebag.

With the growl, chances are, the mountain lion has heard or seen us and is watching us intently.

While I look one way, Casey looks the other way, and we survey our surroundings.

Another crack of sticks, but this time, it's fast and quick, and I can't find the cat.

But it's moving.

Casey aims the gun at the ground, and we take off in the direction of the sounds.

We fly past trees, broken branches, searching. Still, we don't see anything.

I stop the horse and listen. Casey follows my lead.

Dead silence.

We walk through the forest for a few hours, searching for the cat, and come up empty-handed.

"He's smarter than we gave him credit for," I say.

"I just want to kill the son of a bitch."

"Come on. Let's go. We'll try again tonight."

After we bury the dead heifer, we head back to the barn and unsaddle the horses.

Dad walks into the barn. "Find him?"

"Nah. We heard him and tried to find him. Son of a bitch is fast," Casey says.

"Bastard is killing all of our cows."

"Cal and I will stake him out tonight, Dad."

"Got to be the drought. Less water equals fewer animals to feed off of," Dad says.

"Maybe. But either way, we can't afford for this cat to live," I say.

"All right, boys, I know you'll figure it out." Dad turns to leave but stops. Turns back. He watches Casey and me as we brush out the horses. "We're a hundred percent positive it's a mountain lion, right?"

His statement sends chills down my spine as I try to convince myself against the wrinkle in my thoughts that this could be something else killing our cattle.

"Yeah," Casey says, but it's not as convincing as I'd like it to be.

A mountain lion, or any predator for that matter, catches the hindquarters first because it's usually a chase. The cattle hear the mountain lion and run. But with the heifer that was killed, the only thing eaten was its stomach. I thought it was odd when we got to the heifer but didn't want to say anything because maybe I was wrong. Hell, I'm no scientist or zoologist or whatever. I'm just a cattle rancher, trying to keep my cattle alive.

Dad nods. "I'll check with The Lunch Guys down at Dillon Creek Pizza tomorrow. See if they've heard or seen anything."

I'm quiet until Dad is out of earshot. "It was just the stomach gone. Don't you think it's weird that its hind end was not taken out either?"

Casey casually shrugs, pushing the horse into a stall. "Maybe the heifer just didn't see it coming."

"Maybe. Guess we'll find out tonight," I say and lead the horse into the stall.

"Bottom line is, whatever it is, we need to neutralize it," Casey says, taking his gun from his saddlebag, and we walk inside.

I shoot Camilla a text just to make sure she doesn't need my help. But maybe the text is more about my peace of mind.

Camilla: Nope. All is good.

Me: If you hear a truck pull up late, it will be me.
Casey and I are staking out a mountain lion.

Usually, when a mountain lion is on the prowl, it's an ongoing problem among more ranchers than just one. Camilla hasn't had an issue with mountain lions, only humans, and this makes my gut turn.

Camilla: Calder, we're fine. We'll be okay.

Me: I'd rather be safe than sorry.

Bubbles appear to show she's texting, but they quickly disappear and reappear and disappear again.
And finally:

Camilla: Do what you need to.

Dad, Mom, and I eat dinner together, and I offer to help Mom with the dishes, but when Casey pulls up for our stakeout, Mom touches the side of my face. "Go save the cattle."

In our camouflage hunting gear, we quietly make our way out to where the heifer was earlier and lean against the fence posts separated by five feet of barbed wire. The night sky has fallen upon us, and it leaves only the astrological pictures to contend with.

Cannon Watson comes to mind.

What kind of man is he?

Is he a father?

A husband?

Does he pay his bills?

Own a house? Rent?

Is he here in Humboldt permanently or just an out-of-town guest?

Is he in the marijuana industry, because so many people are involved?

Doesn't seem like an upstanding guy, running people off the road or speeding like an idiot.

But what does he want with Camilla—if he's the one who shot the heifer?

Silence surrounds us as we lie in the field and wait.

A gunshot in the distance makes both Casey and me sit up and look at each other. We wait for the ricochet of the sound to finish moving throughout the valley.

"Sounds like it came from the east," I whisper to Casey, who's looking through his night-vision binoculars. I made fun of him when he bought those damn things, and now, they're proving useful even if he did pay an arm and a leg.

Casey stops scanning and motions me to move closer to him. Once I do, he carefully hands over the binoculars. "Six o'clock," he barely whispers, his voice shaky.

I look through the night-vision binoculars. It's a dark spot slithering through the long grass. And before I can comprehend what we're looking at, it unfolds and walks on two legs.

"Holy fucking shit," Casey says.

"Yeah, that's what I was thinking."

"What is that?" I try to zoom in.

"Doesn't look like a mountain lion—that's for fucking sure."

"It's bear-like." I pull the binoculars from my eyes and try to see it with my naked eye, but I can't see anything because it's too dark.

"Does a bear slither?" Sarcasm bleeds through Casey's tone.

I shake my head. "We have to follow it." I hand the binoculars to Casey, quietly stand, and put my backpack on.

"Shit. I knew you were going to say that," Casey groans.

He puts everything in his backpack and stands, and we follow the dark figure into the night.

7

Camilla

I back my truck in on Washington Street, just off Main Street, next to Tipple Motors.

"Just a bit farther, Camilla!" I hear a familiar voice call out before I see her face in my rearview mirror.

It's Nellie Greenwater, a local farmer with the best cucumbers and raspberries west of the Mississippi. At least, that's what I can conclude. Nobody locally or even down the coast can top the sweetness or fiendishly juicy taste of Nellie's raspberries. It's perfect every time.

I wave out my window as a thanks, put the truck in park, and hop out.

"Just look at those strawberries, Camilla. Better get me down for a flat. Can't keep enough strawberries in the house with all those grandkids running around."

"Suppose I can put an order in early for those cucumbers?" I eye them on her truck.

"You bet."

"And the peonies?"

"I can do that. The damn deer ate up my roses last week. Left the gate open to the greenhouse, and they waltzed in there like they owned the place and ate me out of house and home. Neil caught it all on the deer cam." Nellie shakes her head. "But I was able to save my peonies at least."

I think it's cute that Neil is married to Nellie.

Nellie always says, "How could I not marry Neil when our names were destined to be together?"

She retreats to her truck and begins to set up her stand for the farmers market held on Thursday afternoons from June through October.

"How's Luisa?" I ask, pulling the raspberry flats from my truck.

"Oh, about as good as a two-headed horse. That girl doesn't know which way is up."

"I'm sorry to hear that."

Nellie sighs. "She's always been my problem child. Always dying of this or that. I thought a good education would give her some perspective, but instead, it turned her into a goose who's lost its flock." She can tell by the look on my face that her metaphor will need further explanation.

Nellie is like me. She's not from Dillon Creek; she's a transplant that moved here by way of first Nebraska, then Maine, then Alabama, Florida, China, Wyoming, Utah—Neil was in the military. And she and her husband have been in Dillon Creek for about twenty-five years now.

So, I think her sayings are a collection of all the destinations she's been to.

"One time, we were in Utah, waiting for a train to take us to—well, I don't remember where. But a goose was waddling down the sidewalk, honking at each person it passed, mad at the world." Nellie laughs. "I'd like to think it eventually found its flock, but, boy, was he mad and just searching for someone to give him direction." Her eyes get lost in the memory. "Enough about me. How's Malik?"

"He's good. Without school, I think he's happy to have some extra time on his hands."

"I told you that boy is going to be president one day." Nellie struggles to reach her last box of cucumbers from the tailgate, so I jump in and hand them to her.

"Thank you. My body just doesn't work like it used to." She takes the last box and sets it under her pop-up tent. "Heard about the dead heifer at your place."

"Yeah. I'm sure it was just some dumb kid trying to be macho or something." I try to brush it off. But deep down, I know Nellie doesn't fall for things like that, but she lets it go anyway.

After Nellie and I set up our booths, Yolanda sashays by as though she were some sort of royalty with her wannabe prize-winning heirloom tomatoes in a small basket. "Well, hello, Nellie and Camille."

"Camilla," I clarify for the third week in a row and make a concerted effort not to roll my eyes.

She remembers my name.

"Well, hello, Yolanda. Those sure are beautiful tomatoes," Nellie says.

Her eyes light up. "Would you like to try one? I'm giving free samples to all the vendors."

"I sure would," Nellie says.

Yolanda hands Nellie a smaller heirloom tomato, and she takes a bite just like someone would an apple.

Nellie chews and chews and chews and finally swallows her bite. "Wonderful."

Yolanda curtsies and holds out the basket toward me.

Reluctantly, I take one, smile, and say, "Thank you, Yolanda."

Yolanda eyes me curiously. "You're the only one who says my name correctly. Most people pronounce the O as an A."

When Yolanda finishes with us, she continues her one-woman parade down Washington Street to visit with all the vendors.

"My goodness. Her tomatoes sure are beautiful on the outside, but they taste like shit," Nellie whispers under her breath. "That woman is doing herself no favors—that's for sure." Then, she takes the tomato from my hand and tosses hers and mine into an old paper sack. "I'm saving your time and your life, sweetheart."

From the corner of my eye, I see Calder and Malik approaching. I try to push down the butterflies that ignite in my belly. Malik runs to Nellie and hugs her.

"There's my favorite twelve-year-old. Shh. Don't tell my grandchildren."

"Nellie," Calder says in his deep voice. "Mil." He tips his cowboy hat. "Can I take Malik to Eureka to look at new cleats?"

I look down at Malik, whose head is resting at my side with puppy-dog eyes. "Chores are done?"

"Yes, Mom."

I look to Calder and try my hardest not to get lost in his sea of deep blue eyes. "That's fine. And, Cal?"

"Yeah?"

"Malik pays half."

Reluctantly, Calder nods and says, "Let me know when you're done with the market, and I'll come by and help you clean up."

It's then when Yolanda all but runs to Calder and throws herself against him. "Hello, cowboy," she purrs.

Calder is used to women throwing themselves at him, but he'd never say this. He's kind, and he always let them down easy. "Those look like great tomatoes, Yolanda."

"I'd love for you to try one of my tomatoes." She winks at Calder.

Gross.

He takes one from her basket.

"Well, you'd better get going to Eureka," Nellie says, pushing Calder and Malik back the way they came before whispering, "Don't eat the tomato."

As they walk away, Yolanda sighs. "Why that man is still single, I will never know. And yet"—she laughs—"I wonder why I'm still single," Yolanda sighs and goes back to her rightful spot at the farmers market.

Nellie eyes me, and she's careful with her words. "Honey, can I ask you a rather personal question?"

I toss a crate in the back of my truck. Hesitantly, I say, "Sure."

"Why haven't you and Calder made things official?"

"Official?" I ask.

"Well, clearly, he's in love with you. And when you look at him, the world seems to shift inside you, like ... like everything just might be okay. While I won't speak for you and what you love, it sure does remind me of myself at that age when I met Neil."

My chest grows tight, and I hold the butterflies that begin in my stomach hostage because I'm sure if I let them out, I just might smile. "Nobody wants a widow with a son. Besides"—I shrug—"I just need to focus on Malik until he's raised. Maybe then, I'll consider something more ... permanent."

"Permanent?" Nellie laughs. "Honey, it's not a business transaction. This is your heart we're talking about."

I'm not sure what to say.

Nellie's next words are gentler. "You're afraid. I see it in your eyes, your body language, when he comes around. Your eyes might say one thing, but your body says another."

"What could I be afraid of, Nellie? He's just a man." *Albeit a very handsome man, but stripped down, he's just a man.*

"Can I be honest?"

I cross my arms over my chest. "I'd never expect anything less."

"You lost a man you loved deeply. But I don't think you trust God or life enough to fall in love again. You're afraid if you start down that rabbit hole, you'll lose sight of what's important, and I also think you're worried about what people will think. A widow falling for another man. Well, honey, in my book, that makes you human."

My hands loosen from around my elbows, and I try to settle in with Nellie's words. Pick them apart. Rearrange their order to find a different meaning, but all I come up with is fear.

"I knew Joe Crane well, and I know he'd want you to be happy. He'd want a man like Calder to take over with you and Malik where he left off. And it seems like Calder has done that with Malik. It's just you who's holding back."

I blurt out, "He hasn't even tried to kiss me."

"That's out of respect for you. Have you shown him any interest?"

I think back to the other night. Him in the moonlight with his shirt off, his bare chest, and me in my T-shirt, my bare legs, and it takes my breath away. "No."

Nellie's eyebrows slowly rise, and she steps closer. "A man like Calder Atwood has hung on this long because he loves you. Joe's been gone for years, and yet Calder is still waiting like a gentleman—because that's how his parents raised him."

My skin begins to tingle as I swallow, and I want to hide among the fruit, become a wallflower because what Nellie just said makes me feel too vulnerable.

Is that true? Is that why he's hung around so long?

Committed—that's what I've always chalked it up to be. And, maybe, my cooking.

But could it be more?

I hush away the words and the thoughts of Calder and me and see the possible truth in what Nellie just said.

"Afternoon, Nellie and Camilla." Chief McBride approaches our stands.

I turn away and pretend to be busy as fear starts to build in my stomach. *He's not here for you, Camilla.* I try to calm myself. *That was a long time ago. A different lifetime.*

"Morning, Chief," I say over my shoulder.

"Camilla, can I have a moment of your time, please? Official business, you know."

Pain starts in my chest, making it hard for me to breathe.

"Sure," I manage, but I know he hears the quiver in my voice as we move to the front of my truck, away from everyone.

Chief McBride clears his throat and stares at the ground for a moment. When Joe died, Chief McBride delivered the news. I'm not quite sure what I said or what I did, but that day, my heart broke into a million little pieces, and the chief held me until I could gather myself. But I know that's not why he's here now. He's here to ask me a question, and I can tell because he's searching for the right words.

"The dead heifer," he finally says.

"The one that was shot recently?" Relief spreads throughout my entire body.

He's not here about a body the Salinas PD found.

"No, today."

"No, there was one the other day. None today."

Chief McBride pauses, confused. "Have you talked to Calder?"

"Well, yes, but ..." We didn't discuss another dead heifer. We discussed whether Malik could go to Eureka, but I don't tell the chief this.

"Anyway, I'd like to encourage you to file a police report. This ... this doesn't seem like just a random act of tomfoolery."

A slow tremble begins inside me. "I'll come down to the station tomorrow."

"Good. I hope you do that, Camilla. The last thing this town needs is another tragedy."

"Excuse me?" I ask.

"Let's just put it this way. This happened once before in the early 1900s, and it didn't end well for several women in Humboldt County."

"A serial killer?"

Chief McBride scans our surroundings. "Let's just say that I've alerted other departments in the county, and I have room to be concerned for your safety and the safety of Dillon Creek."

"Why didn't you tell me, Calder?"

"And ruin the farmers market for you? No. You look forward to that every week. Besides, I took care of it, and I was going to tell you the second you got home." He sighs and stares down at the floor in the kitchen. "Do you know a Cannon Watson?"

I replay the name in my head several times. "Name doesn't sound familiar."

"That's who the black SUV is registered to. After a Google search, I found several mug shots from as far away as Tennessee to Southern Humboldt. Anyway, Denton is checking on a few things."

"You think he's behind this?"

"It's not often that you find an SUV speeding on Waddington."

"Was the same black SUV found today?"

"No. But same result. A dead heifer."

Sighing, I say, "I told you to let me handle this, Cal."

Guilt starts to turn in my gut, and I want to tell Calder what I'm doing because the only person that knew was Joe. But I can't tell Cal because I need to protect him and the operation of what I started. Cal deserves a good life with a wife and kids and a white picket fence and slow Sunday mornings.

"Let me know what Denton comes up with?" Panic starts to consume my chest.

"I will."

Later that night, I tiptoe into my bedroom and quietly shut the door behind me. Grab the burner phone from between my mattress and box spring and dial the number I never said I would, trying to forget what happened that night when the moon left the sky and the stars bid their farewell, before hope and innocence vanished when the sun rose the next morning.

I peek out the window just in time to see Calder climb in his truck.

"I told you to never call this number unless it was an emergency," my sister on the other end of the line whispers.

"It is an emergency. Is the body still there?"

Silence sits on the line like a surging power line.

"Yes," the voice hisses.

I hang up the phone, able to breathe a little deeper. I walk out into the back, toss a few logs on the outdoor fire pit, throw gasoline on top, light the match, and watch the pit erupt with a whoosh of hot flames.

I pull up a lawn chair and watch the fire burn just as the back door shuts, and Malik comes out to join me.

He will never see that side of me.

"Hey, honey."

He pulls up a chair and watches the flames with his new cleats on.

"Breaking them in?" I smile.

"Calder says it's best to break them in by wearing them, but not on concrete. Don't want to ruin the spikes."

I nod as the fear slowly leaves me with the flames that break and move and dance. "You good, bud?"

He nods. "I'm good. Sometimes, I just wonder if Dad can see me."

I lean into him. "He sees you. And he's in awe of the wonderful young man you're turning out to be."

Footsteps come around the side of the house.

"You guys okay?" Calder asks. "Saw the smoke."

"We're okay. Come on, join us," I say.

"Nah, just enjoy each other." Calder turns to go, but Malik stops him.

"Come on, Calder. Tell my mom that story of the king snake named Ed."

Calder smiles. "I don't think your mom cares for snakes much, Malik."

I don't, and he remembers this. I realize at this moment that I don't know if Cal likes snakes or cheeseburgers or ranch with his French fries.

"Please, come sit," I whisper. "We could use the company, and I'd like to hear the story."

Calder wanders over, hands shoved in his pockets, and sits across the fire from us. "One time, Ed took down a rattlesnake purely with his speed and watchful eye. The rattler was going after one of our pups, and Ed was not having it. While Ed slowed the rattler, it gave Colt enough time to grab a gun and shoot it in the eye."

"Isn't that cool, Mom? See, snakes can be good."

"Some, yes. But it doesn't mean they still don't scare the you know what out of me."

"Do you know what you do with a rattler's head when you kill it?" Malik asks me.

"Bury it?"

Malik's mouth drops open. "How did you know?"

"I had a life before you. I was raised in the country, and rattlesnakes were everywhere. That's probably why I hate snakes so much."

"Yeah, but why do you bury the heads?"

"The venom in the fangs can still be lethal to other animals and small children."

Malik looks from me to Calder and back to me, his mouth open. He shakes his head and stands. "Can I go in and play the Xbox for a while?"

I nod. "Not too late though."

Calder high-fives Malik as he heads inside.

That leaves the fire between us and the stars to hold up the night sky.

Nellie's words wander in and out of my head, and I pretend, just for a moment, what it would be like to be in Calder's arms, to feel him against my body.

"Why have you stayed with us, Calder? All this time, why have you stayed?"

While the flames dance across his face, I have no idea what he's thinking.

8

Calder

"Are the blankets sufficient?" Camilla asks.

I agreed to sleep on the couch tonight and only at Camilla's request. She said it kept her awake at night, thinking about me in my truck, uncomfortable with my long legs hanging out the passenger window.

"The blankets are fine. Thank you."

Camilla nods as I find my rightful spot on the couch. She turns out the light. "Good night, Calder."

"Good night, Mil."

I hear her quietly open Malik's door and peek in, and then she walks to her room. I wait for the door to shut, but it doesn't, and this makes my body stir. Something inside me ignites, like a ticking time bomb.

What does it mean that she kept the door open? She doesn't normally sleep with the door open, does she?

Maybe she's doing it for Malik. Maybe she's doing it for us, or maybe it's just a simple gesture of openness. Or maybe I'm overthinking the whole damn situation.

Go to sleep, for Christ's sake, Cal.

I set my phone down on the coffee table, pull my shirt off, and settle into the leather. I stare up at the ceiling and listen to the outside buzz of the summer night.

This is much more comfortable than my truck. I agreed to sleep on the couch because the second dead cow threw me for a loop.

Now, I know these instances aren't just coincidences and that there's something more going on. There has to be. Two dead cows in a few days aren't normal. The second heifer though wasn't shot and killed. But why did someone kill Camilla's cow? A threat? A promise? Proving a point?

I don't think Camilla would know who's doing this and not tell me.

Would she?

That's not her style. Maybe she's scared to tell me. Maybe she doesn't want to bring me into the mess? But I'm already in, and there's no way in hell I'm going anywhere. But maybe she doesn't know. She'd said she'd make a few calls—whatever that means. Who's she calling? I need more answers than she's giving because if there is something that happened in her past that's coming back to haunt her, we need to take care of it.

My phone buzzes on the coffee table. It's Denton from the PD.

Denton: Got a minute?

I jump up, take my phone, walk outside, and call Denton.

"Got some hits on your man. Turns out, he's only five foot four. I found that to be very interesting because, usually, short men drive lifted trucks with big tires and go by nicknames like Bruiser or Brick—something, well, big and tall."

"Denton, I need the facts, man."

"Oh, right. Well, he's got several cars registered to him in his name. Some are from Tennessee, and some are from California. Turns out, he's got several felonies on his record. He's done some prison time."

"For what?"

"Let's see … drugs."

Why would a guy wrapped up with drugs go around killing a woman's cow? None of this makes sense. I feel my jaw tighten when this thought enters my head.

"What about aliases?"

"Aren't you the detective?" Denton snorts. "Let's see." Then, Denton laughs. "Known aliases are Chewy, Captain, and Superman. There it is … his little stature has caught up with him. Superman." His voice trails off. "He's had addresses in Fortuna, Alderpoint, Honeydew, and several places in Tennessee and a PO Box in Garberville. But from his rap sheet, it looks like Watson has been here in Humboldt for quite some time."

But what is the link to Camilla?

Hell, we don't know if he's the one who's been creating the havoc, but it just seems too coincidental that one man was seen speeding away from the direction of Camilla's house. But he can't be that stupid. He's a career criminal.

"Last known address?"

"Come on, man. I shouldn't be telling you this shit in the first place."

"Address."

"What are you going to do, Calder?"

"Address." And I say only this, so he won't get in trouble.

Denton gives me the address, and we hang up.

The ringing of the house phone rips through the darkness. Camilla answers it from her bedroom, and I jump up and walk to her bedroom and stand in the doorway.

"Who is this? Stop calling my house."

I storm into her bedroom and take the phone. "Who the fuck is this?"

Silence.

"Oh, I see, you're a coward. You're willing to threaten a woman, but your pussy ass can't step up to a man? I see how it is. Who the fuck is this?"

Then, "Who's this?" The voice on the other end is slow, methodical, and calculated.

"Calder Atwood. You'd better make sure you stay as far away from us as you can because if I see you, I will hunt you down and kill you, Cannon Watson. Got it?"

A chuckle moves through the phone line. "How do you suppose you hunt someone that you can't find?"

And then the line goes dead.

Angry, I hang up the phone and catch Camilla's eyes. Her knees are tucked up to her chest. I sit down on the edge of the bed and pull her to my bare chest. I feel her heart pounding against me, and I know she's terrified, though she'd never admit it.

"Don't worry, Mil. I will catch this asshole if it's the last thing I do."

It's the bacon smell that wakes me up.

My eyes shoot open, and I realize I fell asleep in Camilla's bed last night. *Fuck.* I jump out of bed when I see Camilla's spot is vacant. I throw on my shirt that's lying on the couch as I walk past and head into the kitchen.

"Hey," she says.

"Good morning."

"There's coffee."

"Don't mind if I do." I pour a cup. "Malik still asleep?"

"Yeah."

I look back at the kitchen door to be sure he's not on his way in. "Listen"—I lean against the counter as she stands at the stove—"I didn't mean to fall asleep in your bed last night. I'm sorry, and I won't let that happen again."

Camilla doesn't turn around. She doesn't look at me. She just simply nods and keeps cooking.

The silence that sits between us pushes us further apart. I want to walk up behind her, put my arms around her, and let her know that she's safe, but I know I'd be overstepping my bounds, the commitment I made to myself and Malik and Camilla. I'm not willing to risk losing both of them for my selfish needs. I push out of my mind the thoughts of my hands slipping under her T-shirt and taking her full breasts in my hands.

"Morning," Malik says groggily as he shuffles into the kitchen.

Shit. I almost spit out my coffee. "Morning, kid."

He sits down at the kitchen table, and I sit down next to him.

"Who called last night?" he asks.

"Wrong number," I say.

Malik nods as Camilla walks over and slides two plates of food in front of us.

"Eat, boys." She smiles, but the smile is short-lived when she looks over at me only for a second.

"Can we practice hitting and pitching today, Calder?" Malik asks with a mouthful of bacon.

I look at Camilla. Slightly, she nods.

"Once chores are done. Yeah, we'll do it this evening."

I don't know where this kid puts all of his food, but he's done in seconds before he shuffles off to his bedroom to get dressed.

Camilla sits down and looks at me as if she needs to tell me something but hesitates.

I don't ask what or push her to say anything she isn't ready for, so instead, I say, "Denton called last night and got some updates about our friend Cannon." I fill her in on locations of where he's lived and arrests.

"Alderpoint?" Camilla clarifies.

"Yeah. You know anyone who lives out there?"

"Me ..." She stalls. "Before Joe. Before Dillon Creek," she sighs.

I can tell there's more she needs to say to me, but the phone rings, ripping through the silence and the tension in the room.

We both flinch.

9

Camilla

If fear could sit in a room and command attention, it certainly would be present and felt at this very moment. Slowly, I pick up the receiver and look back at Calder, who's on alert.

"He-hello?"

"Camilla? It's Mabe. Listen, I have a quilt I was hoping you could top-quilt for me. I know you usually do this in the winter, but I'd like to give it as a gift to Scarlet for her wedding. Of course, it's already late, but better late than never—that's what 1 always say."

I let out a huge breath and drop my head. Look back at Calder and shake my head. His body bows in relief as he walks past me, so close that 1 can smell his leftover woodsy smell from yesterday, and I try to focus on Mabe's words.

"I'll see you later." He briefly touches my elbow with his fingertips, and it sends chills down my spine.

"Camilla?" Mabe says, trying to get my attention.

"Yes, I'm here, and I'd be honored to do the work. I'll stop by and pick it up on my way into town today."

The front door shuts.

"That will be wonderful. Thank you, Camilla. How's that sweet boy of yours?"

"Malik is doing good. Fifth grade was tough, but he did well. He's been busy around here and playing baseball every spare moment."

"That's great. Remember, these years go by so fast. Be sure to hang on to all the moments you can."

They do, Mabe. They do.

"All right, honey. I'll see you this afternoon then."

We exchange good-byes, and I hang up the phone.

There's a knock on the front door. My nerves are on edge, and my heart almost explodes.

Calm yourself down.

I peek out the window and see Wyatt's truck. I walk to the front door and open it.

"Mrs. Crane." He tips his hat. "Didn't want to forget to give this to you. It's a check from the auction yard for the sales."

"Thank you, Wyatt." I fold the check and shove it into my back pocket. "Give me a hand, checking the cattle this morning?"

"I'll saddle up the horses."

Not twenty minutes later, we find the herd down by the creek, eating, drinking, taking life a day at a time. And for a moment, I'm at peace. It reminds me of the rides Joe and I used to take on cool, crisp fall mornings when the sun slowly made its rise into the starlit sky.

We take stock in trade and survey the animals. Check for limps, injuries, pregnant cows, and the overall health of the herd.

"They look good."

"Yeah, checked them last week." Wyatt rubs the back of his neck. "Mrs. Crane, I don't mean to jump in your business, but did you find who shot 3701?"

"No. But I'm just thankful you weren't here."

"Just so you know, I always carry a gun with me when I'm out with the cattle, so you don't need to worry about me."

"I don't worry about you, Wyatt. And I'm glad you do that, as I know you can handle yourself."

"Did you hear about the mountain lion issue at the Atwoods'?"

"No. What's going on?"

Calder never mentions anything that happens at the Atwood Ranch. I suppose it's his way of keeping the line drawn, and I have to respect that. But at what point do we cross over from being colleagues, in a sense, to friends?

"Mountain lions. I'm wondering, too, if there's more than one. Course mountain lions travel alone, but that's an awful lot of cattle to wind up dead, even for two mountain lions."

"I'll have to ask him about it. We don't talk about things like that."

"Why?"

I shrug. "I guess it's just not what we do."

Wyatt looks up from his horse and to me. "No disrespect, Mrs. Crane, but I thought you guys, you know, were an item."

My horse stops. I give him a soft kick, but he won't move.

Wyatt's horse stops too.

And neither of us moves.

"What's that dark spot down past the creek? Down low behind the rocks?" Wyatt points.

It's hard to see because it's so far.

"I don't know." I try to make out the black outline that's low to the ground.

Wyatt pulls out his binoculars from his saddlebag and focuses on what's watching us. "Run, Mrs. Crane!"

My heart rips through my chest as a popping noise starts, echoing through the valley, and two stray bullets fly past my head.

The horses and cattle get spooked and take off in different directions.

Chaos ignites.

Wyatt pulls up the rear and tries to keep the cattle together, and I take the other side.

"Get them out of there safely!" I yell to Wyatt.

We move them closer to the house as quickly as we can and get away from the creek, operating on fear and adrenaline.

It's only about a minute before the herd is close to the house and we're behind them.

We catch our breath and look back at one another.

"Did you see the man?" Wyatt pants.

"No."

"The black spot was a gun. Suppose it"—Wyatt tries to catch his breath—"was a man in a black beanie and all black clothes. I—" He takes a big breath in. "I couldn't make out his face because that's when the bullets started flying."

"Shit!" I call out in frustration and hop off the horse, leading him back to the stall, and Wyatt follows.

"Do you think it's the guy who's been killing the cattle?"

"I don't fucking know, but I'm done with this asshole. Come on, Wyatt. Come inside. I don't want you anywhere near there."

Once we're inside, Malik is getting out of the shower, and by the look on my face, he knows something is amiss. "What's wrong, Mom?"

"Listen to me. You will not go outside unless it's with me or Calder. Understand?"

"But, Mom—"

"Don't talk back!" I snap. Close my eyes and drop my head. "I'm sorry, Malik. Please just trust me on this, and I will tell you what's going on as soon as I have a minute to think."

Don't shoot my cattle.

Don't shoot my people.

I call Calder as I load my gun, but he doesn't pick up, so I hang up.

"Wyatt? Stay inside with Malik. I'm going to go find this son of a bitch."

"But, Mrs. Crane—" Wyatt attempts.

"That is an order, Wyatt."

"Yes, ma'am."

"Mom—" Malik's face changes to fear.

"Don't worry, honey. I will be right back." I look back at Wyatt. "Lock the doors."

And with that, I walk out the front door and sneak around to the barn. I grab a horse and jump on.

I spent years fighting off my father. Years running from the nightmare he'd created for my sister, my mom, and me. It wasn't until I was ten that I realized normal fathers didn't do to their daughters what my father did to us.

I will not fall victim again.

I give the horse a soft kick, and we take off to the north side of the property line and weave in and out of the trees, trying to be as quiet as possible. But I pull back on the reins slightly when I hear footsteps.

I hold my breath.

My heart slams against my chest, and I hear the blood pulsing in my ears.

I cock my handgun and scan my surroundings. With the tree close and directly behind me, I know at least my back is covered.

The footsteps sound again, and I aim, slowly moving and waiting for the trespasser to come out. "I swear to God, I will shoot you where you lie if I find you."

It's then that a deer takes a few steps away from a big redwood tree.

I sigh. Drop my gun and my head. Take a big breath in. After a few seconds, I un-cock my gun and slip it back into my beltline.

I creep closer to the spot where the shooter lay, and when I finally arrive, there's nothing that I can see, so I hop off my horse and take in all angles from where the man lay.

What were you doing, asshole?

Before I know it, I'm down in the same position the man was, against the rock, holding the gun just as he was, trying to put myself in the shooter's mind. But when I look down, I see a single black hair about an inch and a half long.

"Bingo."

I pinch it between my fingers, and that's when I hear the man's voice behind me.

IO

Calder

I *haven't been up here in years.*
I take in the beauty of the layered mountains, covered by infinite redwood trees. On top of the world is how I remember this view as a kid. It eventually ends up back on Highway 101 or Highway 36, depending on the route you choose. As a kid, when we had out-of-town visitors, this drive was always on the list. It's a beautiful drive, but the road hasn't been maintained for as far back as I can remember. There's no center divider to tell drivers exactly where they're supposed to be or how fast they're supposed to go. It's just a black stretch of asphalt with potholes the size of boulders. But if you can stand a slower rate of speed, the occasional abandoned car, and a good dose of Dramamine for some, then you'll see some spectacular views along the way.

Some call this Murder Mountain, but locals don't. Sure, a few television shows were made about Southern Humboldt, dubbing it the Wild West of the twenty-first century, where marijuana growers and those living up here took the law into their own hands.

Law enforcement, road construction crews, and county employees don't come up this way unless it's imperative.

It's out of the way. It's desolate. And at night, it can be too quiet.

I pass the old oak tree with all the abandoned shoes hanging from its branches.

I remember the cases that drew the national media's attention.

Like the time a thirty-year-old San Diego man went missing. Told his father he was moving up to Humboldt to work on a marijuana farm.

There wasn't a day when you didn't see a law enforcement vehicle heading up this way, and I know this because the local media covered it. Every day, law enforcement searched, and every day, they came up empty-handed, but they never stopped showing up.

It was just that nobody was willing to talk to the police yet.

It wasn't until eight local men of Alderpoint—the Alderpoint Eight, as they're called—took matters into their own hands and followed the whispers of locals to a man, who they kidnapped and shot twice until the man led the Eight to the remains of the slain thirty-year-old kid. The man still hasn't been arrested for the murder. I think the Alderpoint Eight did it because some of them were fathers. And if their son were missing, they'd want to know where he was even if it was just a shell of a body of a soul that once existed.

Or the time that a known troublemaker—addicted, in and out of jail, well known to law enforcement in Humboldt—was warned by those up on the mountain that if he kept stealing things from other people, he'd wind up dead. Well, that's exactly what happened. Still to this day, nobody knows who pulled the trigger, and nobody has been charged with his murder. The case has been closed. The residents up here take care of their own.

It's hard to find and see the growing marijuana from the road. They're done veiny, narrow roads and over creek beds and around boulders and No Trespassing signs. They're among tall redwoods, and alders, and behind electric fences.

I hit another pothole that brings me to the present moment. It's the mile marker I'm looking for, and I take a right down off Alderpoint Road, comparing the map on my phone to the address I scribbled down from Denton. Alders protect the dirt road from the hot sun that beats down on the land. My shirt sticks to my body with a layer of sweat. The summer heat in Southern Humboldt is brutal compared to Dillon Creek. With an hour and some change south, it's at least twenty degrees warmer.

Dogs bark in the distance, and I can't tell if it's from this ridge or the next ridge over because of the sound that travels through the valley.

But I know a gunshot when I hear it.

A succession of shots fired makes me ease on the brakes, coming to a complete stop. I listen. They're distant enough to put my mind a little more at ease, but it doesn't stop me from moving forward to find this asshole who's threatening those I care about. I printed out his mug shot to show people.

But down the road a little farther, I see a black truck moving toward me. I feel for my handgun in the back of my beltline and let off the brakes, so I crawl forward.

As the truck approaches, a man holds out his hand to stop me completely. I do. I am on someone else's property. When we're window to window, I see two men sitting inside the cab with an automatic rifle on the dashboard. I'm not sure if that's more of a fear tactic or if they use it on a daily basis, but I don't scare easily. The two men have bandanas over their mouths and sunglasses, so even if I were questioned by police for whatever reason, I wouldn't be able to give an accurate description of their features.

"You lost?" the driver asks.

"I'm looking for this man." I hold out the printed picture of Cannon Watson. "You seen him?"

"Who wants to know?"

"Got some business with him."

The driver looks at the passenger and then back to me. "What kind of business?"

"That's between him and me." I set the picture back on my dashboard, playing it cool even though my heart is pounding out of my chest.

The driver sizes me up for a moment. "You're on property that you don't own, in a place where people get shot and killed for much less, and you won't answer a simple question?"

"He's threatening a woman I know."

The driver eyes me closely. Looks again to the passenger and back to me.

"Watson isn't here. The fucker had better never show his face up here again either. Don't worry; we're looking for him too."

We establish a very simple layer of trust based on a mutual agreement that Cannon Watson deserves what's coming to him; however, my retribution would not be murder, and I can see by these two men that they wouldn't think twice about putting a gun to his head and pulling the trigger.

"You can turn around and go back the way you came right there." The driver points backward with his thumb—a subtle way of saying my time is up here and it's time to leave.

I give a slow nod and stare back at the two men. I pull forward and turn around, and they sit there and watch me drive back the way I came. I don't let my eyes leave the rearview mirror for a second. They were alerted, whether it was from a camera or a silent alarm, to get me the hell off the property.

I pull back onto the main road and head back down the mountain. Surely, Watson won't be showing his face in these parts because he's caused too much trouble, it sounds like. I don't take all growers for honest people, but the two men I ran into had no reason to lie about wanting to track down Watson too.

Driving down the mountain, I pass an older couple, followed by a woman in a big, fancy gray SUV, probably in her early twenties. She probably lives up here with her three kids and her husband, who owns property, and it's probably laced with the leafy green substance. She probably didn't go to college, and she met her husband only after he made millions of dollars on dope money. And they'll continue to reap the benefits of drugs until, well, who knows?

But the older couple, they most likely live up here, but out of the way, and they're probably parents of one of the lifers out here. Maybe they, too, grew up in Alderpoint, and for all they know, he's probably making his money by cultivation or building water lines or tanks, and that's all they want to know. Sure, they know what Southern Humboldt is known for, but that's why they paid one hundred grand in college tuition for an Ivy League school on the East Coast, so he wouldn't get involved in the drug trade. But even so, the elderly people have grown accustomed to big houses and fancy cars and two-week vacations to Europe. At their lunch dates and dinner dates in Garberville or Fortuna, they sweep under the rug what their son does.

Twenty minutes later, I'm off Alderpoint Road, off the mountain, and I hit Highway 101 toward Dillon Creek and try to remember the last time I was this protective over a woman whom I wasn't sleeping with, not dating. Hell, I haven't had a girlfriend in years. Not since I met Camilla.

In the beginning, right after Joe died, I had a woman friend in Eureka who met my needs. Nothing too serious, just someone to pass the time with—dinner on the weekends, sex in the evening. There were no strings attached, no hurt feelings. It was just time we gave each other. She was finishing her master's degree at Humboldt State University. From the San Diego area originally, she planned to go back home once she finished at HSU and work somewhere in marine science. Kameron is her name. Occasionally, we'll text each other with memories, something that might remind us of our time spent together, which was usually contained between four walls and most always involved two naked bodies. She's younger than me, but not too much younger. She loves the outdoors, something we never got to. I never brought her to the ranch or to meet my parents, my brothers. She was just a good woman who wasn't Camilla. But once Camilla called me to help her one day, Kameron faded from the image of a woman who I could eventually settle down with. She wasn't Camilla, and I didn't think it was fair that I strung her along, so I let her go.

And to think, if something happened between Camilla and me and it ended badly, I'd not just lose Camilla, but I'd lose Malik too. I'd miss these texts from him, the cat memes and the baseball stats on Shane Bieber, his favorite pitcher in the league.

I'd miss all that, and that's not a price I'm willing to pay.

My phone vibrates with a text.

Malik: Calder, you need to get to our house now. A man's shooting at my mom and Wyatt!!! Please.

Immediately, I pick up the phone and try to call Malik, but the call drops. "Fuck!"

I grip the steering wheel with one hand and try again. Still, the call drops. My heart begins to race as I try to push away all the scenarios that spin through my head right now. I hit the steering wheel with the palm of my hand when I see my service has disappeared.

How the hell did Malik's text come through if I don't have service?

"Fuck!" I say again, and stare at my phone and the road, praying I get a few bars to make the phone call.

Finally, a few bars pop up, and I make a call to Camilla's house phone.

"Crane residence." I hear a quick, panicked voice say.

"Wyatt! What the fuck is happening?"

He tells me the story.

"Where's Camilla?"

The line goes quiet.

"Wyatt?"

"Well, she, uh, took off on horseback to find the shooter."

"AND YOU LET HER GO?"

"Cal, someone has to stay with Malik."

Wyatt isn't wrong.

"I'll be there as fast as I can." I hit End and drive as fast as I fucking can.

II

Camilla

"Thought that was you."

Lance Belotti is on foot, walking toward me, his rifle aimed at the ground.

I suck in a deep breath of relief.

"Camilla, are you all right?"

My thoughts start to spin out of control with all the what-ifs. What if it was Lance who was out tending to his back field, minding his own business. With his age, he's not as quick on a horse as he used to be. He could have been killed.

"Somebody was shooting at us. They were on my property and shooting at us," I say, trying to convince myself that the words I speak are true because it's almost too much to believe.

"Calm down, Camilla. It's all right. You're okay. Where's Malik?"

I bend over and try to catch my breath, to slow my heart rate down. "He's at home with Wyatt."

"Good. Good. Come on. Let's go search for this asshole."

With the thin hair between my fingers, I don't dare drop it in hopes that someone can do lab testing in Humboldt County. I keep a tight grip as Lance and I search for any other clues.

"Here," Lance says. "A boot track."

I grab my phone and snap several pictures of it.

"Do you know why this guy is after you?"

We haven't found anything, except a man named Cannon Watson with a rap sheet but no facts linking him to the crimes to make him the suspect. But maybe it is my subconscious tickling the back of my mind that says if I answer no to Lance's question, that would be a lie. I don't tell Lance about the phone calls that I received only because I don't want to involve him or cause him more worry than he's already feeling. Lance has been a wonderful neighbor. He would have been a great father. One who wouldn't hurt his children. A man who should have been blessed by children but wasn't.

So, instead of answering his question, I pretend I didn't hear him, and he doesn't push.

We take a few more laps around the area, searching for any clues that will lead back to the shooter, but aside from the single piece of hair and the shoe print, we come up empty-handed.

When I come riding up on the horse toward the house, I see Calder's truck barreling down the driveway. He flies out of the truck, runs inside, and then runs out the back door just as I'm hopping off the horse.

He clears the fence and runs to me with force and worry and fear. He picks me up in his arms and holds me tightly against his chest.

With the hair still pinched between my fingers, I slowly allow my head to rest on his shoulder, and I feel the slow shake that starts in his arms.

"God," he chokes out. "That scared the shit out of me."

"Cal, we're fine," I whisper.

Slowly, his grip loosens, and he sets me down on the ground.

"I got a piece of hair from the shooter—I hope." Trying to relieve him of the fear I see in his eyes, I smile.

He takes the strand of hair between his fingers. "I'll get this to Denton and see what he can do with it. In the meantime, you will go inside for the evening, and then you and Malik are coming to the ranch."

"Leave here?" I step back. "No, Calder. I'm not going to leave my ranch. I'm staying put. Malik is staying put. We aren't running from this asshole." Even if the two issues—the caller and the person, maybe Cannon, threatening my ranch—are connected.

Calder's jaw tightens. He's never told me what to do, put his foot down, or spoken to me in a tone that is anything but respectful.

But I know it's the fear in him. I know he's scared and he feels helpless.

"Mil," he whispers and takes a step closer to me, "when I got the terrifying text from Malik, my world ... my world crumbled right before me." He pauses. "I've never in my life felt so helpless. Not even when my brother died. But this, right now, I can control. I can help keep you and Malik safe."

But I can tell he's holding something back. Something he wants to say.

"Sometimes, you can't control the situation, Cal, no matter how hard you try," I whisper. "I'm not leaving this ranch because I've spent all my life running. I ran from my hometown. I worked in an unsavory job when I met Joe. It was a quick way to make cash, and I needed it to get as far away from my father as I could." I swallow the pit of emotion stuck in my throat. "I ran from the grow I used to work on because it was easier. But I'm not running again. So, if this asshole wants to come to get me, he'll have a fight on his hands."

I don't tell him what I took when I left Nathan's grow operation in Southern Humboldt. It would put too many lives in jeopardy, including his.

Calder searches my eyes. I see the helpless feeling. I know the helpless feeling. It's the same feeling I felt every time my father crept into my sister's room at night. In those moments, as a child, I felt helpless because my father was so strong and I was so damn little.

"Okay," he says, "but I'm staying too."

I nod. "Fair."

After dinner, in the kitchen, Calder is honest and tells me about the ride he took up to Alderpoint Road. Malik is in the living room, setting up a movie for us to watch.

"Please, Cal. Just … just let me handle things," I plead. The last thing I need is him getting hurt on my account.

Calder shakes his head. "I was searching for Cannon Watson."

"Where'd you go?" I sigh, knowing I won't win this.

Cal takes a paper from his pocket and pushes it across the kitchen table.

I nod when I see the address. "That's the Rochester place."

"You're familiar with them?"

"Everyone knows everyone out there. What outsiders don't realize is that it's a community—albeit a dysfunctional community, but everyone looks out for one another."

"Which grow did you work on?"

"It's not important."

Calder sighs. "How can I help you when you hold back?"

I nod. "The second I drag you into that world, it puts you at risk."

"Why would that put me at risk?"

"When you work for one of them, you're saying, in so many words, that you'll never reveal locations, names, the operations. Not everyone who works on these outfits knows the whole deal, but I did. I paid attention. I was smart. I kept my head down and got my job done, but it doesn't mean that I didn't know what was going on."

"Do you think this money thing is connected to Joe? To where you used to work?"

When is lying ever okay? I've spent the last several years taking what doesn't belong to Nathan. Taking what he took out of greed. And I will take this secret to my death bed until the job is done.

"Could be."

"Come on, guys!" Malik says from the living room. "It's family movie night!"

I watch Calder's breath catch when he hears Malik say this.

"What?"

"I just … I've just never heard Malik refer to us as a family."

"Well, if you didn't know we were family by now, Calder, I guess we just aren't vocal enough about it." Slowly, I reach out and take his hand. "Come on. Let's get watch the movie."

On the kitchen table, we leave the printed picture of the boot print that we were able to capture and the bagged strand of hair and try to forget about today—even if it's just for a little while.

12

Calder

"How'd you sleep?" Camilla asks when I walk into the kitchen.

"How'd you sneak past me this morning?"

She sets a cup of coffee and a plate of food in front of me. "Thank you."

"You were out like a light." Camilla goes back to the counter to retrieve her coffee and sits down with me at the kitchen table. "No, really, how'd you sleep?"

She smiles, resting her cheek on her closed fist, looking up at me with her big brown eyes. Strands of her hair hang down around her face, and I wonder how God could make someone so beautiful, both on the inside and the outside.

"The last time I looked at the clock, it was three in the morning. So, sometime after that." I take a big drink of coffee.

Camilla gives me a look. "What?" I ask.

"I'm worried about you," she says.

"I'm worried about you." I shove a bite of eggs in my mouth and wash them down with my coffee. "I'm going to run the hair sample and the boot print down to Denton today. He's going to ask why we didn't call the police."

"Don't give him a reason to ask."

I nod. "Hopefully, the *Dillon Creek Echo* doesn't get the word about what happened."

Camilla shrugs. "Nothing died. We all survived." But then she laughs. "Who are we kidding, Calder? Of course, the *Dillon Creek Echo* will find out. Of course, word will get out."

It's then that the phone rings, and both of us tense.

I stand and walk to the phone and answer. "Crane residence."

"What on God's green earth is happening over there? Are Camilla and Malik all right? My goodness. They must be a mess," my mom, Laurel, says.

"They're fine, Mom. Everyone is fine." I rub the stubble on the side of my face.

"Honey," she sighs. "It's on the front page of the *Dillon Creek Echo*."

I look back to Camilla, who's already clearing my plate and starting on the dishes.

She looks back at me from behind her shoulder and says, "Tell your mother I said hello."

I nod and watch her as my mom reads the article to me over the phone.

"*Shots fired at the Crane residence again …*" she begins.

There's a knock at the door.

"Mom, I have to go. I'll be home soon."

"Okay, son. Give Camilla and Malik my best. You know, wouldn't it be better if they both came here and stayed with us, just for a little while?"

Camilla wipes her hands on a dish towel and goes to the door.

"Mom, I have to go. I'll be home soon." I already know the answer to that question because Camilla was adamant that she's not leaving her ranch.

It's Chief McBride.

"Come on in, Chief," Camilla says, opening the door. Her shoulders draw up toward her ears.

The chief takes off his hat and steps in. "Camilla, Calder." Malik walks out sleepily. "Morning, Mom. Calder. Chief?"

"Morning, kid. How's that pitching arm?" the chief asks.

"Good, I guess." Malik pads off to the bathroom.

"Can I talk to you both for a moment?"

Camilla leads the chief to the kitchen and pours him a cup of coffee. He sits down at the table, setting his hat on the back of his chair.

"Are you hungry?" Camilla asks.

"Oh, no, thank you, Camilla."

But she sets a plate of food in front of him.

And for as long as I've known the chief, he's never turned down homemade food.

The chief looks down at the end of the table and notices the evidence we collected yesterday and looks back at me as Camilla refreshes my coffee and hers. He doesn't say anything about it, only, "Look, we can't protect you two if we don't know what's going on. Why didn't you call me yesterday when this all went down?"

"What could you guys do? Besides, you're already running thin on officers," Camilla interjects, as if she already prepared a statement.

"We can help. What's that?" He nods to the end of the table.

Camilla reaches across the table and puts the evidence in front of the chief. "Evidence I collected on the scene yesterday. I'm hoping that the single strand of hair and the boot print is our shooter."

The chief's eyebrows rise as he grabs his glasses from his breast pocket and examines the evidence. "Were you able to get a look at the shooter?" The chief's eyes dance between Camilla and me.

"Not really. Through binoculars though, I saw that the shooter was fair-skinned. He was dressed in all black. He didn't have a great shot though because from the range he was shooting, he should have hit one of us—or at the very least, one of the cows."

"I'd like you to file a report with our office, Camilla." The chief is genuinely concerned for her safety.

She nods and looks at me, and her eyes grow shifty. I've always sensed a level of distrust for the police when it comes to Camilla. Why? I'm not sure. Why she hasn't wanted to involve them, I can't quite figure out. And the line of bullshit she just fed Chief McBride about the number of officers, I know the chief doesn't buy that for a second, but he also doesn't force the issue.

The chief sets the evidence back down on the table, takes off his glasses, and puts them back in his breast pocket. He quietly eats the plate of food that Camilla set in front of him and doesn't say a word.

"How did you guys find out?" Camilla finally asks.

The chief smiles. "Lance was madder than a wet hen when he called me at home last night. News travels fast." He shrugs. "He was mad at me for not taking care of the issue," he sighs. "Camilla, if you don't ask for help, I can't help you. I need to know what's going on, so you and Malik are safe."

Camilla stares down at the checkered tablecloth, lost in her thoughts.

"How'd the *Dillon Creek Echo* get word?" I ask.

"Hell if I know. I don't like the way Michael is running that paper these days. I'd much prefer Ike to his son any day. When I called Michael this morning, I think his words to me were something like, 'Sir, if it bleeds, it leads.' "

The chief wipes his mouth, and Camilla takes his plate to the sink and stands there with her back to us as she looks out the window.

"Can you take those for processing?" I ask the chief.

He looks at Camilla. "Is that okay with you?"

Camilla slowly nods.

Malik pads into the kitchen and takes a seat next to me and I ruffle his wet hair with my hands.

"How's my favorite baseball player?" the chief asks.

"Good."

And when she hears that, Camilla turns from the sink and slightly smiles. I see the wall of distrust slowly come down, only a little.

She walks to the oven and grabs another plate of food and sets it in front of Malik, kissing the top of his head. "Eat."

The chief, Camilla, and I don't talk about what happened yesterday because of Malik. Maybe it's also because we'd rather just not remember what happened yesterday even if it is for a few minutes.

"All right"—the chief stands and takes the evidence from the table—"I'd best be getting back to the station. Lord knows we're probably receiving phone calls this morning about this whole thing."

We walk him out.

Before Chief McBride walks to his patrol car, he turns to Camilla and says, "You're one of us, Camilla. You and Malik are part of our community, and it is my job to protect you. I hope you'll let me do my job."

Camilla nods, soaking up his words.

Badly, I want to reach for her and take her in my arms and tell her everything will be all right. But that wouldn't be the truth because I'm not quite sure everything will be okay. But I will die trying to protect her and Malik, just as I know the chief and his officers will do the same.

Back at the Atwood Ranch, Ed is sunning himself on the porch again when Brooks, the mischievous one of the dogs, gives the snake a hard time.

I call them off.

Sal and Wanda Toddwell come up the drive. Already, I picked out a red tri Australian shepherd for Malik, and this must be them delivering.

I rest my hands on my hips as Mom comes out of the house with a dishrag in her hands.

Wanda gets out of the truck, holding an eight-week-old pup.

"Well, isn't he the cutest thing you've ever seen?" Mom says.

"He's the star of the show—that's for certain." Wanda hands the pup to me.

I reach out to shake Sal's hand with my free hand. "Mr. Toddwell."

He nods. "Your dad around?"

"Barn."

I hold the little guy up, so I can get a good look at him again. "Hey, little man."

He looks down at me, his ears in his face, and gives me a puppy growl.

I laugh, lowering him to my chest. "A man that knows what he wants."

He licks my chin and smells my face.

"Don't let that puppy imprint on you, Calder Atwood. You'd better wait for Malik," my mom says.

"I know; I know. Come on, little man. Let's go introduce you to your main man."

The pup sits in my lap as we make the drive over to Camilla's. Williams looks over and scowls, none too excited about the pup who's taken up residence on my lap. If you want to see an Aussie pout, get a puppy.

"Come on, bud. You were little once too. Besides, you need to show him the ropes." I reach over and give his ears a good scratch.

Camilla is hanging laundry on the line, and Malik is at the back fence.

Before I let the puppy down to meet his new family, I give him a pep talk. "All right, listen. This is your family. You must protect your family and love your family and always know what is right and wrong for them. Understand? They're very important people to me. And that little boy will love you just as much as you love him."

The pup twists and turns in my arms, and I know that he understands what I just said because when I set him down, he bypasses Camilla and runs straight for Malik.

Camilla gasps, covering her mouth, and then she looks back at me and smiles.

When the puppy reaches Malik, he tumbles down a slight slope.

Malik looks down and says, "What in the heck is that?" He looks back at me and his mom.

"Your mom thought you could use a companion."

Malik runs down the slope, scoops the puppy into his arms, and slowly walks toward us. I see the tears in his eyes when he looks at his mom. "It's mine?"

"Happy Birthday, Malik. I know he's a little early, but we couldn't wait. Besides, Ed doesn't need another pup trying to give him a hard time."

Malik gets lost in his newfound best friend. "I don't know what to say, Mom and Calder."

Camilla reaches in and rubs the puppy's chin. "It was Calder. Not me."

She looks back at me, and her big brown eyes get me every time.

"What are you going to name him?" I ask.

"Him?" Malik clarifies.

"Him."

"Red."

Malik runs to me with such force, puppy in hand, and throws his one free arm around my waist. "Thank you, Calder."

Emotion gets caught in my throat, and I can't speak, so I don't say anything. I hug him.

Williams slowly makes his way out to us in the back, sits at my feet, and watches Malik play with Red. "Don't worry, bud.

Give him time." I turn to Camilla. "I thought you were going to make him pay half."

Mil smiles and watches the two of them. "I decided I would pay. It is a birthday gift after all."

"You don't have to. Again, Mil, he was free."

Camilla's phone starts to vibrate across the picnic table in the back, and she walks to the table and answers. "Chief McBride?"

He talks, and she listens.

"We will be right down." Camilla hangs up and looks at me. "Chief McBride has something he wants to show us."

13

Camilla

"You're certain your mom doesn't mind?" I ask Calder as we drive to the Atwood Ranch to drop off Malik and then head to the police department to meet with Chief McBride.

"Are you kidding? She wanted grandkids the second my brothers and I all turned twenty-one because eighteen was a little too young for her kids to have babies."

This is the first time both Malik and I have ever really been to the ranch on personal matters. Sure, I've stopped by to drop off things for Laurel or Calder, but I've never asked them to watch my son.

The fire whistle sounds in town. Red starts to make this tiny little howling sound, and we all start to laugh. The howl sounds more like a yelp. I look to the backseat to see my son laughing, the wind from the open window in his hair. He's at peace. Even with what is going on, he's at peace, and I believe that's all due to his trust and his faith in Calder and me, knowing that we'll always keep him safe, no matter the cost.

Calder's hand extends on the seat behind me, and this simple movement makes my body hot and my stomach grow with butterflies. I look over at Calder, who's staring over at me, but when I look back, he moves his gaze to the road again. I notice my sundress is closer to my waist than it is to my knee, and I leave it be. For once, I follow my heart and not my head. Again, I look back at Calder, who's stealing a glance at my thigh before moving his eyes back to the road.

After we drop off Malik and Red and I thank Laurel profusely for watching Malik and his new puppy, we make our way on Waddington to the police department.

The low hum of the tires against the road is soothing. The setting sun beats through the windshield. The smell of summer. And we're alone in the truck. Man and woman. Friends. Longtime friends. Maybe it's my heart, finally ready to move on after Joe, or maybe it's a momentary lapse in judgment. Perhaps I see more of what life could be like as a family of three, not just two.

I take a deep breath in and rest my elbow on the window frame, trying to get right with my mind and my heart. There are things I want in life. There are things I need as a woman. But what is more important is doing right by Malik. I have to remember this. My needs and wants will always come second.

"Hey, you all right?" Calder asks. His arm doesn't move from the back of the seat, his big, calloused hand just inches from my bare shoulder.

I nod, uncertain of anything these days. "Do you ever feel like you're damned if you do and damned if you don't?"

"All the time."

"About what?"

Calder's jaw tightens, his eyes on the road. He won't look at me. Maybe he won't look at me because he's scared of what he'll say, what he'll do at this moment. And quite frankly, I'm scared of the same.

"Are you afraid to say it?"

He nods and laughs nervously. "Not that I'm afraid to say it. I'm terrified of the outcome."

That's when his eyes move to mine and burrow into my heart. His look is both forlorn and electric, and I know he wants to reach out and touch me. So, with a deep breath, I reach up behind me and move his hand to my bare shoulder, and with that small move, Calder's eyes change from electric to full of need. He looks away, and yet his fingers spread, as if he's trying to hold the pieces of me together—the broken pieces, the whole pieces, the pieces of me that I don't much care for.

I reach for his hand and slide it to my chest, so he can feel my heart hammering. With the warmth of his hand on my hot skin, he looks from the road back to me, his eyes hooded, almost dangerous, and I realize there isn't a place in the world I'd rather be right now. It's as if God had made me for this moment. As if I've surmounted all the bad that's happened in my life to get to this moment—the way life is supposed to be. This, indeed, is the heart side of me. Not the practical single mother side of me.

My breathing becomes quick as I stare back at Calder. I want to tell him to pull over so that I can feel his hands on every inch of my body. Allow him to do things to me that I've only imagined.

"Mil," he whispers.

"Yeah?" One word, so raw and so full of want.

He doesn't dare move his hand from my chest to the lower region because then it will be on my breast—and I can't say that I don't want that.

"We can't do this," Calder says.

"I know."

But his look says something so different. "Damned if you do, damned if you don't."

He looks back to the road, and we've made it to town.

"Something like that."

I do something brave. I move his hand from my chest to my thigh and open my legs only slightly, resting his hand there. I don't ask him if this is okay or if this is right. I just let his hand be.

Calder sighs and gives a little laugh that is low and throaty. "Camilla Crane, you will be the death of me."

Just as we pull up to the police station, finally, I ask him, "Why don't you date women?"

He doesn't withdraw his hand from my thigh; it only tightens as his truck idles in front of the station. "Because you are the only woman I need."

I want to pull him to me, feel his skin against my skin. I want him and only him to alleviate the ache between my thighs.

I see the conflict in his eyes before he hesitantly removes his hand from its rightful spot.

Get your mind right, Camilla, I hear a voice in my head say, and I try to snap out of whatever is happening.

When Calder turns off the truck, he sucks in a deep breath and says, "Come on. Let's go inside, okay?"

"Yeah," I say, pulling my sundress down.

We make our way inside the station, Calder's body only inches behind mine. I feel his hand on the small of my back, and I secretly wonder what Calder's hands would feel like against my bare hips, his naked body behind mine, joined by our sexes.

In my ear, he whispers, "Follow my lead," as he moves in front of me and reaches for my hand.

"Afternoon, Calder and Camilla," the receptionist, Tandy, says. "The chief is in his office."

"Thank you, Tandy," I say.

She nods with her bright pink nails and her beehive hairdo. "You're just as beautiful as the day is long, Camilla. I'm sure you get that all the time."

I feel Calder's hand tighten around mine, his way of agreeing with Tandy.

"Well, I don't know about that, but I'll take the compliment, Tandy. Thank you."

We make our way back to the chief's office.

"Calder, Camilla," the chief greets us, and we take the chairs in front of his desk.

The chief types something into his computer. Turns his computer to where we can see a mug shot.

"This guy is Cannon Watson. Denton said he gave you the report from California Highway Patrol. Does he look like the guy in the ski mask?"

I look at the man on the screen and try to visualize him in a black ski mask, and I just can't be one hundred percent sure that it's the shooter in the field. "I can't say for sure. I'm sorry, Chief."

"Does he look familiar?" the chief asks.

"Yes, a little bit." I remember my time on the grow, the time I'd rather forget.

"Calder, what about you?"

"Yeah, looks familiar to me."

We've both seen the same photo before. Calder printed one off, and I saw it in his truck, but I never asked questions. I'm not trying to lead the chief off the trail, but I have a sneaking suspicion that maybe Cannon Watson doesn't have much to do with this.

The chief turns his computer screen toward him again and prints out the picture of Cannon Watson, and he hands it to us. "Take this with you. See if Wyatt or Lance might be able to positively identify him."

"Absolutely," Calder says even though he's been to Southern Humboldt in search of him.

"And please, stay safe. I'd prefer if you and Malik didn't stay alone at the ranch, Camilla. With this guy's rap sheet, there's no telling what he'll do."

The hairs on my neck stand at attention as the color drains from my face.

"You already know how to protect yourself?" the chief asks me.

My mouth goes bone dry, and I nod.

"Good." The chief stands, and we follow him out.

When we get outside, Calder is already deep in thought when he pulls the truck door open for me.

"What?"

He shakes his head. "I'm sleeping in the house from now on."

After the dishes are done, I pull out Joe's old scotch from the cabinet above the stove, two small glasses, and sit down at the table.

Calder walks in and doesn't hesitate when he sees the bottle of scotch. He sits down next to me, opens the bottle, and pours half an inch into both glasses.

I take a slow sip. It burns the entire way down, exploding in my stomach as hot comfort.

I want to tell Calder about my father and what happened all those years ago. I'm not scared of what he'll do with the information. I'm more afraid of what he'll think of me.

"Listen," Cal says, "I'm driving back to Alderpoint tomorrow." Cal takes the glass of scotch and puts it to his lips. I watch as his Adam's apple bobs as he swallows, his eyes focused on me.

"I'm going too."

He shakes his head, setting the glass down on the table. "And what if something happens to both of us? What would happen to Malik? He goes to live with your family?"

"No," I spit out.

Calder can feel the disdain that slithers across the table and up to his arms from the tone in my voice. "How come you never talk about your family?"

"There's nothing to talk about."

"Do you talk to them?"

"Yes."

"How come Malik never goes to visit them—your parents?"

I sigh and run my fingers along the smooth glass of the bottle that sits in front of us. *Be honest, Camilla. With someone. You can't carry these secrets forever.*

"My father wasn't a good man. My mother followed his lead, and my sister and I still carry the burden."

"Was?"

"He died."

"How?"

I allow the brown elixir into my mouth to water down my heart and the fear that starts to creep up, created by the memories I carry with me, and acknowledge the honesty that is creeping up.

Minutes pass.

Calder reaches for my hand, and my eyes move from the table to his.

"I killed him."

14

Calder

If she killed a man, it was right, it was just, and most likely, it was in self-defense.

I squeeze her hand.

"There is only so much you can take before the rage explodes." She pours a little more scotch into each of our glasses. "He'd make sure the bruises were in places no one would see. While my mother wept in the other room, he'd beat us for a bad grade on our report cards. He'd use his fists to let us know who was in charge. My mother could have helped." Her eyebrows rise with hope. "But she never did. Being the older sister, I made sure I took the brunt of his abuse. I'd always make sure he got to me first so she only got pieces of it."

My hand tightens around hers.

"And some marks leave scars that are unseen, and of those scars are just memories that I cannot seem to shake." Camilla lifts her T-shirt to expose her toned stomach.

Cigarette burns.

My vision becomes clouded by thoughts of rage, and my throat becomes dry. I trace my fingers over the scars, my hand unsteady. I try to contain my feelings. Not out of need or want, but mostly out of me wanting to kill anyone or anything that would do this to a woman.

My eyes meet Camilla's again, and I can't read her face. I don't know what she's thinking. And not because this asshole did this, but because she keeps her secrets so well hidden. I can't manage to say anything. I remove my hand, not wanting to make her feel uncomfortable.

Camilla drops her T-shirt. "I'd just turned eighteen, and one night, I knew something was off. I felt it—here." She puts her hand over her heart. "My father had gotten more aggressive as my sister and I got older, trying to prove that he was in control, no matter how old we got. My mother was the submissive one. She always cowered down to him. My sister started to follow in my mother's footsteps. Just accepting what he did like that was the way it was." Camilla shakes her head and looks down at her hands. "But I couldn't just accept it. So, when I went to my sister's room and found my father next to her …" She pauses. "I think I stopped something from happening. He knew he'd never be able to get away with that with me. But, Calder, I saw red. I held up the gun … and I fired until the gun ran out of bullets."

I pull her up into my arms, and she falls into me, choking back sobs, trying to quiet herself because of Malik.

"You did the right thing." I kiss the top of her head.

When her cries become quiet, I slowly release her, but I don't let go completely.

She looks up at me. "You're the first person I've ever told that story to."

"It's safe with me—you know that, right, Mil?"

"Maybe this is karma."

I pull her back to me. "Camilla, listen to me. You killed your father in self-defense, and don't you ever believe anything different."

All the years she and her sister endured the abuse while her mom stood in the shadows, too terrified to help.

After a few more minutes, I tell Camilla that I'm going to lock my truck, but really, I just need to go outside and clear my mind because all I'm able to do is see red. While Camilla cleans up the kitchen, I walk out to the back, and a light I see down by the creek catches my attention.

"Come, fucker. I will break you."

Quietly, I grab my handgun from my truck and sneak along the tree line slowly and quietly toward the spot I saw the light.

There's a rustle in the trees in front of me, and I stop and listen, taking protection behind a tree. Another rustle. But when a skunk makes its way out, I breathe out a sigh of relief.

I continue toward the light, and when I reach it, I'm caught off guard. It's a flashlight that's on, and it's resting on a note.

I hope this light reminds you that I'm always watching.

Cute pup, by the way.

I don't dare touch a thing, thinking we might be able to dust for prints. Searching for leaves, I find a few and pick up both the note and the flashlight. I know testing takes forever in Dillon Creek because they must send it away, but even so, it's worth it.

I set the note and flashlight on the back step and run inside to grab a Ziploc bag.

"Where did you go?" Camilla says, crossing her arms over her chest.

I grab the Ziploc and bag up the flashlight and the note.

Camilla follows me out.

"I saw this light shining there." I point down across the field. "And this note."

Camilla takes the bag and walks inside, studying it closely, thinking. "Cal, do you think he's been inside my house?"

My limbs begin to tingle. "I think it's time we go to my parents'."

Camilla bites her lower lip for a moment, deep in thought. She stares down at the Ziploc bag and its contents and crosses her arms over her chest. "Don't you see, that's what he wants? He wants me to run, Cal. He wants to know that he scared me."

I know she's right. "But at what point is your ego worth your and Malik's safety?"

"Ego?" There's an edge to her voice. "There's nothing about this that is ego-driven." She drops her arms to her sides.

"Then, what is it, Mil? What's keeping you tied to this ranch if it's not ego?"

"How is running going to make this situation any better?"

"It will keep you and Malik safe. Someone can be with you at all times. I can keep better watch. My brothers too."

"Oh." She smiles only slightly. "Then, it's about your ego. It's about you saving the day."

I let a mouthful of air escape me, and I stare hard at Camilla.

She stares back, and I know she feels a tinge of guilt for what she just said because she follows with, "It will only drag your family into it. I can't have that."

"My family got involved the moment you called me to help." *Low blow.* I sigh and lean against the counter, dropping my head. "That's not how I meant it."

"No, you're right. I shouldn't have called. I should have dealt with this on my own." And she says it in a tone that makes me believe her.

She's not trying to be sarcastic or spiteful—not that the woman could be. I don't think she has a mean bone in her body. She's tough, but not mean.

"I know when I'm wrong, Calder. Well, sometimes, I don't, but most of the time, I do, and I have no problem admitting it. We've had this discussion before about us leaving our ranch to go to your parents'. It's something I won't do, and it's not out of ego, but I must teach my son to stand up, even when it's hard, even when it's scary, even when the odds are not in our favor." Her hands are fisted at her sides. She looks down at the floor and then up at me. "With that said, I'd like your parents to take Malik, if they would? Just until we can get this sorted out."

I nod. "Of course."

The corners of Camilla's mouth turn upward. "I think they call that a compromise?"

"A compromise."

Camilla sticks out her hand. "Agreed?"

I stick my hand out, and we shake on it. Our hands linger together far longer than they should.

She whispers, "We'll tell him tomorrow at breakfast."

Red whines from his crate.

"Go to bed. I'll take him out."

"Malik should. It's his dog," Camilla says.

"I think he's been through enough these past few days, don't you?"

"I suppose you're right."

With a long-lasting look, I peel my eyes away from Camilla and go retrieve Red from his crate. "I'll lock up."

But when I come back, Camilla is fast asleep on the couch, and a note is on the coffee table.

Sleep in my bed. You could use a good night's rest.

I smile and look down at her sleeping. Her eyelashes are so long that they touch her cheeks. Her dark hair lies around her, and she looks like an angel. If there were ever a woman that God built for me, it would be Camilla Crane.

I want to kiss her temple, but I know it might wake her, and I don't want to do that. So, instead, I steal a few more seconds with her and quietly take a look in Malik's room to make sure he's fast asleep. I peek down at his face. I think he looks like his mother. Same cheekbones. Same long eyelashes. The only difference between Camilla and Malik is that Malik has an incredible mother who is willing to fight for him at all costs.

Walking back to Camilla's room, I turn off her bedside lamp, pull off my T-shirt, climb on top of the covers, and try like hell to get some sleep.

Somewhere in the middle of the night, I hear the toilet flush and hear footsteps in Camilla's bedroom. Barely do I open my eyes, and I see her small figure make her way toward her bed with a blanket in tow.

My body tenses.

Guilt. I should wake her up. She doesn't remember that I'm in her bed.

Want. I try not to picture her body next to mine.

Protection. I feel better with her next to me.

I stare up at the ceiling and contemplate what to do. When I go to get up, her hand slides over my middle, and she softly moans. The moan reaches spots in my body that it shouldn't. I reach for her hand to move it, so I can climb out, but her whole body moves toward mine, and her leg curls around mine.

Immediately, I begin to sweat. *Please don't get hard. Please don't get hard.*

But it's when her head moves to my chest that something sweeter, something lighter, comes over me. The need to provide protection. Camilla says she can do things on her own, and I know she can, but she's never had anyone to protect her before. Sure, Joe stepped in. But he wasn't alive long enough to finish the job. Camilla has always done the protecting—with Malik, her sister, and her mother.

So, instead of climbing out of her bed, I move my arm around her waist and hold her, and ever so lightly, I kiss the top of her head.

15

Camilla

I jump awake when I hear a truck pull up outside. I glance over at the clock.

"SHIT!" I jump out of bed. "SHIT!" *How the hell did I get in my bed last night?*

I throw my hair up in a ponytail and quickly wash my face and brush my teeth in the bathroom. Then, I walk into the kitchen to find Calder cooking breakfast, Malik playing with Red, and Wyatt sitting down at the kitchen table, coffee in hand.

"Morning, Mom! Look what Red can do!" He looks at his puppy. "Sit."

Red sits.

"Good boy!" Malik gives him a good rub.

"Hey, bud, why don't you feed him?" Calder says from the stove.

"Morning, Wyatt," I say.

"Morning, Mrs. Crane."

I walk to Calder and stand close to him and whisper, "I'm so sorry for getting in bed with you last night."

The bacon fries.

The toast pops up.

The eggs wait.

Calder looks down at me, and there's nothing more to his look. He simply says, "You were tired."

"Thank you," I whisper and begin to make plates of food for Malik, Calder, and Wyatt.

After breakfast, Wyatt heads out on horseback to check the cattle with Calder while I sit down with Malik at the kitchen table.

"Listen"—I reach over and take his hands in mine— "things have been weird, right? A little scary?"

Malik shrugs. "I guess."

"You're going to go stay with the Atwoods for a while so Calder and I can figure things out here at our ranch."

Malik's eyes grow soft. "But, Mom, I want to stay here with you. Who's going to protect you?"

"You listen to me, son. It is not your job to protect me. It will always be my job to protect you, do you understand me?"

"At some point, Mom"—he smiles—"I'll have to protect you because you'll get old."

I smile at my strong boy across the table. "You might be right. But in the meantime, let a mother do her job, okay?"

"Okay." He stands and walks toward the living room. "When do we leave?"

"An hour."

"And, Mom?"

"Yes?"

"You're the strongest person I know."

I nod, smile, and turn toward the sink. "Go get packed."

When I hear his footsteps retreat into the living room, Red at his heels, I look out the kitchen window at our ranch. The ranch that Joe built with his own two hands, knowing our son would be just as strong and just as brave as he is.

"Joe," I whisper, "I hope to God I'm doing the right thing."

"Thank you so much, Laurel," I say as I hand Malik his bag in the kitchen.

"Please, Camilla, it is the least we can do. Thank you for allowing us to keep watch over him." She turns to Malik. "How would you like Calder's old room, Malik? He's got baseball posters everywhere."

"Thank you, Mrs. Atwood. I would like that very much," Malik says as he picks up Red.

Daryl says, "Follow me, kiddo."

"And I cannot tell you how much I appreciate you taking Red too."

"Are you kidding? This house, this ranch, has seen more puppies than people in its day."

My throat tightens. *You're leaving your child with people who are not family*, I hear in my head, though it's disguised as my father's voice. I ignore it.

"Mom, make all the good stuff," Calder says, reaching over and hugging his mother.

Laurel laughs, holding her grown son for just a small moment.

She is a good mother. A strong mother. A woman who would never back down from a fight. She makes me think of my mother and her cowardly ways. How stuck in fear she was of my father. And I can't help but love Calder's relationship with his mother.

"May I talk to you alone, Laurel?" I ask.

Calder holds up his hands. "I get it—mom to mom. I'll be outside."

The door shuts behind Calder.

"I know we haven't spent a lot of time here. I know you don't know me or my son very well, but I want you to know that this favor you're doing for us means more than you know. And I will repay you."

Laurel's head tilts. "Honey, you might not have spent a lot of time here at the Atwood Ranch. You might not know all of Calder's brothers or his father, but you are family. Do you hear me? You never ever owe family favors.

"And that boy of mine out there, he's an incredible man. I know you know this. And I think he's met his match with you because what you're doing for your son is selfless and an act of courage, and if I were his mama, I'd be doing just the same." Laurel reaches for my hand.

A big ball of emotion lodges in my throat, and I'm afraid to speak, for fear of what will come out, but somehow, I do. "How come it feels like I'm giving my son away? That I'm giving in?"

My eyes meet hers, and her hand tightens around mine.

"We have to do what's right, even when it's hard. The guilt is just your ego telling you things it ought not to." She leans in. "Go tell it to fuck itself."

We laugh.

"Some people think I don't use *that* word, and I normally don't—only when it's appropriate." Laurel pulls me in for a hug.

"Thank you, Laurel."

"Thank you for trusting us."

Calder peeks in the back door. "Mil, when you're free, come here. I want to show you something."

After Laurel and I exchange good-byes, I follow Calder outside toward one of the barns. Malik comes outside with Red at his heels, following along the way puppies do—a step and a tumble at a time, just trying to get from point A to point B.

Calder slides the barn door open, and in an empty stall, in a box with a heat lamp, is a mama cat with her eight kittens lying by her side, curled around her belly. "That's Star and her kittens."

"How old are they?"

"About four weeks."

Red slowly, cautiously creeps toward the box. He sniffs at the air and then lowers his little nose to one kitten. Star, the momma cat, watches Red curiously, and it's almost like she knows he's a baby, too, that he's no threat to her kittens.

Malik watches intently. "Can we hold them?"

Calder shakes his head. "Not yet, bud. Star's got to do her thing first. Feed them, take care of them. We don't touch barn cats until they eat solid food."

"Will your mom keep all of them?"

Red looks at Star again, almost for approval, and carefully makes his way inside the box.

Star doesn't budge at this. Doesn't move. Just watches him.

Red sniffs each one of the kittens and then lies down next to Star.

"I wonder if Red thinks he's a kitten too." Malik laughs.

"Maybe." Calder bends down to pet Red. "We thought Star was a mister cat until she had this litter." Calder picks up Red, careful not to touch the kittens.

"She seems so patient." I bend down and admire the eight perfect little kittens.

"Dad was pissed when she showed up. Told Mom we didn't need any more barn cats. But something about Star stuck with Dad. She's an incredible hunter—from birds to moles to rattlesnakes. She might be petite, but she can handle her own." Calder looks down at me. "Like someone else I know. When the kittens are about eight weeks, she'll teach them how to hunt and fend for themselves, and then she'll kick them out, let them go out on their own."

"At eight weeks?" I clarify.

Calder shrugs. "If she doesn't, she'll only be hindering them in the long run. She has to let them go, so they can learn to fly."

Calder is trying to tell me I'm doing the right thing with Malik without telling me I'm doing the right thing with Malik.

I smile and pull my son against my side. "What do you think, bud, about staying here for a few weeks?"

"I'll get to see you, right?" He looks up at me.

I don't want to tell my son that I can't come by every day in case we're being trailed. So, instead, I say, "I'll come by as often as I can. We just need to lie low for a while." I know this is the right thing to do to keep Malik safe, and I know the Atwoods will keep him safe. "We will talk on the phone every day."

I make a mental note to buy throwaway phones in case the lines are tapped. That's one thing I learned on the grow. *Always cover up your tracks.*

When we go to leave, I give Malik a tight hug and tell him how much I love him. I want him to know everything I do is for him.

But he already knows this because he pulls away from my embrace and says, "Mom, don't worry. I'll be fine. Besides, I need to learn to hunt."

He grins, and I laugh.

I'm floored that my son picked up on Calder's metaphor.

But instead of letting go of him, I pull his face to mine and kiss him on the forehead. "I love you, Malik. Forever and always."

"Love you too, Mom."

We exchange hugs with the Atwoods and drive away, leaving the Atwoods and my son in a dust cloud, and I watch in the rearview mirror until they become nothing.

Calder stops in town to pick up a few things, and I follow along.

"I'm going to walk down to speak with Michael at *Dillon Creek Echo*," Camilla says.

"Okay. I'm going to run into Nielsen's real quick to grab a few things," Calder says.

And we say this as if we'd been together for years. As if time and comfort were measuring sticks for love.

When I push open the door to the newspaper, the bell above it jingles.

Michael looks up from his computer. "Hello, Camilla. What can I do for you?"

I lean on the counter. "I'm glad I caught up with you. Listen, I'd like you to stop publishing articles about my ranch, please."

Michael is taken aback. "But, Camilla, it's news."

"These articles that you've run on the cover of the *Echo*, you never once asked me any questions. You never interviewed me. And your facts aren't quite on point."

Michael crosses his arms on his chest. "Like what?"

I shrug. "Like the bullet holes. When the heifer was in front of my house, there were two bullet holes in the heifer. In the article, you stated three. The truth is, there was a shot that dropped the heifer and then my shot that I fired to put the heifer out of its misery. And when I shoot, I never miss." I wink and turn to leave.

"Is that supposed to be a threat?"

"Oh, no. Not at all. Just stating the facts. Good-bye, Michael."

And with that, I let the door slam behind me. If Michael is going to keep running the stories, it will only attract more bullshit. Maybe encourage a psychotic man to keep doing what he's doing. We can't have that on my ranch or anywhere near Dillon Creek. I'll hold myself personally responsible if anyone gets hurt.

16

Calder

This time, I drive to Alderpoint Road without an intended destination. My goal is to drive up and down this road until I find Cannon Watson.

Whether I have to stake out the road, camp, or hide, I'll do what I have to do to find who I need to find.

Wyatt is at the house with Camilla, and Casey said he'd stop by, too, which gives me some peace of mind.

After several hours of snaking through the hilltops around the big alders and pothole after pothole, I park at a pull-off and back up against the tree line.

The occasional car or truck drives by, but it's the black SUV driving way too fast that makes me put my truck into gear and follow as it flies past me.

I barely catch the tail end of the SUV as it speeds around the twists and turns, and I wonder if this guy has a death wish.

These guys know this road like I know Highway 36. I know that road like the back of my hand. With this road though? I'm not interested in dying today for a douche bag that probably won't live until he's fifty because of the decisions he's made most of his life. But then the SUV pulls over out of nowhere, and a woman climbs out of the vehicle. Though I'm one hundred feet behind her, I come to a slow stop and watch her pace and talk on the phone. A cigarette burns between her fingers. Her short shorts and black tank top and high ponytail tell me she's young.

She's nervous. I can see it in her demeanor. The way she carries herself, the pacing. Her arms waving, as if she's gotten herself into a terrible mess and there's no way of getting out of it. She stops and talks loudly on speakerphone.

She doesn't notice my existence. She hasn't stopped long enough to take in her surroundings, to notice a stranger in a truck that's been tracking her for several miles. That, too, is alarming.

Where's she from?

Why is she here?

What mess has she gotten herself into?

Quietly, I roll down my window and listen.

"They took him! They took him and told me if I told anyone, they'd give me a reason to be quiet!" She stops and takes a long drag of her cigarette. Listens.

"NO! No police. That would get me killed, Natasha. No. Yes. I tried to trail them as soon as I knew they were gone, but I can't find him! And now, I'm freaking out because I know they're going to kill Cannon. He knows too much, and he's pissed way too many people off!"

My phone vibrates on my dashboard, and I reach for it.

Unknown caller.

"Hello?"

There's a long pause.

"Hello?" I say again.

"You the guy who was looking for Cannon Watson?"

"Um, yeah."

"We've got him here. A vehicle will meet you on the road. You'll follow the vehicle until it stops."

"How … how did you get my number?"

"Don't worry about it. How far out are you?"

"About five minutes."

"Perfect."

I look ahead at the woman. "Can you give me ten minutes?"

"I can't guarantee he'll be alive when you get here, but it's up to you."

Then, *click*.

I get out of my truck.

The woman who's a nervous wreck stops pacing and flicks her cigarette down to the dirt.

"That could be a fire hazard with this heat and that dry grass," I call out.

"You the fire captain of Alderpoint, fucker?"

"Why are you out here?" I ask. "Shouldn't you be starting college or something?"

"Who the hell wants to know?"

I shrug. "Just concerned, is all. You aren't from around here, are you?"

She shakes her head.

"Well, I suggest you forget about the guy you're chasing."

The woman finally brings her eyes up to meet mine. Maybe she's got too many drugs in her system to focus, but what I just said makes her stop and think.

"What do you know about the guy I'm chasing?"

"He'll get what he deserves."

This woman knows who took Cannon. She knows it wasn't me, but she also knows I know more than what I'm telling her.

"Go back home to where you came from. Start a life for yourself because staying out here will get you nowhere. And quite honestly, if you continue the way you're going, you won't be far behind Cannon Watson."

She lights another cigarette and then stares me down. "You know where he's at?"

I turn and walk back toward my truck, not saying a word.

"Hey, fucker! Will you tell him I'm pregnant with his kid?!"

I freeze and drop my head, but I don't turn back to the woman who's throwing her life away. I just keep walking, climb back in my truck, turn around, and head back down the mountain to the mile marker I found the other day.

An old gray 4Runner pulls up just as I'm about to turn onto the dirt road I'm looking for. The driver flips around and allows me to follow.

The dirt road winds downhill, and it goes on for a few miles before we come to a massive house. Surrounded by a canopy of alders, the house sits on a stretch of green grass, and there's a little girl in the front yard with her mother. But instead of going toward the house, the 4Runner takes a sharp left down another dirt road. When the land opens up, it's covered with several white tents and a large barn. The 4Runner parks to the left of the barn, and I pull up next to it.

The driver gets out, and I notice he's the passenger from the other day. He motions for me to follow him with his finger. Before I get out of the truck, I feel for the steel against my flesh under my T-shirt.

I play all the scenarios.

Am I being lured here?

Am I being set up?

As I get out of my truck, I look at my phone to send Camilla a pin of my location, but no luck. I don't have phone service.

I follow the man behind the barn and into the tree line.

Beyond a few trees, there's another smaller barn.

The man in front of me doesn't say a thing. He doesn't try to build a rapport, he doesn't pat me down for weapons, and he doesn't even acknowledge my existence until we reach the barn.

He stops and turns to me. "You got weapons?"

My heart is already pounding out of my chest. "Yeah."

He puts out his hand, and I grab for my gun and set it in his hand.

Fuck.

The man, no older than twenty-five, draws his eyebrows together. "Nice choice," he says, referring to my gun choice, not my ability to keep honest.

"Any more?"

I shake my head.

He laughs to himself. "You wouldn't survive a night out here."

And with that, he pushes open the door to reveal a man sitting in a chair, who matches the picture of Cannon Watson. Though this time, his left eye is swollen shut, and he's bleeding from his mouth. I look down at his boots.

The other man, the driver from that day on the road, greets me with a grunt and says to Cannon, "Tell him your name."

Cannon smiles, and I see the blood in his teeth. "Fuck you. I ain't talkin' to no one."

The man brings down a punch so hard to his face that it knocks Cannon over in the chair.

When he falls back, I see the soles of his boots. Similar to the tracks we found at the ranch. Probably couldn't prove it though.

"Get up," the taller man says to Cannon.

With a few winces, coughs, and blood that seeps from his mouth, he rolls over onto his stomach, pulls his legs up, and slowly climbs back into the chair, sits down, and stares back at me. A slow grin appears across his face at his recognition of me, but he doesn't say a word.

"What the fuck do you want with us?" I ask.

"I—" He coughs and uses the back of his hand to wipe his mouth. "*I* don't want a fucking thing."

I don't need a DNA test to prove that it was Cannon the whole time, threatening Camilla, shooting her cattle.

"Why'd you do it?"

"Fuck off." Cannon spits blood at my feet.

I look down at it. "Saw your girlfriend on the road. Black tank top, shorts. Blonde hair tied up on her head. She's cute."

Cannon's eyes flicker with rage, but he doesn't say anything. He knows what I'm trying to do.

"You know, she told me something very particular, something you'd want to know. I mean, I guess any man would want to know. Except maybe for dirtbags like you, who threaten women and steal. Turns out, you don't have a good name in these parts. And I guess this"—I motion to the current situation—"proves why you're in this spot right now."

Cannon stares at me, but I can see his wheels are turning.

"I'll ask you again, why'd you do it?"

Still nothing and then, "Go. Fuck. Yourself."

It's then that the tall driver smacks him upside his head. "We don't have all day, asshole. Tell him what he needs to know, so we can speed this shit up."

Cannon gives the tall man a dirty look, and his eyes fall back to me. But he doesn't say anything.

"Let me see. You were probably the fat kid who was picked on. You didn't have a lot of money, growing up. You're from Tennessee, right? You probably lived on a farm that stopped performing, so your dad beat you up when the cotton didn't grow. You thought you'd show him by becoming some psychotic asshole who holds no limitations on death or murder or women. And your conscience is probably buried somewhere underneath that layer of *I don't give a shit*—until, of course, I mention a child."

Cannon breaks eye contact, and a slow stream of blood drips from his eye as it begins to puff and swell.

"I think that we become the people we're raised by. But I also think we can find our way out of the chaos. But you didn't want that way of life. You were attracted to the danger of it all, the chaos of it all, because that's how you were raised. Am I getting somewhere, Cannon?"

Still nothing.

"That girlfriend of yours says she is pregnant," I say again.

That is when I see it. A tiny ounce of compassion. Though it's almost hidden by a tough exterior, I still see it.

That's also when the shorter of the two men raises *my* gun and puts it to Cannon's head. "Your time is running out, Atwood. We've got work to do today."

Cannon meets my eyes for the last time and says, "You got one part of the story wrong." He pauses. "I was born a psychotic asshole. I didn't become one."

And with that, the gunshot is fired into Cannon Watson's skull, and he falls to the ground with a thud.

The shorter guy says, "Remember, if you talk about this, it was your gun that was fired." The shorter guy hands me back my gun and motions for me to follow him out.

17

Camilla

I'm in the barn, organizing my vegetables and fruits for tomorrow's farmers market, picking through the bad ones, keeping the good ones, when I hear Calder's truck pull up outside.

Having not heard from him all afternoon, knowing where he was headed, created a type of fear that I tried to keep at bay all afternoon. Tried to busy myself with work around the ranch and the garden and called the Atwoods twice to check in on Malik and Red.

I played all the scenarios in my head—from calling Chief McBride, to setting up a search party for Calder, to planning a funeral. So, when his truck pulls up, my stomach drops, and my heart finds a slower pace—maybe that's the feeling of relief, reassurance, gratitude.

His footsteps draw nearer to the barn door, and when he stands in the doorway, he fills it. His chest, his broad shoulders, his long legs.

"I was worried," I say as I move a good tomato to the sellable container at the makeshift table.

"I'm sorry," he says.

I look up, and there's a shadow on his face, but I can't tell if it's from his hat or something more sinister.

"Cal?" I focus on his eyes, shades darker than they were this morning. "Are you all right?"

He doesn't budge. "I will be."

But something is off. Something is wrong, and I drop what I'm working on to go to him. Unsure of where to put my hands, I stuff them inside my apron as I try not to look so concerned. After all, Calder is a grown man. I know he can take care of himself.

"Matched the shoe print to Cannon Watson."

"You found him?"

He nods.

My hands move to my hips as I begin to ponder what I will say to the asshole.

"No need for DNA to confirm it was him. I know it was him."

"And?"

Calder shakes his head. "I asked him why he did it."

"And?"

"He wouldn't answer the question."

"And?"

Calder rubs the back of his neck, his eyes hooded.

"Calder, you're starting to scare me. What happened?"

"They found him."

"They? Who's they?"

"Two men. The last time when I went up, I somehow ended up on their property. Told them I was looking for Cannon Watson and said if they found them, they should find me. They said Cannon didn't have the best reputation in Southern Humboldt."

"Who are these men, Cal?" My heart begins to pound.

"Growers. I'm not scared of what these men could do to me. I'm more scared of what I witnessed."

My breath leaves me, and I reach for his hands, taking them in my mine and holding them tight. "What did you witness, Cal?"

"They shot him, point-blank in the head with my gun. Said if I talked, to remember the gun is registered to me, so it will fall back on me. But I don't care about anything like that. I know it's my word against theirs, and it will all shake out in the end. But I watched a shitty human lose his life over shit he'd done, but did he deserve to lose his life over it?" His chest rises and falls quickly.

I step closer to him.

"He had a baby on the way. The man got tired of the pace of how things were unfolding, and he just killed him, easy, like he was asking for directions or asking for the time ..." His voice trails off as he stares at the ground. "I don't know how someone can take another life so simply, so matter-of-factly, as if it were just another thing to do on a to-do list." His eyes move to mine. "But he won't be bothering us anymore."

Hesitantly, I move my hands from his and take him by the shoulders and hold what I can of him, my tiny frame against his six-foot-five-inch frame. He folds into me like a wounded man, and I feel his heart hammering against mine. I give him everything I have at this moment. I'll give him everything if it just stops the memory, the pain I see in his eyes.

His arms curve around my hips, and his hands press on the small of my back.

My arms bend under his, my breasts against his chest. With only thin layers of fabric separating us, I feel him harden against me, and it takes my breath away in all the right ways. I want to tell him I haven't made love to a man since Joe. That I'd be lying if I said I didn't have dreams of Calder having his way with me.

With a hooded look, his eyes dance from my mouth to my eyes and back to my mouth again. He shakes his head and releases me.

"I can't do this, Mil." And with that, he turns and walks away.

With my heart beating at an uncontrollable speed, feeling helpless and wanting to help the only man who has been a constant in my life, I say, "No."

He stops. Turns. Looks at me. "No?"

I move toward him and stand right in front of him. My focus has been Malik, and it always will be, but something inside me tells me that Calder needs me. That no other person, no woman, but me can fill his soul right now. So, while I know what Calder wants, I also know what he needs right now.

It's a funny thing, internal conflict. When you've felt it, you see it in others.

Instead of allowing Calder to walk away, I pull him to me and put my mouth on his and watch as he crumples before me, softly whimpering as my tongue explores his mouth. A deep attraction between the two of us seeps deeper into our kiss, where it's unavoidable anymore.

Our kiss deepens as his hands slip under my sundress, gripping my backside.

My fingernails cut into his back. I try to be gentle, but I'm not sure that I can.

"Stop. Stop. Stop." Calder pulls his mouth from mine.

The sweetness of his kiss still lingers on my lips as he attempts to collect his thoughts.

"Mil, this is spinning out of control. I can't do this with you. No."

He releases me and tries to walk away again. But I grab him by the arm and pull.

"No," I say again, now outside, in the twilight around us. The bullfrogs and peepers do what they can to provide harmony within this moment.

I kiss him.

And he kisses me.

And the most magical thing happens—our hearts begin to find their pattern together.

He pulls away again. I know he's not pulling away for the sake of himself; he's pulling away from me, for us.

"Cal ..." My tone is direct as my heart limps across the patch of grass that separates us to find its other half that exists in his chest.

I see the frustration in his eyes, the anger, as he storms back up to me, and we stand nose to nose.

"Is this what you want?" He takes my body, picks me up, and carries me back into the barn. Flips me around, pulls up my dress, pulls my panties to the side, undoes his jeans, and with one swift movement, he plunges inside me.

I grip the table in front of me and lean over more, so he can have full access to me.

It's not soft; it's not gentle. It's a necessity.

"Is this what you want?" I hear the anger in his tone.

He moves with strength and comes unglued when I say, "Harder," through my clenched jaw.

When he comes, it's quick and hard and loud, and I relish in the fact that I caused him to do this—to just let go.

Still angry, Calder gently pulls from me. Panting, he pulls his jeans up. "Is that what you wanted, Mil?" His voice is tired, sad, and broken. "Goddamn it!" Regret is in his tone. He kicks the barn wall.

I stand, allowing my sundress to fall into its rightful place. I turn to look at him. My cheeks are still flushed, and my body is vibrating from what just happened, an ache still left unmet because it wasn't about me to begin with.

"Is that what you fucking wanted?" he yells, punching the wall, and he leaves me with a wounded stare.

His truck starts and squeals out of the driveway.

"I'll come to get Malik tomorrow," I say to Laurel on the phone from the kitchen.

I'll let Calder fill her in on the details.

They got the guy. Everything should go back to normal.

"All right, honey. Well, you're more than welcome to leave him here for a few more days. Hell, the whole week. We love having another little boy around here to fill the silence in this big, old house."

I smile. "I appreciate that, Laurel. I do. But I miss my boy."

"And I understand that."

To think about what her grown son and I did hours earlier makes me blush, and suddenly, it feels awkward to be on the phone with his mother.

"Thanks again."

"You bet, Camilla. Is Calder there?"

"Um …no. Um … he stepped out."

It's then that a patrol car pulls up to the house, and my insides turn numb.

"Listen, I have to grab something from the oven. I'll talk to you tomorrow, Laurel."

"All right, honey. Good-bye."

And without saying good-bye, I return the phone to the receiver and run to the front door. I open it to see Officer Denton helping Calder to the front door.

"What happened?" I ask Denton.

"Drunk as a skunk. Thought I'd bring him here. Didn't want Laurel to see her son in this condition—you know, with Conroy and all that."

I open the door wider, knowing I can't carry Calder on my own. "No. Please, come inside."

He sets Calder down on the couch inside.

Calder turns to Denton, smiles hugely, and says, "I just fucked her hard. But she wanted it, Denton. What I should have told her was that I'm so angry because now, since we"—he hiccups—"you know, did that, things will change. I won't be able"—he hiccups again—"to be there for her and Malik anymore. Sex fucking changes things, Denton." Calder speaks as if I weren't in the room. "It changes things."

Denton's eyes grow shifty, as if he knows something I don't, and he toys with the rubber band that he's been holding.

He looks at me as Calder falls against the pillow, unsure of what to say or do.

"Thank you, Denton, for bringing Calder here." My cheeks flush from embarrassment.

Denton walks toward the door, and I follow him out.

When he gets to his patrol car, he turns and says, "One time when I was drunk, I made a fool of myself in front of the woman I loved. Made a mess of things. But that won't happen with you and Calder," he sighs. "That man is in love with you."

My interest is piqued. "How do you know?"

"He told me on the way here." Denton shakes his head. "Don't let him slip away. He's one of the good guys." He opens the patrol car door and climbs inside. "That reminds me of a story …"

"Good night, Denton."

We both smile, and he drives away.

I stare at the big, beautiful man passed out on the couch, throw a blanket over him, and lightly kiss him on the cheek. I leave on the small living room light next to the couch in case he starts to spin.

His long eyelashes rest so perfectly on his cheeks, and I wonder if God was trying to be funny when he created two men for me to love unconditionally. Because if I'm being honest, isn't that what's happening? Am I falling in love with Calder Atwood?

18

Calder

I try to roll over onto my side, but the massive headache keeps me in the same spot. My mouth tastes foul, like old tequila. Two pills sit next to a big glass of water on the coffee table. I force myself to sit up and put my socked feet on the hardwood.

Shit.

What happened?

I toss the pills to the back of my throat and take the whole glass of water down.

Regret washes over me as I remember how I took Camilla yesterday against the table. Angry with myself, angry with us for committing an act so personal, so vulnerable, so unthought through.

I should have walked away.

But instead, I gave in to the moment for one minute of sadness and pleasure because I wasn't strong enough.

Next to the empty glass is a note.

Calder,

Breakfast is in the oven. I went to get Malik from your parents' house and then to the farmers market.

Camilla

Fuck.

I lean back against the couch, my head throbbing, my thoughts hazy and hard to reach. I stand, fold the blanket, and put it in the linen closet, leaving no trace of me behind. I eat, do my dishes, put them away, and leave Camilla's.

Great example you're setting for Malik, Calder, I berate myself as I make my way back to the ranch. *I fucked his mom—because that's really what it comes down to—and then got drunk. And how the hell I got from The Whiskey Barrel to Camilla's is beyond me. And I passed out on the couch of the woman, the family, I wish were mine. All so I can throw it away.*

As my head continues to think of all the scenarios of what could have happened, guilt and regret plague my insides like a painful memory. Like the last memory I have of Conroy, the one I keep locked away. The one where he called me to tell me that he loved me, but I was too angry because he'd been drinking and he was supposed to be back at the ranch an hour before to help me load cattle. So, instead of telling him that I loved him, too, I told him to go fuck himself. And that was the night he died.

A pain in my chest moves, and I wonder if this is heartache—a feeling I know Cash is well aware of. He candidly shared his last moments with our brother—on the side of the road in a field full of mustard flowers, waiting for God to take him home.

"Get your head straight, Cal."

I drive down Waddington. A road I could travel in the dark with my eyes closed and with little effort. I've always questioned why the turn wasn't made the night Conroy and Tripp died when both of them know the road so well. Sure, they were both drunk. But even though they were drunk, I still wonder. And that's why I'm almost certain that it wasn't either of them driving that night, which makes me also think, *Was there someone else in the car that night?* But even if I knew, it would make no difference. It wouldn't bring back the two brothers who fought so hard to be here.

And yet, isn't it easier to dwell on other issues than the matters at hand that cause a big disruption in our lives? Isn't it easier to bury down deep the things that make us shy away from life? The things that hurt so deep that there's no way to dig our way out, except to accept, feel through, and move on.

The road veers to the right, and I feel the alcohol still in me from the night before.

I shake my head. *You're such an idiot.* I don't remember the last time I got drunk.

A black car passes me, and it hits me to my core—a reminder that Cannon Watson lost his life yesterday. He wasn't a good man. But did he deserve to die?

My stomach grows queasy as the memory comes alive through my senses.

The smell of heavy gun powder.

The thud of his body hitting the cold, hard concrete.

The color of the blood that poured from his head.

His child will grow up without a father.

I've seen cattle killed, animals killed, but never a human life.

But now that Cannon Watson is gone, Camilla doesn't have to live on pins and needles. She doesn't have to watch out for her livestock. And I don't have to watch out for her. I won't have to disrupt her life anymore by sleeping on her couch.

It will go back to normal.

Now that you've had sex, Cal, it will never go back to normal. Don't be naive.

What I keep going back to is, why Cannon Watson? What dog did he have in the fight? Something deep inside me says it wasn't the money that he was looking for. And if it wasn't his money, then who the hell put him up to it? Or is that me just being some lunatic who wants to find fault, someone to blame—someone living? This makes the hairs on my neck stand at attention.

The threat is neutralized, Cal.

Cannon Watson is dead.

Stop being so crazy about this.

Maybe it's because, deep down, I want to be close to Camilla and Malik every day. Maybe it's my subconscious preying on the feelings that I have for both of them.

Step back, I tell myself. *Let them live their lives.*

When I turn into the ranch, I leave thoughts of Camilla and Malik at the gate and try to find a new normal.

Later that day, when I realize I need a second opinion, I text Casey.

> Me: *Got a minute?*

> Casey: *Weird you just texted me. I've had a funny feeling all day about you. You okay?*

> Me: *No.*

> Casey: *You at the ranch?*

> Me: *Yeah.*

> Casey: *On my way.*

When we were kids, my brothers and I used to play hide-and-seek in the dark in the summertime. That's when we didn't have a life to worry about. Our biggest trouble was whether or not Dad would skin our hides because chores weren't done. Truth be told, he never touched us as kids, but all it took was one look from Dad and the silent treatment for a few days for us to realize we'd messed up. We never wanted to disappoint our parents.

I'm sitting on the fence when Casey walks up, towing a six-pack of Great White beer. He hands me one, and I take it only because of the gesture. Any thought of alcohol makes me want to throw up.

Casey grabs a beer, sets the six-pack on the ground, pops the beer open, and leans against the fence.

We both stare out at the green pasture.

Casey waits for me to speak.

I start with the easier part. "A man was killed yesterday."

He doesn't say anything.

"Cannon Watson. Took a bullet to the head—with my gun."

I feel Casey's gaze move to me. "Your gun?" He's asking if it was me who shot him without asking if it was me who shot him.

I shake my head. "Wasn't me who killed him. He'd pissed off one too many people out there."

"Guy who shot him said if I thought to say anything about what I witnessed, then I should remember it was my gun that shot him."

"Who was it?"

I look down at the cold beer in my hands as the guilt starts to build inside me again. "Doesn't matter."

"So, he's dead?"

"Yeah," I sigh.

"Shit." Casey takes a long swig of his beer.

"Yeah."

I know the truth will reveal itself if it ever needs to. I've always had faith in the truth. "I slept with Camilla last night." I can't say that I made love to her because that's what it wasn't.

I feel Casey's smile spread from ear to ear.

"It's far more complicated." I shake my head.

Casey nods. "You're scared you've fucked things up with Camilla and Malik because you slept with her."

"Yep."

"Have you talked to her?"

The peepers grow louder as if they, too, are waiting for my answer.

"No."

"Why not?"

"Fear, I guess."

"Cal, you've been showing up for that woman since the day Joe died. You don't think she has the same feelings? I'm certain she would have kicked your ass to the curb by now if she didn't want you there."

"It's not that. It's just … what if it doesn't work out? Then, I'll lose both of them for good."

"Just because it *could* happen doesn't mean it *will* happen, dumbass. Listen, I might be your younger brother, but it seems to me that living in the future has always caught me up. I have got to stay in today. And worst-case scenario: you do fuck the whole thing up—not that you will, because you're the golden boy and all. But, dude, that doesn't mean you'll lose Malik. You built roots with that boy. You two will always have a special bond, no matter what." He takes another swig of beer. "I mean, sure, you'll lose the love of your life …"

He laughs and I start to laugh because Casey has the funniest laugh, and it's infectious.

When our laughter dies down, Casey says into the night, "You won't mess this up, man. It means too much to you."

"Look what Cash did with Scarlet," I whisper.

"And look at Cash and Scarlet now," he counters.

Headlights pull into the driveway, and I have a flash of memory.

Me in Denton's car. He's driving, and the headlights are bouncing off the road while I'm professing to Denton that I'm in love with Camilla.

I silently groan and rub my face with my hands.

If I said that, did I say anything about the murder I'd witnessed with my gun? Did I tell Denton everything? Shit.

The headlights belong to Dad, and when Casey and I turn to him, his walk is slow, and his face is drawn to the ground.

"Dad? What's wrong?" Casey says.

Dad picks his head up and says, "It's your grandmother, Clyda. She's dead."

19

Camilla

I unload the truck and put what's left of the strawberries and the green onions out to pasture for the critters. Malik grabs the crates from the back of the truck and puts them in the barn. Red is nipping at his heels, clumsily following Malik.

The barn … where everything went wrong and right.

My phone rings from my apron pocket, and I retrieve it. It's Laurel. I hit Ignore and drop my phone back in my apron. After thirty seconds, it vibrates, indicating a message.

Once the truck is unloaded and the barn is locked up—I'm still locking everything regardless of the fact the Cannon Watson is dead—Malik, Red, and I go inside the house.

I warm up leftovers, and we quietly sit down to eat dinner. Red sleeps at Malik's feet. Farmers market for a pup his size is a big day.

It's different here without Calder, and Malik notices too. "I like it better when Calder's here."

I take another bite of green beans. "How so?"

He shrugs with a mouthful of spaghetti and swallows. "I don't know. I guess … I guess I miss him when he's not here."

"But you have me."

"You know what I mean."

I smile and reach for his hand, trying not to remember the phrase Calder used while drunk with Denton in the room last night. The phrase sends chills up my spine and twists in my stomach. Chills because I think if Calder had had a better opportunity, then he would have made love to me. Twists because I'm not so sure it was the right decision.

But I can't stop thinking about it.

"Go take a shower, and I'll do the dishes tonight."

Malik hops up, and Red comes to life, not knowing which way is up, and then he immediately plops back down and falls back to sleep.

"Don't worry about Red. Leave him in the kitchen with me."

Malik retreats to the shower.

"You know," I say to the sleeping puppy, who's somehow negotiated his way to my feet as I do the dishes, "if you'd slept at the market today, you wouldn't be this tired, sir."

I glance down, and he's on top of my feet now, legs sprawled out. I smile as his little mind drifts into a dream, one where he's running and letting out a low growl.

When the dishes are done and the kitchen is clean, I scoop Red up in my arms and go sit down on the couch, and that's when I see the note. The note I wrote to Cal. But underneath my writing is something different.

Thank you, Mil.

Love,

Cal

"I just fucked her hard." I replay Calder's words in my head. What redeemed him was the part he said after that. *"I won't be able to be there for her and Malik anymore."*

As if sex was never the important part, and here I was, thinking he needed it. I saw it in his eyes, the need for me, for something that only I could provide—or maybe, that any woman could provide. I was trying to give him what he needed, and if I'm being honest, it was what I needed too. And I know I gave him a look he couldn't withstand. I think he was trying to give me what I needed too.

But is he right?

Does it change things?

We haven't talked all day, except through the note.

Malik opens the bathroom door and heads to his room to change.

Red, from my chest, picks up his puppy head for only a moment and drops it back down to my chest.

I stroke his red ears, and his mouth slightly opens. I smile. I don't know what qualifies as better—a sleeping puppy or a sleeping baby. But I'd say both are a win.

"It's late," I say to Malik when he sits next to me on the couch.

"Mom, it's summertime." He takes the television remote from the coffee table and flips on the TV.

My phone vibrates again, but this time, it's from the counter in the kitchen, where I left it. I hand Malik Red and go retrieve it, remembering Laurel's message she left earlier.

I hit Play.

"Hey, Camilla. I just wanted to let you know that Clyda passed away from a heart attack late this afternoon. Anyway, Cal isn't one to ever ask for help, so I just thought I'd let you know. Hope all is well, and give a big hug to Malik and Red for me. Quite honestly, we miss them already. The house is just too quiet. I forgot what it was like to have a boy around here again …" Her voice grows softer. "And I forgot how much I missed it. Be well, Camilla. Good-bye."

My heart sinks, and my stomach drops.

Clyda Atwood? What is the world coming to?

I lean against the counter and stare at the floor. *Should I call Cal or text him?*

Call, Camilla. Don't you dare think you can escape with a text. But don't be too much or too forward. Just a simple wanted to let you know I was thinking about you.

I call Calder.

Ring one.

My heart starts to race.

Ring two.

My stomach begins to churn.

Ring three.

My breathing becomes quicker.

Ring four.

My foot beings to tap.

Ring five.

I begin to bite my thumbnail.

Ring six.

His voice mail picks up, and I wait for the beep.

"Hey, Calder. It's Camilla." *Of course it's you. You don't need to clarify.* "I heard about Clyda and just wanted to pass on my and Malik's condolences." I grow quiet for a moment, uncertain if I should have said *our* instead, as grammar is not my strong suit. Heat rushes to my face. *Just finish leaving the damn message already.* "If there's anything you need, please don't hesitate to reach out."

I hit *End.*

Why didn't he pick up?

Is he avoiding my call?

Does he think last night was a mistake?

Do I think last night was a mistake?

Will we ever talk again?

You shouldn't have called, Camilla.

My insecurities play on me, and I push away my thoughts as I push off the counter in the kitchen and go back into the living room to tell Malik.

"How'd she die?"

"Heart attack."

He's quiet for a moment and then, "What if you die of a heart attack, Mom?"

"Oh, honey, I won't. I'm too stubborn."

"But what if you did? Where would I go?"

I haven't thought of this. I suppose all good mothers should. "Where would you want to go?"

Immediately, his response is, "Calder's. I'd want to live with him."

My breath hitches, and I'm not sure if it's relief that I feel or an overwhelming sense of love for a man who is so good to my son that he'd want to live with him if something were to happen to me. My boy was so shy at the beginning of his life that he could barely mutter two words to anyone, except for me, after his father died. Then, Calder came into our lives, and Malik thrived.

What does that picture look like—the three of us instead of two? The picture doesn't quite fit the American dream, but instead, it's the twenty-first-century dream, where families become melting pots, blended, and the bottom line is love.

"You would?"

"I mean, yeah. He's the one who's always been there. He's the one who taught me how to ride a bike and tie my shoes and play baseball."

Malik has a life as if Joe never existed, and I live as though he were still here.

Not wanting to move on.

Clinging to what he and I had.

Reminders, pictures that captured our lives in a succession of memories, ones well lived, are scattered throughout the house, reminding us that grief never evades our hearts.

I've pushed Calder to the side and focused on my son, not allowing my heart to beat the way it should—in love and full of promise. Secretly worried about what others would think about a widow with a son moving on to a well-loved man in the community.

Malik was so little when Joe passed away. He has no memory of the way Joe looked at him like he was the most precious thing in his life, that this life had to offer up.

"Mom?" Malik asks.

Abruptly, I turn to him. "Sorry."

"Where'd you go?"

"To the past." I smile, trying to reassure my son that I'm all right. That everything is okay as long as we're together.

"You know what I think?"

"Tell me."

Malik strokes a sleeping Red, still quite comfortable next to him now. "I think God brought Dad into your life, and I think he also brought Calder into both of our lives."

A tingling warmth spreads to my arms and my legs. My chest expands as I look at my intuitive son. "When did you get so wise?" I lean my head on his shoulder, not allowing myself to let go of this moment. "Can we just sit here for a minute, you and me, and just be?"

"Yeah, we can do that."

A slow, calm silence slides over us like a warm blanket in the winter, and I can't help but wonder if Joe is with us.

Please, Joe, give me a sign that it's time to move on ... for Malik, for me—for us.

My son's head is now on my lap, both him and Red fast asleep, and I get that life is good. It is moments like this that make me appreciate that if it all falls apart tomorrow, as long as I have my son, everything will be as it should be, and I am at peace with that.

My phone buzzes on the coffee table, and carefully and skillfully, I reach for it.

It's a text from Calder.

Calder: Thank you for the message, Camilla.

I lift my chin at the curtness that I feel through his words. *Camilla. Not Mil. One sentence and nothing more. Six words.* He didn't return my call, and I wonder if this is his way of saying good-bye. So, instead of allowing the feelings in, I push the door shut to my heart. Slam it closed and remember why I do what I do every single day.

I remember what to do next, and that's to survive.

I learned it from a young age, and it's something that's continued to work for me when nothing else has.

I'll get up tomorrow morning.

I'll drink coffee.

I'll make breakfast for my son.

I'll continue living because that's what people do.

Move on, Mil, I tell myself.

Too good of a thing will never last.

Besides, Calder deserves a woman who doesn't have a son that doesn't belong to him. Needs more than a widow whose past is shredded, who has memories she'd rather not have. And who's not a killer.

He deserves to start over. He deserves more.

So, that's exactly what I tell myself until my cell phone rings, this time drawing my attention to the *Unknown Caller* displayed on my phone.

20

Calder

"What do you mean, Grandma didn't want a funeral?" I say as we feed the cattle.

"She said she didn't want people wasting their time. She'd rather see them go about their work or donate time to something more productive than grief over a dead old lady." Dad pauses when he sees my face. "Her words, not mine."

"Did someone call Carl and Mabe?"

"Your mother did. She's at your grandmother's house now."

"Do you know if she called Camilla too? Last night, she called me and left a message, giving her and Malik's condolences."

"Not sure."

I throw several hay bales farther down the fence line and dump a coffee can full of grain.

"You two have a falling-out?"

My dad doesn't do details. He's not simple-minded, he just prefers to keep life simple. And in matters of the heart—*things get too detailed*, as he says.

"No. Why?"

He tosses another hay bale. "You wear your mood, is all."

I was also hungover yesterday, but I don't tell my father this. I've never seen him drunk in my life or my mother for that matter. I've always taken pride in that. While other fathers tie one on in social settings, Dad always has only one beer the whole night and has eyes on us boys and my mother. He's just a good man.

"Wear my mood?"

"On edge," he tries to clarify as he climbs back into the side-by-side, and I slide in next to him.

We take off at a slow pace back to the barn.

"You might think I don't notice, son, but I do. You haven't brought a woman home in years. You dote on Malik, and the way you look at Camilla …" He whistles through his teeth. "I remember those days. Hell, I still feel them. Just because you boys are grown and your mother and I are old, the love hasn't changed for nothing."

We ride back to the barn in silence.

"Son?" my dad says after we park and he's leaving the barn.

"Yeah?"

"Don't *not* do something because you're scared of the outcome, okay? Leave that to the big guy upstairs. More times than not, we just need to have faith that everything will work out the way it's supposed to."

I'm caught by surprise, as Dad doesn't talk about God too often. He goes to church with my mom every Sunday, and that's the extent of it. Most of the time, he just goes because of her.

And with that, my dad turns and walks back toward the house.

Simple is best.

When Dad has the advice to give, he does it best, and I forget that. But maybe, sometimes, we don't ask because we're more scared to hear the right answer.

I get in the side-by-side-and drive it to the back of the barn. In the rearview mirror, I see a sulking Williams wander up to the barn door.

"What's the matter, buddy?" I get out and walk toward him.

He sits at the door and drops his head.

I laugh. "I'm sorry. I didn't take you to the feed today. I promise you'll go tonight, all right?"

I take his face in my hands, and he stares back at me, as if to say, *You promise?*

"You know me—I never go back on a promise."

He barks and pops up and is back to his old self, waiting for what we'll do next.

I walk to my truck and hold open the door, so Williams can jump in.

He sits on his side of the truck. I roll down the windows and make my way into town.

I begin to think about my grandmother and the way she loved Granddad. I think about my parents. They made it through a lot.

Loss of a child.

Loss of jobs.

Loss of faith.

Life detours.

Changing plans.

Different ideals.

Alcoholism.

Hard winters.

Depression.

But no matter what, they persevered.

What could break Camilla and me? What could cause a rift so deep that we'd never be able to recover and I'd lose them forever?

Instead of answering the question, I turn up the music and let Luke Combs take me to a beach somewhere. I know Camilla and I need to discuss what happened between us, but I'm not sure either of us is ready for that.

When I pull up to my grandmother's house, my mom is sitting on the porch with Mabe. I carry the paperwork my mom needs, Williams following me up the walk. I take the steps by two and give Mabe a big hug.

I feel her tremble in my arms, and I'm afraid to let go because she seems unsteady on her feet—because of grief.

She gently pulls away. "Oh, Calder. I'm so sorry for your loss, honey."

"Thank you, Mabe. I'm also sorry for yours. I know how close you and Grandma were."

Mabe eases down into the chair again, staring at nothing, and I imagine that's the grief. "That's life, right?"

But there's something more in Mabe's look, and I wonder if it's loneliness. It's a *what now, God* look. Her immediate family is gone, and two of her best friends have died recently.

I remember when Conroy died. When I woke up the next morning after his passing, I wondered with despair, not knowing what the reality of losing someone so close to me felt like yet.

I remember thinking, *What are we going to do with four brothers? How do you act as a brother of three? Who's going to fill the void at the Christmas dinner table? Who's going to give the sound advice that Conroy seemed to always have, even at a young age? Who's going to be the eldest brother? Surely, I can't handle the job.*

Who will make our hearts better? Or a better question, *What will make our hearts better?*

Without another thought, I say to Mabe, "Death sits at every street corner in every single life. It waits until the exact right time to make its move. For some, it's sooner." I'm referring to her daughter, Francine, and my brother Conroy. "But for most, there are still plans. Things they must do before they're called home."

My mother and Mabe stare at me, wide-eyed.

"What?" I say, looking behind me. I take my hands to my face to be sure there's nothing there.

Both their eyes grow teary.

My mom leans over to Mabe. "He's got Conroy's sense of knowing."

"You got that right," Mabe says.

This is one of the few times I've ever heard my mom use Conroy's name.

We just don't talk about him very often at all. And not because he doesn't matter, but because it's hard to fit grief into a box and tell it to stay there.

Recently, we talked a lot about him when Cash told us about what he saw the night Conroy died. We're all still trying to navigate our grief, I guess. But it was good to talk about it as a family. It's easier to tuck it away, hide it, and go about our days, but eventually, it always catches up with us.

Williams groans as he lies down at my feet, and I remember the loyal love of a dog. I remember how our first dog made losing Conroy feel less lonely. Somehow, it was his excitement to see me that dragged me out of the depths of despair. I kept going because he needed me, he needed us.

Mabe watches Williams and smiles. "He's such a good boy."

I nod, looking down at him. "All right, boy, let's go get our errands done."

Williams perks up, stands, and stretches. He walks the few paces to Mabe's chair and buries his head between her legs, as if to say, *I know you're hurting. I've seen that look before. Things will get better.*

Dogs just have a way of knowing.

Mabe takes his ears in her hands and gives them a good rub, and when she's done, he simply walks back to me and waits.

"All right, bud, load up."

I reach down and hug my mom, and before I pull away, she whispers, "Thank you, son. I don't know how you do it, but you made me feel better." And she kisses my cheek.

"See you, Mabe." I reach down and hug her.

"Thank you, Calder. You're a true gem, and that Camilla Crane is lucky to have such a great man."

All I can do is nod. I don't tell Mabe that we're not dating and that she's not my girlfriend. I just let the information stay where it lands.

As Williams and I climb into the truck, I wonder about her and Malik and how they're doing. What they did last night and how Red is doing. Now that Cannon is gone, I don't worry so much as think about what they're up to, if they're happy, if they need anything.

I pull up to Main Street and park next to The Flowerpot. I leave the windows down for Williams. He'll want to people-watch because that's what he does best. I pat him and walk down to Nelson's. I'm in the fencing aisle when I hear Camilla's laugh. I feel her change of octaves so deep in my chest that it stops me in my tracks, and I wonder who's making her laugh like that. Who's making her smile, who's tending to her needs. Trying to stay focused, I grab what I need.

When I turn and start down the aisle, I see her, and she sees me.

"Hey," escapes me.

She's got a yellow sundress on, and her long, dark hair dances down her back. And I think of what we did the other night, and it makes my body grow hot as I visualize the way she asked for more. And here my heart is, breaking all over again. But I couldn't stop myself. I lost control that night, and it scared the absolute shit out of me. She looks like a goddess.

"Hey," she says behind a shy smile.

And we both stand here, letting our *heys* stay in balance, keeping distance between us and putting our egos in front for all to see. Because that's what we're doing, right? Distancing ourselves?

But I see something change in her face as she takes a few steps toward me.

"Can we talk?"

"Yeah," I say almost breathlessly because that's what Camilla Crane does to me.

"My house tonight?" Her perfectly shaped almond eyes meet mine.

"Yeah," is all I can say.

"Seven o'clock suit you?"

"Yeah."

"Okay." And with the sun on her side, she turns and walks back down the aisle, carrying with her the light that shines within her.

I watch her walk away and think about what she's gone through and how she's willing to face anything that comes at her with dignity, faith, and courage without a second glance backward.

"You guys have a falling-out?" Lance Belotti, Camilla's neighbor, walks up behind me.

"Why does everyone think that?"

He shrugs. "Haven't seen your truck at the ranch for the past day or so."

"Can't two people do separate things?"

Lance gives a low chuckle. "Wish you both would pay attention to the signs that you were meant to be together."

Shaking my head, I walk away, and Lance laughs.

"It's just a matter of time. But don't wait too long—you could lose out on a good woman," he calls after me.

I pay for the barbed wire and leave.

On my way back down Main Street, I'm taken aback when I see Cranky Carl on the bench in front of the Blacksmith Shop.

I throw my barbed wire in the truck and let Williams out of the truck.

"Hey, Carl. Room for two?" I say, motioning to the empty side of the bench.

But he doesn't answer me. Lost in thought, he's staring at his hands. It isn't until he sees Williams sitting at his feet that he lifts his head to find me.

"Calder," he says breathlessly, emotion straining his throat. "I-I'm so sorry to hear about Clyda."

I sit down. Hesitantly, unsure of how he'll take this, I gently rest my hand on his shoulder. "How are you holding up, Carl?"

His deep blue eyes fill with tears. "I—" He rubs his hands together.

I place my hands on my lap and take a big breath in. "After Conroy died, there was this old cherry tree that was dying on my grandparents' property." I pick at the calluses on my hand, wondering how my hands don't look rougher. "One day, my grandma handed me just a handsaw and asked me to go cut the tree down. So, I took the handsaw and headed to the old cherry tree. You should have seen the girth at the base of this cherry tree. Carl, it was huge, not your normal cherry tree. I was certain that I wouldn't be able to cut down the tree with only the handsaw. I knew it. So, I went back to my grandma and told her that I couldn't do it and that I was going back to the ranch to get a tractor to pull it out. She responded, 'Oh, no. You will cut it down with the tool I gave you. Now, get to it.' I went back to the cherry tree and took full stock of its base, its roots, its branches. There was no way in hell I was going to be able to cut this thing down with just a handsaw. I went back to my grandma, and do you know what she said to me?"

"What?"

"She said, 'Calder Atwood, I didn't say it had to be cut down in a day. I didn't say it had to be cut down tomorrow. Hell, I don't care if it takes you a year—as long as you keep showing up to do the work. Eventually, the tree won't seem as big as you thought. Time always shows us where we were. Death is always inevitable in what lives, but to grow anew, we must keep showing up.'"

Tears start to fall from Carl's eyes.

"My grandma was tough. She was old school, and she was wise. She knew I was struggling with Conroy's death, but I was more worried about getting it done in a hurry. What she was saying was, grief is a process, not a destination."

Carl looks up toward the sun with squinting eyes. "Sometimes, I forget." He nods, as if trying to accept the memories of his first wife and my grandma as they come.

Williams leans into Carl's leg, letting him know to lean on him.

Carl gently puts his hand on Williams's head and gives a slow chuckle. Carl side-eyes me. "How are you doing, son?"

"I'll be all right. I just keep showing up for life."

"Heard you had a falling-out with Camilla?" Carl says, still stroking Williams's head.

"Yeah? Who'd you hear that from?"

"Lance, down at Dillon Creek Pizza."

I laugh. "Got to love small towns, Carl." Standing, I reach out my hand, and we shake hands. "Good to see you, Carl."

"Take care of that family of yours. Enjoy every minute, Cal, because before it's over, you'll realize that all those minutes were life passing you by."

21

Camilla

Just before seven, I look in the mirror one last time and dash to the kitchen to check on dinner. I decided that I'm not going to tell Calder about the Unknown Caller who called again after Cannon was murdered. We thought that business was already taken care of, but I will handle things on my own. He doesn't need that right now. He's just lost the matriarch in the family, and my stuff is the last thing he needs on his mind.

I won't own up to what I did. I just can't—not out of selfish reasons, but because what I'm doing is the right thing. And I won't stop until every last woman is rescued.

I replay the conversation in my head.

"I don't have your money."

"Where's Joe?"

"He's dead. He died several years ago. It has nothing to do with him."

"Well, someone took my money, and I want it back. I don't care if you have to sell that ranch. That was my fucking money, and you'd better get it back to me, or there will be major hell to pay."

"Who is this?" My voice grew angry.

"Don't play stupid with me, Camilla. Nathan sent me. Remember the guy who played with that tight ass and perky tits? Don't fuck with him this time. Give him what's owed, and we'll back off."

"I don't have that kind of money," I whispered.

"Not my problem, sweetheart. Listen, when you round up two million, call back at 707-498-4422."

And now, I know the two situations are related.

Nathan Amben wants his money back.

The money I took and the money I spent.

There's a knock at the door, and I shut off the memory, blinking it away, and take the casserole out of the oven.

I hear Malik run to the door, followed by Red's little claws tapping against the hardwood floor.

"Calder!"

I casually peek my head in the doorway from the kitchen, act like everything is normal, that we didn't have sex and that he didn't say he was in love with me. "Hey."

Calder looks up at me, and I see his mind searching for words as he stares at me for several seconds before Malik says, "My mom looks pretty, doesn't she?"

I smile at Malik, and Calder smiles at me.

"Malik, take Red outside to go potty?"

"Okay." Malik scoops up Red and walks him to the back door, the screen shutting with a slam.

"Come in," I say to Calder and make sure I can see Malik from the kitchen window.

I feel Calder's eyes on me, but I don't say anything, feeling like a big, dirty secret sits between us.

Before Malik dashes in, Calder says, "Mil, you look beautiful."

And just as Calder finishes the sentence, Malik runs back in, and I'm relieved for two reasons. One, my son is safe inside, and two, it breaks up the heat, the uncontrollability between Calder and me. Because if I'm being honest with myself, Calder's collared button-down shirt, the sleeves rolled up just enough to expose his defined forearms, make me think things I shouldn't.

I put the casserole, the dinner rolls, and the fresh salad from the garden on the table.

Malik lights the candles that he said had to be on the table. "It's a mood," he said.

"So, Malik, how's Red coming along?" Cal asks.

"Good." Malik looks down at his feet to see his puppy waiting for table scraps.

"If Malik could stop feeding him from the table, he wouldn't beg—that's for sure."

"Mom, I can't stand the puppy eyes. He acts like he's starving."

I roll my eyes as I take a bite of my salad.

Malik looks to Calder. "I love him. And when the strange man drove up to the house the other day, Red barked like he was going to attack him."

"What? What strange man?" I say, setting down my fork.

"I dunno who he was. He just asked for you, and I told him you were out, feeding the cattle with Wyatt."

Sharp pain sears my chest, and my stomach drops. I feel as though I can't breathe. "When?" I bark.

"Today. I just forgot to tell you."

My eyes dance from Malik to Calder and back to my food. I try to play it off, but I have no poker face, and now, I'm ready to call the number that was given to me, so I can tear Nathan's face off. How dare he—or whomever Nathan sent to do his dirty work—come to my property and speak to my son.

I glance up at Calder, and he doesn't seem shocked because he doesn't know what I know. As far as he's concerned, the threat has been neutralized, and I intend on keeping it that way. Maybe he's counting it as a man who's interested in me —I don't know.

"So, you're enjoying Red?" Calder says so casually, taking a drink of his water.

"Yeah," Malik says.

"And how about you, Mil? How was the farmers market the other day?"

I try my best to fight off my anger. "Good. It was good." I shovel food in my mouth, so I don't have to continue talking.

We dance around the issue between Calder and me and what happened between us. We dance around the issue that Calder hasn't been here in a few days and try to find our way through it. We dance around all of it.

"You know what I was thinking about, Malik?" Calder asks.

"What?"

"I was thinking about starting a travel baseball team. Where we have some really good athletes and we travel around California to play other travel teams. What do you think?"

Malik's eyes light up. "YES!"

"It's a big commitment, time-wise. We would play ten months out of the year. Think you can commit to that? That is, with your mother's consent."

I hear a phone buzzing and eye Malik. "I told you not to bring that to the table."

"I'm sorry, Mom. I forgot." He pulls it from his pocket and looks down. "Can I stay the night at the Andersons'?"

Instinctively, I'm ready to say no because that means he will be away from me, and I can't control what happens if he's away from me—or for that matter, I can't control other people.

But a tiny voice inside me says, *Say yes. Let him be a kid. Let him get away from what's going on here.*

Usually, I'd ask Calder if that was okay only because he's here, visiting the both of us, but I don't because I'm pissed off about the travel baseball he brought up without asking me. "That's fine. Go pack your stuff."

Calder and I are finishing up the dishes, and Red sleeps, as puppies do, in the middle of the kitchen floor.

I feel the tension in my shoulders, my back, needing to tell Calder what's on my mind.

He puts the last of the dishes away as I wipe down the sink.

"Listen," we both say in unison.

"You first," he says.

I nod. "First, please talk to me before you bring up something as big as travel baseball. Cal, I can't afford that."

"I never planned on you paying a dime for it."

"His primary focus should be school. Not sports. That's secondary. You know that."

"I'll make sure of that."

"You need to talk to me before you say things like that to him. You can't just drop it at the dinner table."

"I'm sorry. You're right."

This reaction catches me off guard. Not that I'd expect him to be argumentative, but I expected more of a reaction, I guess.

"Okay then." My eyes move from his to the kitchen floor, to Red, and back to him. "Also, what we did the other night in the barn, I thought you needed that." I'm too embarrassed to admit that I needed it just as much as he did. "What I didn't realize was that it would put you in a position to stop speaking to me. Making things awkward between us. I mean, sure, sex changes things. I ... I don't know what I was thinking." I shrug. My eyes fill with tears. "I just wanted to fix your heart."

Calder rests his backside against the counter, listening.

A long silence rests between us.

Cal finally says, "Do you know what I'm terrified of?"

"No."

"I'm terrified of losing you and Malik. I like what we have, Mil. I like spending time with the two of you. I like being here. I like dinners together—as a family. And—"

"What?" My voice is low and gravelly and wanting. I want him to admit he's in love with me without the booze, without the truth serum.

He meets my eyes.

The low hum of the refrigerator takes up the silence.

Finally, I say, "I love having you here with us. I love our family dinners together. I love that Malik loves you. But I'm just as equally scared of losing you. I cannot put Malik through that again."

He picks up his head. "Mil, you didn't have a choice in the first place. You didn't cause Joe to die. You didn't put Malik through anything. And sex messed things up for me, Mil."

"Oh."

He shakes his head and gives a little laugh. "It really messed me up." Cal takes a step closer to me and meets my eyes. "I knew from the second I met you that I got the memo late. The second Joe brought you to town and I laid eyes on you, I knew you were different. And I knew that I would have to find someone else. That I'd have to settle for someone else because it was Joe who had won your heart over. And then you got pregnant."

I see Cal blush a little.

"I couldn't imagine another man making love to you because I wanted to be that man. I wanted to be the man who went to bed with you and made love to you every night. I wanted to be the man who kissed your fears away. Who held you when things got tough. I wanted to be the man who fixed your car and changed your light bulbs. I wanted to be all of that."

Wanted.

Kissed.

Fixed.

These are all past tense words.

"And then Malik was born and Joe died, and I knew I couldn't be that man because you both needed a constant in your lives. Someone who would be there, no matter what. Someone who would take Malik to baseball, coach his team, help you at the ranch. And I settled for the guy who was a constant because that meant I could keep you both in my life forever.

"But then I messed up. I couldn't control myself the other night. The way you looked at me, the way your hair danced around your face. You ... you're this beautiful, bright light. Every time I tried to push you away and you told me no, I felt like my heart was breaking a little more, and I felt trapped. Like no matter what decision I made, we were on course for a collision.

"So I went with the choice that would make me feel better in the moment. I wasn't thinking about you, and that ... that scared the living shit out of me, Mil." Calder's glance falls to the floor and comes back to me. "I will never put us in a position where I put my own needs above yours or Malik's. I might have asked you if that was what you needed at the time, but it was more about me. And I will never let that happen again."

I tremble, and my bottom lip begins to quiver—not out of sadness, but out of disbelief. My eyes fill with tears because I know Calder Atwood is in love with me, and I understand where he's coming from. "So many times ..." My voice wavers, and I pause. "So many times, we think the act of love is flowers, and sex, and romance. So many times, people get confused about what love is—to put your whole life on hold forever to be next to someone and not with someone." I choke back tears. "That is an act of love." Whether I want this or not, I have to respect his wishes.

But I won't tell him about the money I took.

And if this puts a rift between us, then so be it.

I'll have to accept it, no matter how hard it is.

Because in the end, it will all be worth it ... even if my heart breaks.

22

Calder

What if things between us get to the point like it did the other night when I just can't take it anymore? That I can't control myself.

Then what, Cal? Do you think you can withstand her again? Or will you give in and fuck her again? No. You remember how you felt after that happened. So distant and so broken and so out of control. No, you won't let that happen again because you love her too much. No, you finish the job and do whatever you have to do so that doesn't happen again.

Careful not to wake her, I stand and walk into the kitchen. What we didn't cover last night was how drunk I had gotten after what happened between us. How Denton brought me to Mil's house. I've slowly been able to fill in the blanks as my memory returns.

I start breakfast.

"Morning."

I hear her footfalls across the kitchen floor to the back door as she takes Red out.

She just has a T-shirt on, and I try not to stare at her bare legs. Try not to visualize what she has on or doesn't have on underneath the T-shirt. I try not to picture her bare breasts rubbing against the inside of her shirt.

God, you need to get out of the house.

It's easier when Malik's here. I don't think about her body, or the memory of me pushing into her, or her calling my name, or her telling me she needs more.

I shake my head and take a cup of coffee outside for her.

"Thank you," she says and takes the cup of coffee.

It's foggy this morning.

"How'd you sleep?" I ask.

"Honestly?"

"Honestly."

She takes a sip of her coffee and stares out over her ranch. "Better when you're here."

I smile. "I sleep better when I'm here."

"Liar. You sleep on my couch. How can that be better than a bed?"

"Peace of mind is more comforting than physical comfort."

She nods. "Should have known you'd say something like that."

"What's on your agenda for today?"

"Sort through some fruit and help Wyatt treat some of the cattle for pink eye."

I nod. "I can help Wyatt."

"You have your own ranch to run, Cal."

"I can do both."

"I can handle it."

"Suit yourself."

"Listen, I ... I haven't been entirely honest with you, Cal. There are reasons I haven't told you things, and those reasons have nothing to do with me or you, but they have everything to do with the lives at stake. While I can tell you some things, I can't tell you everything. You just need to trust that I'm making the right decisions. No police."

"What—what are you talking about, Mil? Cannon Watson is dead."

Camilla shakes her head. "He is. But he's not the problem anymore. Now I know who we're dealing with."

"Mil—"

"Before, I wasn't so sure. Quite honestly, it has been so long that I thought he'd never find what I took and what we're doing."

"You took?"

Camilla leans forward and rests her forearms on the fence. "It's much more than you think, Cal. So much more and such an ugly picture."

"Who is he?"

"Nathan Amben."

"Doesn't ring a bell."

"Runs one of the biggest drug cartels in Humboldt. It was his grow that I worked on before Joe and I …" She leaves the sentence where it's at. Her stare is sharp when she looks over at me. "This conversation will involve time. I want to be able to answer all your questions, and I want to do this the right way. You deserve to know everything. And quite frankly, I told you this, so I could hold myself accountable and not back out." She takes one last sip of her coffee and looks back at me. "My family is being threatened, and it's about time someone stands up to Nathan."

Nate's name draws no recollection in my memory. You'd think with his reputation, there would have been newspaper articles about drug raids, murders, arrests, felonies. But if a drug lord flies this under the radar, he must have several levels of management, several people taking the fall for him. He's probably so far removed from the day-to-day operations that he has no idea who's doing what.

"When can we talk privately?"

"Tomorrow night. Malik asked to stay the night at the Andersons' again."

"And you're okay with that?"

"I can't put him in a bubble, Cal. He's got to have a normal life. Besides, Nathan won't touch Malik. He's not like that. He's dirty and greedy and ego-driven and underhanded, but he wouldn't take a child. He'd kill an adult without a second thought, but not little children."

"How do you know?"

"I almost married the guy. I know his weaknesses."

"You almost married the guy?"

"Again, a conversation for tomorrow night, Cal." She touches my arm, looks up at me, and walks back inside the house.

"Do you have some sort of other life that I'm unaware of?" I call after her.

She stops, turns, and slightly smiles. "Something like that."

The killing of Cannon Watson is fucking with my mind. Regardless of the guy he was, he was a human being. Regardless of what he did, nobody deserves to die like that. Well, maybe some do. Pedophiles. They deserve to die unimaginable deaths.

But not small-time criminals.

What I keep replaying in my mind is the look on his girlfriend's face when she told me about his unborn child, and the thud of Cannon's body against the ground. I've never seen fear and regret play so vividly on someone's face, so clear that you could hold it in your hands.

I wonder where his girlfriend is.

I wonder if she'll go through with the pregnancy.

I wonder if she'll stay in Alderpoint and raise the child on her own.

I brush the horses and put them back out to pasture for the evening. I watch them run and nip at each other and play. The cattle pay no mind to the fast-running horses. They bend, they chew, they watch. They repeat. And I wonder if that's what I'm doing with Camilla. Maybe I'm allowing her to pass me by, to move on slowly, and I don't even know it because I'm too committed to an innocent idea. An idea that if played safe, hearts won't get broken, and bonds will remain.

Maybe my dad is right. *"More times than not, we just need to have faith that everything will work out the way it's supposed to."*

Maybe I just need to trust that idea.

It's the headlights behind me that make me glance back.

It's a patrol car.

The officer gets out and puts his hat on. "Calder, can I talk to you for a moment?"

It's the chief.

"Yeah." My chest starts to burn as thoughts of Cannon Watson's death play through my head.

I was there.

It was my gun.

But I didn't shoot him.

Will they believe me?

I had a motive.

Denton could attest to that with the threats to Camilla's life.

They could prove that with phone conversations. Hell, they probably have it recorded in the station.

Chief McBride takes in our land, scanning from one side to the other. "I've always loved it out here." He places his hands on his hips. "But that's not what I'm here about." His look is heavy. "We got a call from the Salinas PD about a body being dug up on the property of Harvey and Mildred Mastavoy, which, turns out, are Camilla's parents. You ... you wouldn't happen to know where Camilla is, would you?"

My mouth goes dry. "Did you call her cell?" I play it off. "Does she know?"

"The body has been there for quite some time. Salinas PD just wants to talk to her. I guess her sister is having a tough time, and they had to sedate her. The mother was committed to a home."

"Home?"

"Crazy house."

163

"Oh."

"Anyway, when you talk to her, would you have her give me a call or stop by the station?"

"Will do, Chief."

The chief turns and walks back to his car. Stops. Turns back. "And, Calder?"

"Yeah?"

"If we're on the same page, I need to know everything. It's my job to protect this town and its innocent people."

"A-absolutely."

Beads of sweat begin to form on my forehead as Williams comes out from the barn, seemingly from a long nap, like, *What'd I miss?*

When the chief's car is no longer in sight, I make a call to Camilla.

"Hey," she says, a calmness to her voice.

"Did the chief call you?"

Silence.

"Mil? Did he call you?"

"I'm checking my phone. Yes. I missed the call. Did he say what he needed?"

"Mil, they found a body on your parents' property." I don't get into the specifics on the phone, just in case the line is tapped or the police pull phone records.

"What?"

I know it's her father.

"Your sister, it sounds like, is in a bad way, Mil. And your mother has been committed to a home."

"What?"

"That's what the chief said. That's why the police need to talk to you."

"I have to go."

And the line goes dead.

23

Camilla

I start throwing clothes in a bag and call Calder back. "Can you watch Malik for me? I need to go down to Salinas and figure things out."

"Of course. Do you want me to go with you?"

"No. I need you to take care of Malik."

"Okay, Mil. Look, whatever it is, it will be okay. I will watch over him."

"Thank you."

"Mil?"

"Yeah?" I throw two more tops in my bag.

"I love you."

I stop and stare at my bag and try to figure out what Calder means by *I love you*. But there's no time.

"Yeah. Okay. Thanks, Cal. I'll drop Malik off to you in about fifteen minutes."

"Or I can just come there?"

"Okay." Then, "Bye, Cal." And I hang up.

It's not more than ten minutes later when Cal's truck pulls up, and I'm carrying my bag out to the truck.

Cal gets out of the truck with Williams and takes my bag, puts it in the truck, and stops me dead in my tracks. My head is spinning in a million different directions.

"Listen"—he takes my cheeks in his hands—"I love you, Camilla Crane. I'm in love with you, and nothing will ever change that. Do you understand me? So, whatever happens down there, Malik and I will be here, waiting for you at home, where you belong. Do you understand me?"

I nod. Will he say that when he knows it was me who took the money from Nathan? Will he listen to the whole story before he knows it was me who put our lives, his family's lives, in danger? And in the end, I know I will ask myself if it was all worth it.

But for now, I make my way down State Route 211 to Highway 101, weaving through the magnificent redwoods among the evening splendor, and pray to God I'm making the right choice. Not the easy choice, but the right choice.

I'll confess to killing my father.

I know Malik will be taken care of.

Cal will find the note I left for him.

And I know, when he's older, Malik will understand all the reasons of why I did what I did.

Yes, I was protecting my sister.

Yes, we had endured years of abuse.

And, yes, if I had the same choice to make all over again, I'd do it just the same.

I truly believe that things work out the way they're supposed to.

I believe I was supposed to go to Humboldt.

I believe I was supposed to work for Nathan and discover his dirty little secrets.

Nathan has connections all over the world—with corrupt cops, with the Mafia on the East Coast, with the dark corners of the world, where he traffics young women and sells them and thinks of it as a long-term investment—not human lives being destroyed. Though this has never been proven, I saw the look on the young girls' faces, barely eighteen, full of hope that being in America would give them the start they needed. And fear. Fear if they said something wrong, or did something wrong, or broke the picture of trust that Nathan created, then they'd somehow be sent back to where they came from. Most of the women spoke broken English but worked hard. They were filled with broken promises of a better future for themselves, for their families, and then they disappeared. Sent off to another politician, another wealthy man who lived in his sick secrets. I knew all of this was so wrong. It felt wrong, and I didn't realize it until I was in too deep.

One night, Nathan whispered in my ear promises of big houses, lots of money, children, and dreams. And when he brought the needle out, he said it was just for fun. Something we could do together. And I almost believed him until one of his goons came barging into the bedroom and told him that something was wrong.

Nathan hid the needle beneath the mattress, and I followed him out, out of the big and lavish house, out of the yard, and down to the barn, where a woman shook on the floor uncontrollably, foam coming from her mouth and a needle hanging from her arm.

Nathan looked at one of his men and nodded—some sort of agreement between drug dealers, comrades, business partners.

And I ran.

I ran as far and as fast as I could, and then Joe found me. Joe found me hidden in the trees on Alderpoint Road, begging life for a second chance, knowing I'd made wrong choices, maybe tried to take the easy road—which ended up being the harder road. But sometimes, it's hard to see the road when hope stands in the way —hope that I'd find what my father couldn't give me. Hope that Nathan would take care of me this time.

The night Joe found me, I knew he was meant to be there at that exact time. That I was supposed to be there for him to find. That fate had other plans for me.

But guilt twists in my gut because I left girls, women, behind. Maybe I took the money, but it wasn't for my purposes; it was so that Nathan, one day, could no longer steal women from their families and use them as a tool.

And now, Nathan has discovered my little secret.

24

Calder

It's noon the next day when Mil calls. We're branding some new cattle, teaching Malik how it's done. Dad even bought a few extra at the auction yard for Mil, so she could replace what she'd had to sell to make ends meet. How he knew, I have no idea. I suppose he talked to Wyatt.

I jump out of the shoot and take a few steps into the field. "Hey," I answer.

"Hey," she says. "How are you guys?"

I glance back at Malik, working with my dad, and I'm filled with a sense of goodness, as if the world has righted itself all on its own. Maybe this is the world telling me that no matter what, everything will be okay.

"We're good, Mil. We're doing okay. I, um, talked to Malik last night about what you were doing. Gave him the details I could for a twelve-year-old. The kid is wise for twelve, Mil. Too wise."

She lightly laughs into the phone. "Yeah, he is."

"How are things there?" Nerves start to build in my stomach, hands start to sweat, as I think of what Camilla went down there to do.

"Going to the police station today to speak to the detective who's in charge of my father's case."

"How're your mother and sister?"

"Sister is okay, and my mom is doing okay too."

"What is it?"

"What do you mean?"

"I hear it in your voice."

She sighs into the phone, and I visualize her smile. "It's nothing."

"A man can never know a woman too well." I smile.

"This isn't the first time my mother has been committed to a state hospital. Not that she's crazy. She's not. But she's had nervous breakdowns—several—but this one … this one put her into a catatonic state for a while. My sister broke down because she'd never seen our mother like that. And I think that's what scared her the most."

"But they're both all right now?"

"For the most part. Today anyway."

"Are you nervous?"

"Actually, no. This has been weighing on my conscience for far too long. I'm sad, yes. Malik, you—" Her voice breaks.

"Listen, Mil, you are coming home. Do you hear me? You're doing the right thing, and your father was a violent, awful man. Things don't happen by accident." I don't say he deserved what he got because Cannon's death plays in my mind once more.

But do people like that deserve to die? Men who hurt women? Once a man hurts a woman, I don't think they ever go back to being normal. I think it's embedded in them. Triggered from a traumatic childhood or whatever. They had witnessed behavior that told them it was okay to do what they were doing—or maybe it's something they can't control. But it's never okay to hurt a woman. And so, maybe the only way to stop a monster is to kill him.

"Hey, I've got to run, but I'll call you back as soon as I can, okay?"

"Yeah. Okay."

"Cal?"

"Yeah?" I run my hand through my hair and look out at the ranch.

"I love you."

I smile and feel her words inside me. "I love you too, Mil."

"Tell Malik I love him."

"Absolutely."

"And, Cal?"

"Yeah?"

"Thank you."

"Bye, Mil."

We hang up, and I walk back over to the shoot to help with the branding.

"Hey, Dad," Malik says.

When I look up, I expect to see Joe, and I know he's dead, but for some reason, that's what I picture. But I meet Malik's eyes, and he's looking straight at me.

"I'm sorry. I hope it's okay that I call you that."

It takes my breath away, and for a moment, I just stand here and stare back at him.

Finally, with a lump in my throat, I say, "Yeah. Yeah. That sounds pretty fantastic, coming from you, kid."

I reach over and take him into my arms. This skinny twelve-year-old kid, who's mostly outgrown hugs, is hugging me back. Ninety percent of kids don't get to choose who their fathers are, but some do, and Malik chose me.

25

Camilla

"Hey, Sam," I answer the phone.

"Camilla, I need you to meet me in my office in ten minutes. Can you make that work?"

"Well, to be honest …" I pause, breathing in my choice. "I was just heading down to the police department."

"About that. Stop here before you go there."

"I suppose I could."

"Perfect. I'll see you then." Sam hangs up.

My sister stares out the window at the crime scene tape still up at where they discovered my father's body. Nothing left behind but remnants of a story told through the eyes of the law—and not through two children who suffered for years at the hands of a man who couldn't get well.

"I called Sam," my sister, Kamden, finally says. "I couldn't just let you confess to killing a monster without a second opinion."

Sam Fulton is a childhood friend of mine. She spent time here at our place as a kid, saw things she probably shouldn't, and she pushed it under the rug, just like we did.

Survival is a funny word. It makes us do the very same thing we shouldn't. *Run and hide.*

We never talked about it.

There was a day she just stopped coming over without an explanation as to why. But I knew why. I could pinpoint all the times that Sam felt the same terror that Kam and I did.

"I called Grace, your counselor."

My sister turns to me.

"You'll start early next week again." I smile weakly.

She nods. "It's probably for the better."

"When did you stop seeing her?"

"I don't remember."

We both stare out the window, and I gently place my hand on her back and rest my head on her shoulder. "It's time we stop running, Kam."

"I don't want to end up like Mom," she whispers to the window.

"I know. That's why you need to go back to Grace."

"I know. Do you need me to go with you to talk to Sam?"

"No."

"I figured. Then, I'll go see Mom."

I pick my head up from her shoulder, kiss her temple, and try to put out of my mind what could happen by the end of the day.

It's Sam's assistant who asks if I'd like coffee or mineral water. I tell her I'm fine and take a seat in the ridiculously comfortable chair in the waiting room.

In the corner, by the floor plant, is a painting of three little girls holding hands, their backs to the viewer as they make their way down a dirt road. On either side of the girls are rows and rows of lettuce. The path doesn't veer; it doesn't split. It simply disappears into the horizon, where the sun is rising.

"Camilla?"

I jump and turn to see Sam in a black blazer, a cream-colored blouse, and black heels, and immediately, I feel underdressed. She looks beautiful and well rested and as if she eats mostly vegetables and fruits and all things green.

We stare at each other for a moment and try not to remember what happened that day, try not to allow the memories to take up space. And as soon as the moment is over, we walk to each other.

"It's been a long time," I whisper as we embrace.

"It's good to see you, Camilla," she softly whispers into my ear. "Come inside my office."

I want to ask her about the painting, but I don't. It feels so familiar to me, but I can't put my finger on the memory. I do, however, take a seat in front of a big mahogany desk. A canvas photograph to my left hangs on the wall of Sam, two children—one about ten and the other about fourteen or so—and a husband, and I realize that we've lived a lifetime apart.

I took the seedy route after everything happened, and she went to law school, the framed juris doctor degree with her maiden name etched in black ink—*Samantha Wooley*. Now, Samantha Fulton. Just as I left Salinas, Sam started dating the Fulton boy. I heard whispers that she was pregnant at a young age, but I was too caught up in myself to acknowledge it.

I like the picture of her family, of her successes—pictures with state leaders, past presidents—better than the painting out in the waiting room.

I tuck my hair behind my ears and pull at my sundress, feeling uncomfortable in my skin. "You haven't aged a bit, Sam," I say.

"I drive ten minutes out of my way on my commute home so that I don't have to pass your parents' place." Sam has never been a sugarcoater. She's a *to the point, just the facts, ma'am* type of woman, and it seems as though nothing has changed.

I nod. *I would too.*

Sam stares at me from behind her desk.

"It was a no-brainer when I started college, Mil. It was a no-brainer that I was going to law school and that I'd become an attorney. I love the intricacies of the law, and I also love that there are so many loopholes. But what I love more is proving the truth with facts and evidence. I always envisioned myself working for the state of California in the district attorney's office. And I did. After two years, I became good at what I did. I never anticipated that I'd want to work as a defense attorney. But"—she sighs—"it was a calling that I had to answer. I couldn't tell you why or how. A push inside me told me I had to open up my practice with virtually no money. That I had to help those who were wrongfully accused. Those who had a story that wasn't being told. I had to find all the pieces, put them together, and construct a puzzle that was truthful and accurate and defendable. And I had to be able to sleep at night, knowing I was doing the right thing." Sam nods as she looks down at her hands in her lap. "Now, I know why all this happened." She brings her eyes to me.

"What?"

"You."

"What?"

"Do you know what happens when a body lies in the ground for ten years?"

"Decomposition."

"Right, and also, the bugs, everything under the sun, eats away at the flesh, so all that's left is a big pile of bones. And the most important and internal part?"

"What?"

"Because the body was in the ground for ten years and everything did its job—the bugs, the insects, everything—the coroner cannot determine a cause of death."

"What?"

Sam shakes her head, clasps her hands together, and stares straight at me. But she's not the woman she's become. She's the little eight-year-old Sam, terrified. "What that man did to you, your mother, and Kamden was not right, Camilla. The bruises, the beatings, the late nights spent cleaning the floors because of spilled milk, where he made me watch you guys clean until your hands turned red and began to burn. The bleach he'd dump over your heads, where it got into your eyes, and the cuts he created—that is not right." Her voice grows shaky. "I remember."

Sam's eyes are full of tears. But mine aren't.

I remember, and I feel the bleach sliding from my hair to the sides of my face and into my eyes. Into the cuts that burned so badly that I wanted to rip off my skin.

"It wasn't you who killed your father. You and I both know it."

I held a gun out.

I aimed.

And I fired and fired and fired until the gun simply continued to click.

But I hadn't done it. I'd fired over his head, and it was my mother who had fired the shot right between his eyes.

We three girls didn't have time to react hysterically. While my mother stood there, holding the gun, trying to come to grips with what she'd done, I got my sister from underneath my father's body and put her in the shower. Sam and I rolled my father's body up into a rug and placed it on his wheelbarrow, and in the dead of night, we buried his body and set the rug on fire.

And nobody ever asked any questions.

And I blocked the memory too. My mother had killed my father. I remembered the day just as I needed to.

It wasn't me who had killed my father. It was my mother, and I needed someone from that day, who had witnessed it all, to remind me of that.

Oftentimes, we remember things how we want to see them instead of how they happened.

"The painting in your waiting room," I ask. "Who painted it?"

Sam's eyebrows furrow. "What?"

177

"The painting—who painted it?"

"Mil, you did. Don't you remember?"

"I painted it?"

Sam hesitates. "You … you don't remember painting it? Do … do you not paint anymore?"

"I—"

"Kamden's never asked about your paintings?"

"No …"

I've kept my two lives separate. Those years with my sister and mother and father and those years afterward with Joe and Malik. I've never intermingled the two. Perhaps it was my way of keeping my childhood away from the most beautiful parts of my life—an attempt maybe to never revisit what happened. And maybe letting go of painting was one of them.

"We'll block out some of these times or most of these times to cope," Kam said to me after one of her counseling sessions with Grace.

"Did I enjoy it?"

"Yes. I … I think you painted as a way of coping through it all, Mil. You don't remember any of this?"

Survivor's guilt: when a person believes they have done something wrong by surviving a traumatic or tragic event when others did not, often feeling self-guilt.

And maybe it was the easier way—or so, I thought.

Running.

I ran from home.

I ran from Nathan.

And finally, I found a home, a family, where peace and love existed, and I would fight to the death to keep what we had. In doing that, maybe I found my solace with my family and tried to push out any memories of what life had been like before, and that's where I left the painting—in memory, flushed away with a different lifetime. But I remember the strokes of the sunrise—the angry orange, but the vibrant reds and yellows, my shaking hand that painted our outlines, our shadows in the dirt, as we left the past in the past.

I remember now.

I remember the painting and how it felt against my heart and how I cried with hatred for my father. Tears of sadness, or gratitude, or relief—maybe all of it after it was all over.

The painting is of Kamden, Sam, and me, walking away from the body that we'd buried beneath the old oak tree next to the field of lettuce. And we were walking toward faith. Faith that we'd made the right decision. Faith that no matter what, we'd be taken care of. None of us knew that day when someone would come looking for my father, but nobody ever did.

"I—" My voice is raspy. "I remember now."

"Faith."

"I'm sorry?"

Sam points to the young lady in the canvas photo on her wall. "I named one of my daughter's Faith. I knew one day, this would all come to a head, Mil. And I know in my heart that it was the right decision. And I will defend that decision until I don't have to anymore."

26

Calder

"When's Mom coming home?" Malik asks.

The kid has had macaroni and cheese for three nights in a row and hasn't complained once. My mother offered to send dinner with us, but if I'm going to take care of this kid, I need to do it on my own. And I've got to learn more about cooking.

"Soon, buddy."

He nods, pushing the noodles around his plate, his eyes downward. I know he misses his mom.

Williams and Red are piled up in the doorway of the kitchen, sound asleep.

I change the subject. "Red and Williams seem to get along well."

Malik looks over at the dog pile. "Yeah. Can I ask you something?"

"Shoot, kiddo." I wipe my mouth with my napkin.

"Did my mom kill my grandfather?"

My stomach drops, and I try to prepare a logical answer, but there is no logical answer for a daughter killing her father, except the truth but it's not my place. "You'll need to ask your mom about that, Mal."

"Why can't you tell me?"

"It's not my place, nor is it my business." I sigh when his face drops. "But listen, if your mom had to decide that, I know it must have been a really tough choice, but it was probably the right one."

Malik nods, still pushing his noodles around his plate. "I heard you and my mom talking one night—about—that."

I don't know what to say so instead of deceiving Malik, I say, "Bud, you don't need to finish your plate."

He nods again and still pushes the noodles. "I love being with your family."

"Our family," I correct him.

He smiles sightly. "Our family."

"It's a big family."

"That's what I love about it. For a long time, it was just me and mom. I like that Casey calls me Mal and that Tess always pulls me in for a side hug. I love how your mom always kisses the top of my head and that your dad always calls me son. Like I fit in just as if I had the same blood even though they haven't spent a lot of time with me."

I'm afraid to speak because I'm afraid Malik will see the emotion that's caught in my throat right now. So, I wait a minute, clear my throat, and say, "You are part of our family, Malik. Whether you like it or not, you're an Atwood."

"I like that."

Malik finishes his macaroni and cheese and mushy carrots that I steamed because he'd told me last night—by accident—that his mom always makes him eat his vegetables, and I realized that I hadn't been feeding him a whole lot of vegetables. But truth be told, if he didn't want to eat his mushy carrots or his soft broccoli, I wouldn't make him.

"Can I ask you something, Malik?"

"Yeah."

"I practiced this speech a million times in my head, just wanting to get it right, and I never did, so here goes. Malik, I love you and your mom more than cheeseburgers, a prime rib, and ranching. I love the way you're protective of her and how you still kiss her good-bye when she drops you off at school. I love how you always think of others first, yourself second. I'd love for us to spend the rest of our lives teaching each other things, fishing and hunting together, and sharing our love for baseball. I promise to always be there for you and your mom every single moment that I breathe. I'd love to ask for your permission to marry your mother, if you'll have me?"

Malik turns the corners of his mouth up and nods. "I'd like that a lot."

"Good. Okay then. Let's go pick out a ring, you and me together, in Eureka tomorrow. Sound good?"

"That sounds good."

I try not to worry that I haven't heard from Mil this evening yet. Once we hit play on the movie, my phone rings, and thank God it's her. I put her on speakerphone.

"Hey, Mom!"

"Oh, my baby boy, I miss you so much." I hear the strain in her voice, and I wonder how everything went today. "How are you doing?"

"Doing good, but we miss you."

She sighs into the phone. "I know. I miss you guys too ... more than you know."

"Is Cal there?"

"You're on speakerphone, Mil. Hang tight." I switch it off. "Hey, bud, want to run Red outside to go potty real quick?"

"Yep."

Williams pulls up the rear. Williams knows his job, and that's to watch over Malik and the pain-in-the-ass puppy that chews on his ears all the time. But I think he remembers being a puppy once, too, so he puts up with it.

"Hey," I say lower.

"Hey."

"Everything okay?"

"Everything is okay. There's a lot to talk about, but I know everything will work out the way it is supposed to."

"Did you go to the police department today?"

"No. That's what I'd like to talk to you about. But I'll be on my way home tomorrow, so I will fill you in when I get home."

"Okay. What time will you be leaving?"

"Early."

"I'll make sure to have dinner ready."

"Dinner?"

"Yeah, macaroni and cheese and steamed carrots." I laugh. "I made them for Malik, and he seemed to like it."

"What? He hates steamed carrots and macaroni and cheese."

"He does?"

"Yeah."

"But he ate the whole thing," I say in disbelief.

Mil laughs lightly into the phone. "Quite honestly, I'm sure it was just because he was being polite."

"All three nights ..." I groan, wishing he had told me. "And thinking back, when I mentioned macaroni and cheese last night, he gave me a cheesy grin, and I thought he was just trying to be funny."

Camilla laughs, and it's beautiful and broken and tired, but it's still Mil, and she's still laughing, so I let her laugh as long as she'll do it.

"All right, I will see you tomorrow, Calder Atwood."

"Drive safe, Mil."

"I will. I have two very important people I need to get back to."

"I love you."

"I love you too."

The dogs start to bark, but Malik shoos them in quickly, a look on his face like I've never seen.

"Mal, you want to say good-bye to your mother?"

I hand him the phone and study his face. The dogs at his feet are growling and looking back at the door.

I peek out the window, but it's pitch-black outside except for the orange hue cast by the porch light. Malik and Mil exchange good-byes, and he hits End.

He looks up at me and says, "Come on. I need to show you something in the barn."

Malik takes the lead into the barn, and when I click on the light, I see the damage.

All of Camilla's fruits and vegetables are ruined, dumped on the barn floor. It's been ransacked—crates destroyed, red spray paint everywhere. Williams lets out a low growl and sniffs around while Red follows with the same cautious walk.

What the hell happened?

I bend and pick up a basket of strawberries from the barn floor, crushed like jam.

It's everywhere.

Suppose the red spray paint was to make sure nothing could be sold or reused.

"Who did this?" Malik asks.

I try to ignore his question by picking up a few pieces of apple. "Grab that broom, would you? I'll go get a few trash bags. Let's get this cleaned up before your mother gets home."

What I want to do right now to Nathan Amben is to murder the asshole. Ruining Camilla's hard work. And then it dawns on me ... the garden ...

I walk outside to the garden and see the mess he's created out there too.

Red spray paint everywhere. Everything dug up and cut and broken.

Malik comes up behind me. "Oh, wow. Mom's going to be pissed."

I fume. "Yeah. Come on. Let's get to work."

It's well into the late afternoon when Camilla's truck pulls up outside.

Malik takes off in a mad dash, and in tow are Williams and Red. I pull up the rear.

When I reach the front door, they embrace, and I can't think of a more beautiful moment in my life than watching the two of them.

Mil doesn't let go of Malik and breathes in his scent.

He squirms. "Okay, Mom," he says, and she lets go.

"Hey." I walk up to Mil, bend down, and kiss her cheek.

"Hey."

Malik asks if we can get Dillon Creek Pizza for dinner tonight, and Mil and I laugh. When he walks inside, I look down at Camilla and slide my hands around her hips.

"I hope this is okay," I whisper.

I put my mouth on hers, and she melts into my arms. I move my hands to her face and toy with her mouth slowly at first, looking into her big brown eyes. Anticipation grows inside me and to areas I'd rather it not right now. She tastes sweet and feels like silk against my skin.

We've never kissed like this before.

We've fucked.

But we've never kissed before, and all I want to do is get lost in her.

"Get a room!" Malik yells from the front porch. "Also, can I stay the night at the Andersons'?"

Mil smiles against my mouth, and I go in for one last kiss, lingering on her lips longer than I should.

I say, "He's been a really good kid. Didn't ask to stay anywhere while you were gone."

"Chores are done, Mom," he calls.

"But I just got home," she calls back.

"Mom, we're going to have plenty of nights together, the three of us."

Camilla shakes her head, smiling.

"It will give us time to talk," I say.

"Fine. But I get to drive you to their house."

"You just spent eight hours in the car. I can take him."

"No, it's all right." She takes my hand and leads me inside.

After she gets back from dropping Malik off, I'm there at the door.

"Bath." I lead her to the bathroom, where I've drawn a bath for her with some lavender-scented bath bubbles, recommended to me by Anna and Tess.

"What's this?"

Candles line the tub of the bath.

"I hope you like lavender," I whisper above her, taking in her vanilla scent.

I slowly slide the strap to her dress down her shoulder, then do the same on the other side, and her sundress falls to the bathroom floor.

Mil turns to me in her bra and panties, and it takes every fiber of my being not to fuck her against the bathroom wall.

"Get in and take your time," I whisper in her ear.

While she's in the bath, and as suggested by Anna, I run to town and grab some candles. When I return, I light a few candles—also suggested by Anna and Tess—and put them on the table with a pizza box.

After an hour, I quietly knock on the door, but there's no response, so I peek my head in, only to find her fast asleep. I smile and push the door open.

"Mil," I whisper, bending at the side of the bath. "Mil?"

She jumps and opens her eyes. "The bath felt so good."

"Come on. I'll help you out." I hold my hands out for her to take—along with my heart.

She stands, and I see all of her in front of me. Her breasts call out my name. Her hips stall my breathing. And the scars … I want to make it all disappear.

Mil stares up at me. "Make love to me, Calder."

27

Camilla

He dries my body off, slowly sliding the towel from my head to my toes, between my legs, and I breathe deeply when the fibers touch the outside of my folds.

We're in my bedroom, and the only light is from the moon shining outside, peeking around my dresser with soft rays of white light.

I step away from him and retreat to the middle of my bed and watch him watch me.

"Take off your clothes, Cal," I command, resting my hands on my breasts, parting my legs only slightly.

Calder meets my gaze. He pulls his shirt off, and I see his broad shoulders, his chest, his hands in a different light. His broad shoulders that he uses to help buck hay on our ranch. His chest that takes on the worry of our world. And his hands that have held Malik and me up when we couldn't hold ourselves up after Joe died.

"Now what?" he asks.

"Take off your pants and your underwear."

Without breaking eye contact, he does what he was told, and I watch all of him come to life. He springs to attention, and I realize how large he is.

"And now?"

"Come here."

When he gets on the bed next to me, I feel his length at my leg, and I shiver. Slowly, he turns me around so that my back is facing him. Cal peppers kisses across my shoulders, down my back, between my thighs, and down my legs. When I'm on my stomach, his hand reaches my buttocks, and he caresses them. From behind, with a soft touch with his finger on my folds, he feels my wetness and gently pushes on the knot that takes my breath away.

"Is this okay?"

"Yes," I say.

When he slowly moves his finger deeper, I move with him, aching for more. After a minute, I realize I can't take it anymore and roll over onto my back.

"I want to watch you," I say finally.

He moves between my legs, putting my legs on each side of him so he can see all of me. Cal sits forward and caresses each of my breasts with his mouth, pulling and nibbling on my nipples. He moves to my mouth, teasing by biting my lower lip, and my tongue reaches for one last touch.

He moves away and slides his hands down my stomach and to my middle again, sliding a finger into my folds and then inside me.

And I lose all ground. I lose sight of everything and get lost in the way this makes me feel.

He removes his fingers and puts his head between my legs.

Carefully, he pulls my folds apart with his tongue, so he can get to my core. When I feel his tongue pressing against me, I realize I'm powerless over his touch.

I call out, arching my back, and he pushes harder with his tongue, gripping my buttocks with his hands, softly moaning into me.

My body begins to move with tantalizing licks. "Oh my God, Cal."

Joe never did this. Joe never touched me like this.

He looks up at me as I grip both sides of his head and watch.

"I don't want to, not yet," I pant and pull his mouth to mine, feeling his hardness resting against my stomach. "Please, Calder. I need you."

He whispers, "No, wait."

And he drops his head to my lower stomach, panting, going back to my folds.

Cal slides his fingers inside me, and I call out, "CAL!"

Because my body can't take any of this anymore.

I reluctantly push myself up onto my elbows, then my hands, and I get to my knees. I push Calder to the pillow, and a sinister smile spreads across my face. "My turn."

He puts his hands behind his head and watches me take him in my mouth.

Slow and steady, I watch his lips part, letting out a low, throaty groan, pushing my hair from my face.

That's when I crawl on top of him. He can't control anything anymore, and neither can I.

I spread myself over him and Cal pushes himself inside me.

He sucks in a deep breath as we keep eye contact.

I realize that it's his eyes. His eyes have made me feel at home. Almond-shaped with long eyelashes. And it's his mouth. The words that come from it, straight from his heart to mine. I know there isn't any other place I need to be.

I sigh as I feel his length enter me and wonder how my past has brought me here, to this moment, with a man I never expected. A man I never saw coming.

Someone so different from my father, so different from Joe.

Cal kisses my mouth, then my neck, then my breasts as I rock on top of him.

"Camilla," he barely says.

"Yeah?"

"I can—I can't …" He uses his hands to stop me from moving. "Stop," he says.

He looks up at me, kissing my mouth with so much soul that if I were fire, he would be my gasoline. If I were a cold body on a dark day, he would be my warm blanket. If I were his now, he would be my forever, and I realize at this moment that he will have the rest of my tomorrows until the world decides it's time for us to make our final ascent to heaven.

"I love the man you are, Cal. I love what you stand for—family, loyalty, and forgiveness."

He watches me in the moon's light. "I've loved you since the day I met you, and I will forever love you. You are my bright light. And the only one in this world that I would spend the rest of my life with."

Slowly, as we watch each other, we push and pull and show our love through our bodies, and we both climax—me, then him.

He's still inside me until I ease out and take the spot right next to him, pulling the sheets up to my chest and laying my head on his chest, contemplating my next words carefully.

"Have you ever had something in your life happen that you thought went one way, but it went a different way?"

Cal adjusts under the sheet, moving our bodies closer together. He thinks about it. "Tell me what you're thinking." He kisses the top of my head.

"I had to go back to my past with an old friend, Sam, to figure out that it wasn't me who killed my father."

There's a long silence between us, as if he's waiting for me to continue.

"Since I was eighteen, I thought I was the one who had pulled the trigger. So often, I told myself that I was the one who had done it that I started to believe the lie."

"Who killed your father?"

"My mother. And here I was, thinking she wasn't brave and hid in the corner, too scared to protect us kids. And she was scared for a long time. I guess she finally found the courage to do something about it. Now, I can see why she went in and out of depression, and according to my sister, she only got worse when I moved away."

"Guilt can be a beast."

I nod against Cal's chest and run my hand through his chest hairs.

"Who's Sam?"

"She was there. When it all happened. She became a defense attorney, of all things." I shake my head.

"And what about your father's death? Was it ruled a homicide?"

"No. No way of proving what happened, according to Sam."

"Will your mom talk?"

"I don't know. It's up to her. It's her story."

Cal nods and pulls at the strands of my hair. "It's also your story, Mil," he sighs. "You have a way of always selling yourself short. You're always trying to take care of others before yourself. For once, Mil, put yourself first."

I allow Cal's words to float above us in the darkness, and I watch them as they come to rest on my chest …

"So, about your barn …" Cal starts.

I pull my head up to look at him. "What?"

Cal tells me the story about how my work barn was ransacked, how our garden was torn apart. Tells me about the note he found.

"It said, *An eye for an eye.*"

"He'll never find what he's looking for, but I need to settle this once and for all."

Cal laughs. "No way."

"What?"

"Not by yourself you're not."

"Cal, I've survived years without you, and I've made it out fine."

"What are you going to do? Drive up the mountain and demand he stops?"

My eyes search around my bedroom and then fall back to him. "Yeah."

"No. You're not going without me."

I sigh, and my head falls to his chest.

"Do I think this needs to be settled? Yes. But I don't think it's going to be as easy as you think."

I laugh. "Nothing is easy with Nathan Amben. Nothing. There are always strings attached."

It's his turn to pick up his head. "In what?"

"I can't tell you that."

"Mil, why not? Don't you trust me?"

"It's not about my trust in you. It's about putting others' lives at stake, Cal. I can't risk that. When it's all over, you'll know. Until then, I'm going to go to Nathan and tell him that I don't have his money."

"I'm not on board with this plan, Mil. Not on board at all."

"You're not?"

I roll on top of him and trail kisses down his neck, and he hardens beneath me. I grin, and he takes my mouth and kisses me hard.

"Make love to me again, Cal."

And with that, he rolls on top of me and pushes all my fear to the darker corners of my heart while he fills me.

If I'm being honest, I'm scared of Nathan. But now, I'm more scared of him hurting someone I care about.

28

Calder

"Mildred Mastavoy, please." I look around the painfully white walls and wonder if everyone is crazy here.

"Can I ask who is here to visit?" the woman says from a seated position behind the window.

"Calder Atwood."

She slides the window shut and speaks with someone who is most likely a supervisor. The woman slides the window open once more. "Are you Colt Atwood's brother, by chance?"

Rolling my eyes would be rude. Sighing would also be rude, so instead, I say, "No, but I could get you an autograph," in hopes that I'll get my way.

The woman behind the counter unfolds about her son's love for basketball and asks if we can pose for a selfie and if I could sign a piece of paper for her.

I'm not a celebrity. My brother is, I want to say, as I am sure as shit that I didn't sign up for that.

I work the angle I've been given as I slide the piece of paper with my signature through the window, and then I pose for the selfie. "Now, any chance I can get in to see Ms. Mastavoy?"

"Absolutely," the woman says and hits a button that makes a bell ring and a door open. "Room 227. The second floor and the elevator are at the end of the hall, Mr. Atwood."

Through the door and to the end of the hall I go to find the elevator, which I take up to the second floor and then arrive at 227.

I close my eyes and say a quick prayer that this is over quickly and that Ms. Mastavoy says yes to the question I'm about to ask her.

Through the door, I can hear the television.

I knock.

Nothing.

I knock again.

Still nothing.

I pound several times, and the television stops.

Then, it's quiet.

Then, "Who's there?"

"Ms. Mastavoy, it's Calder Atwood, ma'am. I was hoping I could speak to you for a few moments, please."

The door swings open, and before me is a beautiful woman, although time reflects in her eyes. Her slight smile that she puts forth is somehow harder than most women her age, but nothing takes away from the beauty in it.

In a red housecoat with pearls around her neck, she says, "I've been waiting for you, Mr. Atwood. I've heard a lot about you. Please, come in, won't you?" Mildred holds the door open to her windowless space. "It's not much, but it's enough to keep me until the end of my days.

"Would you like something to drink, Mr. Atwood? Coffee?"

"Coffee would be great, Ms. Mastavoy."

"Sorry. They don't allow hot things in our room."

"Oh. That's perfectly all right."

"How about a soda pop?"

"Sure."

"Oh, no, sorry. The cans are too sharp. St. Francis shuns on sharp things—you know, crazy and all." She tilts her head up just so, looking at me tersely, as if waiting for a reaction. "I can offer you water in a Styrofoam cup if you'd like."

"Great. That would be wonderful."

Mildred walks to the kitchen and retrieves the water, walks back in, and tells me to sit in the chair next to hers.

I sit, and she hands me the water. When I take a sip, I realize it's warm water.

"Warm water helps with circulation."

I choke it down and smile and swallow again. "This is fine, Ms. Mastavoy."

"Well, what brings you to my neck of the woods from that haven up in Northern California?"

"Well ..." I set my Styrofoam cup down on the coffee table.

"Use a coaster, dear."

I look around for a coaster, but I don't see any. "Is there one I can use?"

"No."

To make things easier and less confusing, I hold my cup instead. "Well, I'd like to ask for your daughter's hand in marriage."

"Which daughter?"

Which daughter? Well, there are only two, and she knows where I'm from. Camilla mentioned me on her trip down here, or Mildred wouldn't have said she'd heard a lot about me, but I could be wrong.

"Uh, Camilla."

"Ah, yes. She's a keeper, for sure. And please, call me Mildred."

"Mildred, I—"

"No, actually, I changed my mind. Ms. Mastavoy sounds so much better. Less old, you understand."

"Yes, okay, Ms. Mastavoy."

"No, no. You know what? You'll most likely be my son-in-law whether I like it or not, so let's just go back to Mildred."

"Right. Mildred, as I was saying, I would love to take Camilla's and Malik's hand in marriage."

Mildred's eyes grow big. "You'd like to marry both?"

"No, no." I sigh. "I said that wrong. I'd like to marry Camilla and raise Malik as my own."

"No skin off my back. Her first husband—what was his name? George or Joel, or—"

"Joe."

"Anyway, it doesn't matter. He never asked to take my daughter's hand in marriage, and now, apparently, he's left her and the child—Malik, you said his name was?"

"Yes, Malik. And Joe died."

"What?" All the color drains from Mildred's face.

"Didn't Camilla tell you?"

Mildred shrugs, her eyes searching for a new focal point other than me. "I forget things."

I find it alarming that Mildred has forgotten her own grandson's name and the fact that her son-in-law passed on, but instead of sharing this, I empathize. "Are you all right, Mildred?"

"I'm never all right. If I were all right, do you think I'd be locked up in this facility?" She motions with her hands to the essence of the space we're in.

"I see your point."

Mildred smiles. "You're sharp, Mr. Atwood. I like that."

"Please, call me Calder."

"Anyway, Mr. Atwood, yes, I will give you my daughter's hand in marriage as long as you do me one solid favor."

"What's that?"

"Bust me out of this place."

"I ... I can't do that."

"Come on, just for an hour. I just need out for a few hours."

"To do what?"

"Watch the sunset."

"What about your other daughter, Kamden?"

"Oh, hogwash. She doesn't come by but every morning to give me a bath, and then she's gone again."

"Do you think she does that only because it's hard for her?"

"How do you think it is for me, Mr. Atwood? I'm locked up in a loony bin because I killed my husband, and nobody has bothered to ask me how I'm feeling."

"Point taken." And against my better judgment, I say, "Where would you like to go to watch the sunset?"

"Salinas River State Beach."

"Just for an hour?"

"Just for an hour." Mildred takes a coat from her coat rack and lays it over her arm. "I'm ready, Mr. Atwood."

"Please, let me take your coat."

She obliges, and we make our way downstairs to get her signed out for an hour.

We're at the beach, sitting in silence, listening to the ocean crash against the shore in the late afternoon. Casually, I look over at Mildred. She's much grayer than I suspected, much older than my mother. Her eyes closed, she breathes in the salty air.

"It was never my intention to be a coward, Mr. Atwood. You must understand that."

She peeks out of her right eye to watch me.

"It was also never my intention to marry a man who would hurt my children. But as in life, there are consequences to decisions. And when I got pregnant with Camilla, my father forced me to marry a man I didn't love. Sure, it was stupid to have had sex, but I was just a girl, and my mother had never explained to me the ramifications of sex and what went along with that.

"You see, I came from an affluent family. My father owned a bank, and while he worked, my mother took to making sure my sisters and I attended our charm school and were always held accountable for our actions. I was supposed to be the child who succeeded. The one who married well and went far in life.

"But everything changed when I met Camilla's father. He worked for my father, tending to our livestock and taking care of our land. And just to be clear, Mr. Atwood, I was a rule follower. I'd always been a rule follower. But the day Camilla's father started working for us, something had changed in me. I suppose it was the way he looked at me. The way I caught him staring at me through the crowds of people, the way he took up no reservation in expressing his feelings for me. We were from two different worlds, Mr. Atwood." Mildred's voice trails off as she seems to go to a deeper place.

"His father was also a farmer, an alcoholic, among many other things. Anyway, I thought I could help him.

"I wasn't always crazy, just so you know. But some things happen that you push so far and you will them to disappear into your lungs, soak into your skin, so you just won't remember them. A life lived is acceptable if you can just remember to keep your wounds at bay. Bury them until they don't make a showing. But they always make it back to the surface, Mr. Atwood. Always. They haunt your dreams, your waking thoughts.

"My parents had high expectations for their debutante, and here I was, having sex with a farmer's son who would grow up to be just like his father, and there was nothing I could do to change that. No amount of love could change what he did and who he did it to.

"You can't change a man who has experienced darkness in ways that most people wouldn't survive. You can't change a man who just wants to not remember, so he drinks until he can momentarily forget. But the incomprehensible demoralization always comes back. It always returns when the alcohol can no longer do its job."

Mildred looks down at her fingernails, and I'm lost in her story.

"So, you think something will change if you could just be a better wife. If you could just cook better dinners, keep the house cleaner. If you could just love deeper. But like I said, I was never in love with him. I loved him, yes, in the beginning, but being in love and loving someone are two completely different things. And when he hit our girls, hurt them, all I could do was pray. I didn't take the bullet for them. I hid in the corner and watched." A single tear slides down Mildred's cheek. "Because if I'd interfered, he'd have only beaten them harder and longer, and I'd rather just get it over with and begin to heal the bruises, the burns, the scars he left behind.

"Do you hit women, Mr. Atwood?"

"No."

"Do you drink?"

"Only on occasion." I think back to the incident with Camilla and being drunk on her couch. *God, if I'd only known …*

"That's what Camilla's dad said when my father asked him the same questions. Truly, I think Camilla's father was none the wiser. I do believe that was the truth back then. But life changes, right? The scars catch up with your heart, and you begin to feel and remember things you'd rather not. Isn't that how life always works, Mr. Atwood?"

The question is rhetorical because she continues, "We could take the abuse; we could endure it because divorce back in our day was simply unacceptable. After all, I'd witnessed my father strike my mother on two occasions and thought that was acceptable.

"I had a funny feeling that day, Mr. Atwood, like something wasn't right. I believe Camilla and I knew at the same time that something was off. Something wasn't quite right. It was Camilla who entered the room first. And where she got a gun, still to this day, I don't know. However, I took a gun from the gun safe. And while Camilla wanted to shoot her father, I wasn't going to let her. I wasn't going to let her throw away her future as I had. I know what you must be thinking, Mr. Atwood. I had two beautiful daughters from this man. How could I say *throw away*? Well, when you hear something long enough, you begin to believe it. And while my daughters will always be the most important things in my life, it can also mean that my life was intended for more than marrying a farmer's son who was broken from the beginning."

The sun begins its descent.

"Mr. Atwood, would you take me home now? I'm tired."

But the sunset is just beginning, Mildred, I want to say, but instead, I say, "Yes."

I help her back to the truck, and just before we reach the facility, a block away, she asks if I'll pull over.

When I do, she turns to me. "Mr. Atwood, you'll make a fine husband for my daughter Camilla. You have my blessing."

And with that, she climbs out of the truck.

Immediately, I jump out. "Mildred, it's my responsibility to get you back to St. Francis."

"Please, Calder, let me walk the last block. I'll be fine."

Against my better judgment, I let her walk, but I watch her until she makes it to the front doors of St. Francis. Then, I make my way back home up Highway 101 to Dillon Creek, trying to soak in Mildred's voice, the story she told, trying to make sense of it all.

I'm about thirty minutes out of town when my phone rings.

"Hello?"

"Hello, Mr. Atwood. This is Lennox from St. Francis. You're well past your hour mark, and we need Ms. Mastavoy to be returned to the facility."

"I did. I dropped her off a half hour ago."

"Well, you didn't sign the return paperwork."

Fucking shit!

I flip the truck around and drive the half hour back, only to find the police at St. Francis.

"Are you Mr. Atwood?" one of the officers asks me.

"Yes. Where's Mildred?"

"She's in our custody, Mr. Atwood. However, I do recommend you come down to the station so that we can ask you a few questions."

"My name is Sam Fulton, and I will be representing Ms. Mastavoy. What is Ms. Mastavoy being held on?" Sam Fulton appears out of nowhere.

"Murder. She just confessed to killing her husband."

Sam doesn't budge, but instead, she walks to the back of the police car and says to Ms. Mastavoy, "I told you to let me handle it, Mildred."

"It's quite all right, dear. I'd rather go down with the truth than go down with a lie."

The police car pulls away from the curb, and Sam looks back at me.

"What the hell happened, Mr. Atwood?"

Shit. I run my hands through my hair and stare at the ground.

I explain to Sam that Mildred asked to walk home. "I watched her walk to the door and then took my leave, Sam."

But Sam is already on the phone, making her way toward the police station.

What have I done?

29

Camilla

"What do you mean, she confessed, Sam?" I wait on bated breath. "What? What the hell is Calder doing down there?"

"St. Francis said he took her on an outing. Checked her out of the facility for an hour."

"Are you kidding me?" I try to catch my breath, but my throat feels like sandpaper.

"Look, I'll see what I can do, but the police say they have a taped confession."

"Shit! Okay, I'm coming back down."

"No, I'll handle it. I'll call you when something changes."

"You're sure I shouldn't come down?" *She's my mother.*

"Malik needs you right now. Be with him."

I nod into the phone, soaking up Sam's words like water, but my gut turns with guilt. "Okay," I finally say.

"I'll be in touch." Sam hangs up.

Angry, I dial Calder's number, but it goes straight to voice mail, and I leave a message.

"How could you, Calder? How could you not return my mother where she was supposed to be, and why in the hell would you take her on a field trip or whatever and not take her back and check her back in? I can't believe you, Cal," I say in a calm voice.

I pace the house and wait for a callback from Sam or Cal, waiting for an explanation. I walk to the kitchen and fill a big glass of water and take it down, staring out at the ranch. I make a call to St. Francis.

"St. Francis Living. How may I direct your call?"

I ask for the Director of St. Francis. "Lennox Randolph, please."

"Transferring."

"Hello. This is Lennox."

"Lennox, what the hell is going on down there?"

"Camilla, I was just getting ready to call you."

"Why on earth would you let my mother leave?"

"Camilla, she left with Calder Atwood. He signed her out. What was I going to do? My hands were tied."

"You could have called me or Kamden first." I seethe.

"You're right. I suppose I could have done that. But he looked like a good guy."

"He is a good guy."

"Then, what's the problem?"

"The problem is ..." I stall because I realize I can't tell her this part of the story.

"Besides her admitting to a murder?" she says. "Come on. That's not Mildred. It's probably one of her episodes. I'll let you know when they release her."

"They're not going to release her, Lennox." And I hang up.

"Thanks for watching Malik, Laurel." I watch Red follow Malik as he follows Daryl out to the pasture.

"I'll be back later tonight."

"Okay, dear. No problem."

I hop back in my truck and head to Alderpoint to talk to Nathan—to settle things once and for all—before I head back down to Salinas to help with my mother.

Some stretches of Highway 101 down to Alderpoint are straight like a pin while other parts of the road groove around redwood trees. As if God planted them there just so, just to let drivers know that the earth is alive and well.

I suppose I'm supposed to feel the mix of emotions building in my body.

My heart quickly searches for a more comfortable pace.

My skin vibrates with the low hum of my truck tires against the pavement.

And fear uncomfortably hovers in me and through me, making me want to upend and expel all of it—any way to get rid of these feelings.

What if Nathan snaps?

What if he kills me?

What if he has someone else kill me?

But what if I kill him?

I take the Garberville exit off 101 to Alderpoint Road and the fear inside me screams to turn around.

Go back the way you came, Mil. Go back and push everything under the rug and continue to deny any wrongdoing. You did take someone else's money after all.

No, no. Nathan took the money from other people in exchange for the women and the girls, whom he sold in dark places to elected officials, movie stars, and anyone else who was willing to pay top dollar for sex.

Mil, remember the women you've helped save. The women you've sent back to their families. Saved them from a lie that had told them about a future in America. Hope that they might find themselves one day in a beautiful home in a free country with an adoring partner and two children, maybe three.

But the dream got lost between the lines of heroin and unkept promises.

You have three women left.

Three women are still stuck in the chaos of what Nathan Amben brought to life.

Three women left to save, and then I'll alert the authorities.

When I hired the underground group to help save these young women, I surely didn't think they'd be a group of ex-Navy SEALs. Ex-Navy SEALs who have been inside Nathan's compound.

On the dark road, I almost miss the turn to the place I'd rather never go back to, but some monsters are worth fighting.

I haven't had to come up here since I left that day all those years ago.

Before Joe.

Before Malik.

Before my life in Dillon Creek.

Before … Calder.

I push Cal out of my head. *Stay focused, Mil.*

I was able to draw detailed maps of the entire compound from memory. Tell them where surveillance cameras were kept and monitored closely. Where traps were put in place to not just hurt trespassers, but to also kill them.

I drew out underground bunkers and sheds and bunkhouses.

I drew out the unmarked cemetery, where those who were killed were buried.

The dark road continues, and I can only see as far as my headlights will take me.

I continue to tell myself the narrative that no matter what happens, it will be worth it.

After several bends in the dirt road, around alder trees, redwood trees, and life's synchronicity, I move forward.

When I reach the end of the road, I see the light I'm looking for. I park my truck, grab my phone, and contemplate getting the handgun underneath my seat.

He'll find it. He'll take it. He'll question why I had it in the first place, so I'll leave the gun where it's at.

Late into the evening, what's left of the day's heat, remnants of a long summer day, sits and waits for the sun to rise again.

The crunch below my feet against the dirt road makes it nearly impossible to mimic the quietness that surrounds me.

Off the grid.

No cell service.

No help.

I might be walking into a death trap, but I'd rather fight than continue to hide.

Once and for all.

I pull my coat around me tighter, not because it's cold, but more so out of nerves. My steps take me deeper into the trees, into the darkness, and then I walk toward the light that shines through the trees, a dim light that barely makes its appearance known.

But I know the light.

The light I walked away from.

The light that haunts my dreams.

It's the light of Nathan's main house. The big house. The house where death and drugs and addiction don't exist. Because he built it this way. He wanted his house to be pure. He wanted all of his evilness to take place outside the place he lays his head.

When I reach the door of the massive rock wall of a house, I notice I'm trembling. I look through the stained glass. Although dark inside, I know he's there.

With my heart pounding against my chest, ready to cave, I knock.

"I'm glad you're here, Camilla." A voice gently lends itself to the warm summer evening and sends chills up my spine.

The air around me has somehow grown suffocating. Barely, I turn my head to see Nathan sitting in an Adirondack chair, his face in the shadows.

"I'm also very glad to see you finally came to your senses with all the nonsense going on." He motions me over to the chair next to him. "Come sit. Let's chat for a minute, shall we?"

My skin begins to tingle as I slowly walk to the chair next to him. Sit.

We stare into the darkness.

"I just came to tell you that I don't have your money, Nathan." I exhale.

Silence sits between us, and he gently folds his hands in his lap.

The light from the porch illuminates only half his face.

"I killed an eighteen-year-old boy, Camilla."

I know what he's doing, and I don't play into it. I don't question it.

"I thought you didn't hurt children. Or did that change too?"

He looks over at me. "He wasn't a child. He was a grown man. Old enough to vote. Old enough to buy cigarettes. Old enough to go to prison."

My lips part. "Not in his mother's eyes."

Nathan slowly laughs. "You've always been feisty, Camilla. Nothing has changed."

"Where is everyone?" I change subjects quickly because I can't bear to think of the mother who doesn't know she's lost a child yet.

The compound was always crawling with people. But not tonight. I don't know what's changed, if anything, or if it's the time of night.

Trimmers.

Truck drivers.

Workers.

Friends.

"Things have changed since you left," he whispers. "People change, don't they?"

"Not you." I don't give him anything more.

"How so?"

"Monsters are born evil, Nathan."

Nathan laughs. "I suppose you're right. And sometimes, when people change, it isn't always for the better. Wouldn't you agree, Camilla?"

I lean back in the chair and rest my arms on the armrests but don't answer his question. I feel his stare burn through the side of my face.

"You were always a great lay. With your tight nipples and banging body."

He whistles through his teeth, and my skin crawls.

"I'm not here to discuss that, Nathan. I'm here to tell you that I don't have your money."

"You might not have it, but I know you took it. And that family of yours? Your son, Malik, looks just like you. We could have had beautiful children together, Camilla."

I try to see the trees, but my vision grows blurry. I try to shake it off, but I can't. "What did you do to me, asshole?"

Nathan grows into a shadow of a man as he stands above me.

"I know a lot of people, Camilla. You know that. I can make people die and disappear. Never be heard from again."

My vision begins to spin, and the trees become the house and the house becomes the trees. "What—" But I can't speak, and I feel myself slide out of the chair and onto the concrete.

"Go to sleep, Camilla. We'll speak when you wake up."

Please help me.

I feel Nathan's hand on mine as he bends, kisses the top of my head, and says, "I'll be back momentarily."

30

Calder

"What do you mean, Camilla is gone, Mom?" I whisper, looking back to Malik, who's in the living room, watching television with Red asleep at his side, Williams asleep on the other side of him.

"She left, and she left you this letter for you." My mom hands me an envelope and I tear into it.

> *Dear Calder,*
>
> *There is a time in life when we're called to stand up for what we believe in, even at the cost of our families, even at the cost of our own life.*
>
> *I took Nathan's money, and that's what he's looking for. I took the two million dollars when I left Alderpoint for good. I stole it and I think he knows it was me, especially after he found out Joe died. Cal, I saw things that weren't right. I think he sent Cannon Watson to scare me into giving it back. The money is spent and gone and while I can't give the details as to how it was spent, I need you to trust me that I'm doing something right and just with it. I will not subject*

you to the details, as it could blow what I've been working for since I left that place in the past. But you need to trust me.

If something happens to me, my ranch has a buyer. An old friend of mine from Salinas. Her name is Sam Fulton. She'll pay full price, and it will be handled discreetly. Take that money to raise Malik. Joe would have wanted it that way. You'll find the full appraisal in this envelope with the buyer's contact information. I'm sorry this wasn't better planned, and I'm sorry I don't have the money to give you outright. I hope you understand.

And last, I'm in love with you, and I didn't realize it until I was able to let Joe be free—and me, too, for that matter. I believe now that God gave me two men to love unconditionally and replaced one with the other. I just didn't see it. But Malik did.

All my love,

Mil

"She went to settle the score with Nathan." My hands grow sweaty. Panic builds in me.

My stomach drops when I realize where she went. "I ... I need to go." My stare is hard when I find my mother's eyes.

"Where are you going, Cal?"

"I'm going to get Camilla."

I can't tell my mom where I'm going. She'll tell Chief McBride. She'll fold out of fear. And then the whole Humboldt County law enforcement unit will be out looking for us, and we don't need that right now. Not yet.

I grab my jacket and leave my parents' place and make the drive to Alderpoint, not knowing exactly where I'm going.

I drive between eighty and ninety miles an hour until I take the Garberville exit off Highway 101 to Alderpoint Road. I call her cell phone, and it goes straight to voice mail.

"Mil, it's Cal. Call me back, please. We're all worried about you. I won't call the authorities. I just need to know you're all right." I leave a message for two reasons. One, I want her to know I'm looking for her, and two, I want those who might be listening to her voice mail, screening her calls and texts, to know that I'm looking for her.

"Where are you, Mil? Come on. Give me a sign," I say after I hang up.

In the dark, this road is different. It's more haunting. My headlights bounce off the abandoned cars. Cars that have caught fire and are used as houses for transients making their way up the road for summer work.

I'll drive down each road until I see Camilla's truck. That's my plan.

Worry consumes my body in a slow tremble. I try not to live there.

I call her phone again, and once again, it goes straight to voice mail. I swallow the fear that creeps up my throat. The fear that takes me to places I'd rather not visit.

I take a turn down a road off to the left at the bottom of Alderpoint Road.

It ends quickly, but it doesn't stop me from getting out of my truck with a flashlight and a gun. The same gun that I witnessed murdered a man.

"The truth always prevails, Calder," my dad always used to say and still does when he gets the chance.

I creep quietly along the tree line and notice that the property has been eaten alive with berry briars. This isn't Nathan's compound. It's too close to town. Not buried deep enough for the misdoings and evil he likes to create around himself.

Maybe there was an arresting address for Cannon Watson.

But without cell service, I can't look a damn thing up. I make my way back to my truck, turn around, and pull out onto Alderpoint Road again.

You should have left with a plan, idiot. You shouldn't have left without knowing where the fuck you were going. Smart, Cal. Real smart.

Back on the main road, I take another road down off to the left. I could get shot and killed for driving onto people's property up here.

It's a small cabin with a motion light on the peak of the roof, and it illuminates when I drive up. Still not close enough to see if they have cameras, I make sure to park in the shadows. The motion light doesn't stop me from hopping out of my truck while staying in the shadows and peeking in the windows.

Nothing. I guess when half of your sole purpose in life is left in the hands of evil, you don't think. You react and run.

But I'm here, and I can't leave until I come home with Mil.

I try her cell phone one more time, and it goes straight to voice mail. I push the bile down that's building in my throat. I can't rightfully think straight when fear is knocking on the back door. Like an automatic door, I just keep working.

In the dark, I drive farther up the road.

And I drive.

And I drive.

And I dip down another driveway, only to find another dark place.

And another dark place.

And another dark place after that.

Until everything is so dark and so quiet.

I pull over and slam my hands against the steering wheel. "Fuck!"

By this time, it's three in the morning, and I know I'll need sleep for tomorrow.

"Mil, where are you? Please. Just give me a sign."

Hastily, I pull a sweatshirt out from behind the seat and rest my head against it. I focus on a tree branch straight ahead in the darkness.

It's when I finally drift off to sleep that someone knocks on the window.

When I look up, I can't believe whom I'm staring at.

I look around to make sure that my surroundings were as I left them. The tree branch. It's still dark out. Quickly and maybe frantically, I roll down the window.

"Joe, what—how—what are you—how are you here?"

Joe Crane begins to speak, but I can't hear what he's saying. It's still dark out.

"Joe, I can't hear you."

I try to get out of the truck, but I can't. The door is locked, and I can't find out how to unlock it. Joe's face changes. Fear maybe. He still speaks, and I begin to panic.

"JOE! I can't hear you! Please. Talk louder! The door is locked! Can you unlock the door?"

But he doesn't budge. He doesn't move.

Joe's image starts to fade.

"Joe!"

And then Joe's voice yells, "Look for the triangle!"

I jump awake when I hear a loud noise.

The early morning light is shining through the trees, and I push open the truck door, jump out, and suck a few mouthfuls of air, bending at my waist. When I'm back up again, my hands clasped behind my head.

Look for the triangle.

Look for the triangle.

Look for the triangle.

Look for the triangle.

How the fuck am I going to find a triangle?

"Dammit!" I kick the tire of my truck and climb back in.

I pull out onto the main road again and drive.

"Look for the triangle."

My eyes scan from left to right and back again as I drive.

A green car passes me, going the opposite direction, with a bumper sticker that says *Emerald Triangle Fringe* with a pot leaf as part of the brand. I've seen it before, but I can't place where.

Can that be what Joe was talking about? No way it's that quick to appear.

I don't feel as tired as I should. Adrenaline courses through my veins. I take my eyes off the road and notice a few bars on my phone, so I take the opportunity to make another call to Camilla again, and again, it goes straight to voice mail.

"Hey, Mil. It's me. Call me when you get this."

My bars disappear again.

In my rearview mirror, I see a truck gaining on me.

Gaining on me.

Gaining on me.

Gaining on me.

When the truck comes into view, I see that it's Casey.

I pull over and hop out of the truck, and he does the same.

"What the hell are you doing here?" I ask.

"I couldn't let you do this shit by yourself." From behind his seat, he takes his gun and tucks it into his waist. Then, he reaches for a piece of paper on his dash. "I had Denton pull arrest records for Nathan Amben and Cannon Watson." He hands me the records. "Both addresses are in Garberville, and it wouldn't go hurt to look. And whenever you're ready, I'd love the story on how all this shit got started anyway. Get in with me. You're too crazed to drive. Probably tired as hell too."

As we chase the road to the bottom, I fill Casey in on what's transpired with Nathan Amben and what Camilla has told me thus far.

She took the money.

She had good reason.

And Nathan wants it back.

She's now somewhere on Alderpoint Road, the compound she used to work on when she met Joe, telling Nathan that she doesn't have his money.

"She took his money but doesn't have it?" Casey clarifies. "Did she spend it?"

"If she took it and spent it—it wasn't on herself."

"All right, well, let's find her," Casey says.

We drive to the first address, and it's a business, a bail bonds business.

"*Alex's Bail Bonds*," Casey reads aloud as we hop out of the truck. "What do you think you're going to find inside?" Casey asks.

"I don't know, but it's worth a shot."

Casey and I walk in, and the bell rings above the door.

"Can I help you?" the woman behind the counter says.

"Looking for Nathan Amben. You know where I can find him?"

Straight-faced, she looks me dead in the eyes and says, "Can't help you."

"Does he come around here?" I try again, and my body language softens.

"Not anymore." She eyes Casey and me up and down. "You two undercover cops or Feds or what? We're legit here." She takes her framed business license from the wall and slides it across the counter with a screech. "Legit. I know how you guys work. You think all the businesses in Garberville are just drug fronts for something more sinister. But you're barking up the wrong tree," she snaps.

Casey looks to me, and I look to the woman. "Is your name Alex?"

"Yeah. Who wants to know?" she asks, the chip still weighing on her shoulder.

"Look, we're not Feds. We're not police officers. We're just looking for Nathan Amben. We have product we'd like him to take a look at."

Alex's face changes. "Are you playing me for an idiot? Listen, I don't do business with Nathan anymore. Not many of us do anymore." She crosses her arms. "Now, if you'll excuse me, I have work to do."

I nod but not before scratching my number down for Alex. "Call me if he comes back into town?"

She leaves my number on the counter and walks to the back, calling behind her, "He won't. And I wouldn't hold your breath."

When we go to leave, I notice the sticker that says *Emerald Triangle Fringe* in the window of a black truck that sits idle, a man on his phone.

Bingo.

"We'll wait to see where this black truck goes," I say.

"What? Why?"

I can't tell Casey that I saw a dead Joe Crane in my sleep. That he came to me in a dream. So, instead, I say, "It's a hunch."

Casey and I walk back out to the truck, and we sit here and wait. Not fifteen minutes later, the man in the black truck throws his phone on the dashboard, runs into the bail bonds shop, and runs back out with a bag.

Trying to follow the black truck with a safe distance between us, Casey asks, "Why do you think she took the money?"

"I don't know. But Mil always has a reason. She wouldn't steal something from someone if it wasn't the right thing to do."

"You're not wrong. Not that I know her well, but I trust you, and you trust her. But what on God's green earth would persuade Camilla to steal two million dollars from one of the biggest drug lords in Humboldt?"

The black truck takes a left and then a right and another right.

"Let's just see where this takes us."

"Guess I'm just along for the ride, man."

"Good."

The black truck turns on Alderpoint Road.

Hopefully, it will lead us to Camilla.

When the black truck pulls over and the driver hops out, I play it cool, and we continue to keep driving. In my rearview mirror, I see the driver make a phone call.

"Who's he calling?"

"Do you think he's on to us? You think he knows we were following him?"

"Maybe."

The driver hangs up the phone, and without giving us a second glance, he passes us on the one-way road.

I just hope we're not walking into a death trap.

And if we are, then I hope three of us can make it out alive.

31

Camilla

It's been said that redwood trees are not just trees; they're part of a complex community of living things, and the ecosystem relies on the redwood trees for protection. It's proven that redwood trees must have heavy coastal fog to reach their full height and girth. Redwood trees can live between five hundred to seven hundred years, even up to two thousand years. It starts as a seed, and if it survives its first winter and gets the appropriate nutrients from its ecosystem, it can grow into a massive protector.

Maybe that's what my sister and I needed from our father and didn't get. Maybe we had an idea of what a dad should be. A mammoth, a giant to us when we were children. He didn't start out hitting us. That started when his drinking took off.

I remember the first time.

I was four, sitting at the kitchen table. I spilled my cereal, and it was his hand that came up and hit my chin first. My head moved upward so quickly that I thought something had come up from the ground. But when I looked up at my father, my mouth bleeding and the chips of small teeth floating in my mouth among the taste of metallic, I saw anger in his eyes.

What I remember most about that moment isn't that he hit me for the first time; it's the look on his face when I stared into his eyes. As a four-year-old, I could never put a word to his beady eyes, his red face, and the grimace he wore for days afterward. My little four-year-old mind couldn't quite understand what happened that day. I hadn't seen anything happen. I'd felt it, yes. I'd felt it for weeks after, but I couldn't understand what had happened until it happened again.

But it was my mother who had swooped me up that morning and carried me to the bathroom. She grabbed a towel from the rack, got it wet, and cleaned the blood. She didn't say a word. She didn't cry, and I didn't cry, but I watched her. I saw the fear in her eyes every time she turned back to me to see my chin, my face. My mother said one thing once the bleeding subsided.

She said, "At least they're your baby teeth."

And so, I'd thought, *Thank goodness it wasn't worse. Thank goodness it was just this. Yes, maybe I lost teeth, but I was going to lose them anyway. See, it's not that bad.*

But when it happened a third time after I dropped a glass of water, I saw the rage in my father's eyes. I smelled the alcohol on his breath when he gripped my chin so hard that his fingers dug into my jawbone.

He said, "Stupid little brat. Always spilling stuff." And then he let go of my face and walked away. "Clean it up," he barked and walked out the front door.

My mom wasn't home, and my sister was in her room.

And do you know what I said to myself as I cleaned up the water, my heart lying broken on the kitchen floor? I thought, *At least I still have my teeth. It could have been worse.*

At a young age, I began minimizing the way people treated me with, *It could have been worse.* As if I should have been grateful it wasn't worse.

So, from a little girl, I started to think I deserved what I got. That most fathers probably hit their daughters, knocked their teeth out when no one was looking, and nobody said a word.

My mother never told anyone how my father hit her and talked nasty to her. My mother never talked to us about it. I never talked to Kamden, and so none of us ever discussed the fact that we were all being abused by a man who was supposed to protect us. It was just accepted that it was what it was.

At age nine, I remember being with Sam and her family on a vacation. Her father always treated her mother kindly. He never raised a hand to her, but of course, he wouldn't in front of others, right? Because that only happened when others weren't watching.

As we walked out of our hotel and into the parking lot, a man and a woman were fighting, and the man took his fist and hit the woman in the face. It didn't faze me, but when I looked over at Sam and her mother and saw their reaction was of horror and Sam's dad rushed us inside to call the police, I knew from that moment on that my reaction was nothing close to normal. That what we had witnessed in the parking lot was horrific—or that was what I'd read on Sam's and her mother's faces. That I should have been appalled.

Later that night, Sam asked me if I was all right with the situation earlier. She said she'd never seen that happen before and that she was scared. What I found out right there and then was that what was going on at home was horrific and unacceptable. But what was I to do? My father should have been my redwood tree, my protector, but instead, he'd become our nightmare.

It's the morning light that taunts my eyelids, coaxing them with quiet promises of a bright day.

My head begins to throb when I try to turn on my side.

Memories begin to attach themselves to my conscience.

I open my eyes.

It's a bright room.

One I don't remember.

When I slept in Nathan's house, it was always in his bedroom, his lair.

But this room is light and airy. Sheer curtains hang in their rightful place. It's peaceful.

I look down and see that I'm wearing a white nightgown, but I don't remember changing. My clothes hang nicely over the antique chair in the corner of the bedroom.

When I try to sit up, I realize my right arm is handcuffed to the bed.

I remember what happened up until my vision grew blurry. I was to lure Nathan in.

It was the SEAL team who was going to grab the three remaining girls from Nathan's grips on the compound and then come back for me.

My insides grow queasy when I realize why Nathan dressed me in the nightgown. He was doing a body search, and he found what he was looking for. When I reach into my ear, I notice the earpiece is missing—my only communication with Landon, the SEAL team leader.

Shit.

How the hell did he drug me without touching me?

Chemical warfare. Nathan has always been a big fan of that, wanting as little mess as possible. A germaphobe some might consider him.

But he's never messed with Camilla Crane.

I stew and wait and think about what all I will do next and try not to let my heart, which is crashing against my chest, remove the idea that I'll make it out alive.

You need to make it out alive, Camilla. You have a son to finish raising.

And my mind drifts to Calder.

The message I left him. I wince. My regret. I will him to understand that what I said was out of anger and fear for my mother. I was too harsh, and if I have the opportunity to tell him I'm sorry, I'll snatch up those moments as if stealing them from my memory.

You'll think of a way to get out of this, Mil. You always do.

It's then that I remember the words my father spoke a week before he died.

He said to me, "Camilla, if you are to survive in this world, you must meet your enemy's weakness. There's only birth and death in this life—that's the only thing guaranteed." So, he did give sound advice; it just wasn't for the faint of heart. And my father wasn't for the faint of heart.

I survived my father. And if he didn't kill me, I know I can survive Nathan. I know how to take him down. Make him fold, putty in my hands. It might take some convincing, but I know if I'm patient enough, it will work.

I need to raise my son.

I need to tell Calder I'm sorry.

And my mother is in good hands with Sam. Even if she does go to prison, she's the one who had to make her side of the street clean.

And I need to live so that my life story has a happy ending, not just for me, but also for my family.

Three hours later, Nathan knocks on the door gently.

"May I come in?" Nathan says, peeking through the ajar door.

"Absolutely." I move my bare leg so that if he stands at the foot of the bed, he might get a tiny glimpse of what he saw all those years ago. Felt. Licked.

Nathan comes in and quietly shuts the door behind him, as if he were a gentleman. As if he were the superhero of the story.

Nathan, all six feet of him, stands, at a distance from the bedside.

Casually, I look over at him, as if this position on my back, my right hand handcuffed to the bedpost, doesn't bother me. I bite my lower lip and stare back at him.

His eyes graze over my body. "You were always my favorite, Camilla. So slim and perfect." Nathan leans against the dresser, his arms crossed over his big, broad chest.

My stomach turns as his eyes stop at my breasts.

Breathe, Mil. Think about a time when you were relaxed.

Me, Calder, and Malik at the Giants game a year ago. It was the first time I felt whole in a long time. As if the hole in my heart grew just a bit smaller. I could breathe deeper and see more clearly, untainted by handfuls of grief.

"If you hadn't taken my money, Camilla, I wouldn't keep you here. I'd have no reason to keep you here."

What I want to ask is, *Then, why keep me here?* But I don't. It's not part of the plan.

So, instead, I say, "Can I at least take a shower?"

Nathan thinks about it. His gaze meets my eyes. "Five minutes."

He goes to the bathroom, retrieves a towel, sets it on the counter. Then, he pulls a key from his pocket and unlocks the cuff.

"Thank you," I say, taking my left hand and rubbing my right wrist.

Nathan helps me up and stares down into my eyes. "Your eyes, they don't seem as brown as they used to be. Is that what lying does?"

Instead of answering his question, I pull my arms up over my head, allowing him to pull the cotton nightgown over my head.

Once again, his eyes rake over my body.

"Can I shower now?" I ask.

"Yes," slithers from his lips, but not without a slow caress of my hips. "You were the best ride in town, Camilla." He whistles through his teeth.

"Shower with me?" I ask.

He shakes his head. "I'll watch."

Barely, I smile and walk into the bathroom, my stomach turning with disgust. His footfalls are behind me, giving me enough distance to breathe.

One. Two. Three. I exhale.

Nathan steps in front of me to turn on the shower with the glass doors. He throws the towel over the top of the shower and helps me in.

The hot water falls down my back, and I put my head under the steady stream and gently slide my hands over my breasts. I feel Nathan's gaze.

I take the bar of soap and move it along my shoulders, my arms, my breasts for far longer than I should, down my thighs, between my legs, and when I do that, I make sure he's watching. I see what I'm doing to him. I know what he feels like when he's hard against me and inside me and when he hits the point of no return.

"What are you going to do with me?" I ask as I begin to wash my hair.

"I don't know yet."

32

Calder

We followed the black truck back up Alderpoint Road, and when it went down a dirt road, we waited off the main road. Sure as shit, a man matching Nathan Amben's likeness from the arrest photos that Casey brought pulled out onto the main road a few hours ago.

It's nightfall now, and I have Casey drop me off in the dark at the top of the dirt road.

"This is the stupidest thing you've ever fucking done, dude."

I put my backpack on. "What would you do if this were Tess?"

Casey slowly nods. "Point taken. But I was more talking about you going it alone and not letting me go with you."

I shake my head. "No, you have a wife and a baby on the way, Case."

"What about Colt?"

"Same thing. I'm not going to take my brothers away from their families." I shut the truck door and lean in the window.

"What about Malik?" Casey asks.

"That's different."

"How? Because he's not your blood?"

"No, it's different because I'm trying to save his mom."

Casey allows a rush of air to escape his mouth. "What the fuck am I going to tell Mom if you fucking die out here?"

"I don't know."

"No, you know what? Fuck this shit. I'm going with you." Casey rolls up the window that I'm leaning in, turns off the ignition, and climbs out of the truck. But not before grabbing his handgun under his seat.

"You're not going, Casey."

"This isn't up for discussion."

"Stop. No." I meet him at the front of the truck. "If something happens to you, I—"

"Don't worry, Cal. We're not going to die today. God's not ready for two more Atwood brothers. I'm sure as hell that Conroy is up there, giving heaven hell." Casey loads his gun.

I roll my eyes. "Fine. But you're only going to the gate."

"Fuck the gate. I'm going all the way in."

I shake my head as I take the lead, and we make our way down the winding road to Nathan's place.

"Do they have booby traps and shit?"

We walk quietly in the brush.

I shrug. "Not sure. Guess we'll find out."

Casey shakes his head, and we continue to walk for what seems like a half hour. We see a porch light and stop in our tracks. Casey gives me the hand signal to stop—the hunting code we established when we were kids.

We stop.

Listen.

And the only thing we hear is the land, alive with frogs, peepers, and whatever else lives out in Alderpoint on summer nights.

We wait.

Casey holds up his fist to his ear, straining to listen. His eyes lock on mine, as if to say, *Did you hear that?*

But I don't hear anything—until I hear the leaves crunch.

My heart starts to crash against my chest. Holding my breath, I strain to listen and hear the leaves rustle again, like footsteps.

Casey and I lock eyes and quietly move behind the alder that's in front of us.

We listen.

The rustle of leaves comes again, though this time, it's closer.

It's so dark that I can barely see.

But then I see the white stripes of a black skunk. The skunk waddles its way closer to us. Its nose is in the air, taking in the unfamiliar scent.

"Don't. Move."

The skunk makes its way past us.

Once it's out of earshot, I carefully let out a breath. "Come on," I say to Casey.

"That was a close one. I hate skunks. Good-for-nothing fucking rodents."

The blackness draws us in, and we move like we know where we're going.

Just follow the road.

After a few minutes, headlights off in the distance catch my eye.

"Down," I say.

Casey and I drop down into the leaves as the headlights negotiate the twists and turns of the road. After what feels like forever, it finally reaches us and keeps going. I can barely make note of the old-style Toyota Tacoma. The body color, maybe silver. I try to see if there's a license plate from behind, but I don't see one, which isn't unusual out here. Nothing is unusual out here. Nothing's too illegal. Kidnapping. Murder.

"Coast is clear," Casey says.

We stand when the taillights of the truck disappear.

After thirty minutes, we finally see a light, a porch light of some sort.

"That's Nathan's house."

Casey looks at me. "That's no house. That's a goddamn mansion."

That's when Casey trips on something, sending him face-first into the ground.

Then, dogs—big dogs—begin to bark.

"Think I found a booby trap." Casey pulls a fishing line. "And those dogs don't sound like Chihuahuas either."

"Run!" I whisper-yell.

And we both take off in a dead sprint through the darkness.

The dogs' barks are moving closer, and there's more than one. Two, maybe three.

"Here," Casey whispers breathlessly to a set of six-inch boards going up a tree.

"A death trap?" I say.

"And our alternative?" Casey says, looking down from the boards he's already begun climbing.

I shrug and climb up behind him.

I hear the dogs again, closer.

"Anytime, Case."

Casey hops up, and I pray to God the floor of the tree house doesn't fall through.

The dogs snapping and snarling draw closer as I peek out the slits between the boards of one of the makeshift walls.

"Uh, Cal, I'm not sure we're alone."

I turn my head to see what Casey's looking at.

A man sits in the corner. The gunshot wound to the head is fresh.

"Holy—" But I quiet as I hear the dogs gaining on our scent, then voices.

Casey and I exchange glances and check our guns.

Two voices grow closer. It sounds like two men. The dogs' barks grow farther and farther away in another direction.

But the voices become clearer.

"I'm not fucking going up there and grabbing the body. It's your turn, asshole. I did the last one."

Minions, Casey and I conclude. Minions on a grow, doing the grunt work. Hoping one day to be the right-hand men for a drug lord. Mid-level career criminals. Maybe some outstanding warrants for drug sales. Maybe grand theft, but nothing too violent.

"The last time I did the body, I couldn't sleep for weeks, man. Come on."

"Fucking baby," the other guy says.

Their footsteps fall right below us.

"Fuck it. Leave the body. Let's go follow the dogs. Probably another skunk tripped the line again."

After a long pause, the men start to move again, and after several seconds, Casey and I let out sighs of relief. Once the dogs' barks fade into the distance and nothing is heard, except for the occasional bullfrog, we climb down the steps of the tree house.

When we get to the bottom of the tree ladder and plant our feet on solid ground, red lasers appear on our chests.

"Don't fucking move," the commanding voice says.

33

Camilla

It's late into the evening when Nathan returns to my bedroom.

"It's late," he says from the bedroom door, his eyes raking over my body.

He steps into the room and pulls back the covers. "Get in."

I do. "Can you at least uncuff me, so I can get some sleep? Just for a few hours?"

Nathan thinks about it. "You took money from me, Camilla. How can I trust you?" He sits down on top of the covers next to me. Gently takes his hand and runs it over my chest. "Even after childbirth, Camilla, your breasts are still as firm as I remember them."

I want to throw up because all I can think about is Calder. Deep down inside, I feel as though I'm cheating on him. "I remember how perfectly your mouth fit around them," I whisper.

Nathan smiles. "Do you still enjoy your nipples being tugged on?"

I nod, shy.

Nathan pulls back the covers and pulls the nightgown up over my head, exposing my breasts.

Nathan's eyes grow with excitement, though he tries to play it cool.

He leans back and pulls the key from his pocket and unlocks the handcuff, freeing my hand.

"Thank you," I say, rubbing my wrist, as if he'd done a favor for me.

Nathan walks to the chair across the room, unzips the zipper to his jeans, and frees himself.

"Touch your breasts," he says.

I do, taking one and then both into my hands.

Nathan's hand slides down his erection as he watches me.

"Put your finger inside yourself."

Breathe, Camilla. Just breathe.

And when I do, I watch his hand slide up and down on his erection, and for a moment, he closes his eyes.

I slide my finger into my folds again and quietly call out, "Ahhh."

"Yeah," he says. "Just like that." He strokes himself a little faster.

"You know what would feel better?" I say breathlessly.

"Tell me."

"You inside me. Like old times. No one will know. Just me and you."

Nathan shakes his head. "I can't fuck a woman who fucked me over, Camilla. You know that."

His eyes grow narrow as he holds himself in his own hands.

I'm hesitant at first, but then I stand, and step toward him. Another step.

Nathan has never been able to turn down a beautiful woman.

Three steps.

He looks up at me, and I take him by the hand and lead him back to the bed. I bend over at first. I know how he likes to take women from behind.

"Like this?" I say.

I hear his sigh and feel his hands slide to my backside, pulling my thighs apart. His hands move around my ass, and he reaches around to my front, sliding his finger into my folds.

Breathe, Mil. Breathe.

"God, Camilla."

"Wait." I rock against him, not allowing him to insert his fingers inside me. I push myself to the bed and rest my back against the mattress. "I want to watch," I whisper and open myself up to him, spreading my arms across the bed.

Nathan drops his head and grins as he climbs on top of me, putting himself right outside my folds with anticipation.

"Kiss me," I say, my hips moving, waiting for him.

"I can't," he sighs.

"Please," I beg.

Nathan drops his head and stands. He takes his gun and puts it on the nightstand. Throws his underwear and jeans to the floor and climbs back on top of me. He rests his body on my body, and his mouth meets mine. I kiss him deeply and moan softly into his mouth, and he hardens the kiss, biting on my lower lip right when he pulls away to pant. I pull him closer and wrap my legs around his as I retrieve the letter opener from under the pillow and shove it through his back.

He lets out a slow groan. His eyes wide, he looks down at me, and I push myself from underneath him and try to stand. Nathan falls to the bed. He is still alive but can't talk.

"You threatened the wrong woman, Nathan." My voice is shaky with nerves. "I took your money. I was the one moving the women from this encampment, so you couldn't hurt anyone else. I took your money, and I paid for these women to be rescued. While you were trying to ruin lives, I was trying to save them. And now, you won't get another chance to do that. Because it ends right now."

"Oh, dear." I hear a voice say from outside the bedroom door.

"My apologies, Camilla, for not introducing myself sooner. My name is Michelangelo," he says in an accent.

"Who—who the hell are you?" I don't remember a Michelangelo.

The tall man fills the doorway of the bedroom.

He looks down at Nathan, whose back is barely moving. My eyes drift to Nathan's gun on the nightstand, and in one swift movement, Michelangelo beats me to it.

My heart crashes against my chest as I stand here.

Before he goes to Nathan, he tosses me a bathrobe. "Here, put this on."

"Listen." My voice is steady now. "Please let me go. I won't tell anyone about this. Please."

I didn't anticipate someone else. Someone hiding in the shadows. Someone watching. Someone lurking. I can't beat him at his own game if I don't know who he is in the first place.

Michelangelo quickly removes the letter opener from Nathan's back with a grunt. Nathan lets out a soft and sick moan, a gurgle. The dark maroon thickness gathers like a puddle on his back, making its way down the sides of him.

The peculiar thing is, Michelangelo doesn't try to stop the bleeding. He just sits down in the chair, the gun aimed at me, and he watches Nathan's consciousness leave his body. Nathan's eyes were once wide with fear and have changed to hollow, empty.

This reminds me of my father, a tall, willowy man, made for brashness and cruelty.

My eyes move from Nathan to Michelangelo. Unsure of what he'll do next, I tighten the robe around me and ask him if I can sit, say that I'm light-headed, that I've never seen death before.

"Free country," he whispers, still watching Nathan.

"I didn't mean to," I lie. "It all happened so quickly."

After a long moment of silence, Michelangelo stands, walks to Nathan, and whispers something that I can't understand. It's not that I can't hear him; it's because of the language. It's not English, but it flows so seamlessly from his mouth. The words that are strung together sound more like a song, soft and tired, than a sentence. Maybe a prayer.

"Come," he says to me.

"Where are we going?" I ask.

This time, he waves the gun in the direction he wants me to go. "Just come."

I stand and take the lead out the bedroom door and into the hallway.

"This way." He motions with the gun to go left, which takes us back out to the kitchen.

He signals to a tall barstool at the kitchen counter. "Sit."

I do.

Michelangelo sets the gun down on the granite countertop. "Are you hungry?" he asks.

"No, thank you."

"Are you sure? You are very thin. You need food."

Slowly, I nod. "I'm good. Thank you."

"I will make eggs."

Michelangelo turns his back to me.

He turns his back to the gun.

Is this a test? A test of trust?

"You could take the gun and shoot me in the back; however, if you do that, you will not know where the final three girls are."

Bile rises to my throat.

He knows.

He takes the egg carton from the double-sided stainless steel refrigerator, which is more geared to feed a hotel full of people than one single person.

"What do you mean?" I wait, holding my breath.

Michelangelo takes the eggs and a bowl and a fork and sets them down on the counter between us. He opens the egg carton, cracks an egg on the side of the glass bowl, and dumps it into the bowl. "Do you think just because my English isn't the best, that I'm stupid?"

He smiles, takes another egg, and cracks it open against the side of the bowl. After he repeats this process four times, he grabs a pan from below the counter, in a cupboard that I can't see.

"I catch on when girls slowly leave. They just … disappear into thin air." He snaps his fingers and stares back at me while he takes a fork and stirs the eggs. "Do you like salt and pepper in your eggs, Camilla?"

I nod even though I was clear that I'm not hungry.

Michelangelo puts salt and pepper in the eggs and then transfers them to the pan. Moves over to the stove and begins to cook them.

"You will make good for American men." He grins. "You stole women from us."

I don't say anything.

Michelangelo thinks for a moment and grins again. "At first, thought I go crazy. Like, where are the women going? Did I get rid of them and not remember?"

He laughs, as though it were all a funny joke. He bends at his waist, still laughing. Laughing so hard that his face is turning red. Then, his laughter turns to silence that rips through the kitchen, the house, like a trail of gunshots.

"I think, I can't be crazy. So, I set up cameras." His stare is hard. "Do you know what I found, Camilla?" he asks and then turns to grab two plates from the cabinet next to the refrigerator and sets them on the counter next to the pan. Carefully, he separates the eggs onto two different plates. "I found men sneaking around our property. So, you know what I did?"

"What?" I can barely breathe.

"I shot and killed them."

Michelangelo searches my face for a reaction, but I don't give him one.

"What do they have to do with me?"

I see him smile again, and he puts a plate of eggs in front of me.

"Do you like ketchup on your eggs? It's an American thing that I enjoy very much." He shrugs.

"No."

"Suit yourself," he says as he smothers his eggs with ketchup.

He walks over to my side of the counter and sits next to me. "Your mother was very nice to me. Had long talk with her. It had been years since I had seen her last. And your father. He deserved to die for what he did. I don't blame your mother one bit for doing what she did."

Air leaves my lungs, and the large kitchen grows extremely small. A trickle of sweat starts at the base of the back of my neck.

How does he know this?

"Nathan said you would be a good find." He takes a bite of his eggs, nodding. "You still don't recognize me?"

My mind explodes with different scenarios, but I can't focus on any of them.

"Some might call it grooming, you know, be kind, and relate experiences, build friendship and then take her away from everything she knows." Michelangelo wipes his mouth with a napkin. "Would you like a napkin, Camilla?" His eyes pierce mine.

"No." My gut twists.

"You were my first prey. But I just couldn't do it, couldn't put drug in your body, so instead, I offered you a place in Humboldt County on Nathan's farm." He chuckles, pinching invisible crumbs between his pointer finger and thumb. "So, Nathan says to me, 'Michelangelo, send her to me, and I'll show you how.'"

Oh my God.

Phillip.

The hired hand on our farm told me there was trim work in Humboldt County. How could I have been so stupid?

"I know; I know. I look different. Put on a lot of weight, worked out. Skinny back then." He touches his stomach.

"How—you don't even look the same," I whisper in disbelief.

"Nathan got very mad at me. Say I botched the job because I let my heart fall for you. And then he steals you from me right under my nose." He's still smiling. "But now, I see the money Nathan makes selling girls. And it's greed, Camilla. Greed got the best of Michelangelo. I can get three times the amount for you that I'd get for three young girls combined."

"But they're young and beautiful. I'm not as young or as beautiful."

Michelangelo shakes his head and wipes his mouth once more. "No, no, no. Men like seasoned women with beautiful bodies. Women with experience. Old men love. And they are very, very, very wealthy. Leaders of our country. America." Something catches his attention, and his eyes zero in on it. He goes on. "We will do an exchange tonight with a wealthy man from the East Coast." Michelangelo stands and looks at my untouched eggs. "You will need protein, Camilla, for the trip east. Eat."

"No."

He shrugs. Takes our plates, washes them. When he turns his back to me, I grab the gun from the counter and aim it at his back.

Michelangelo laughs. "Are you going to shoot me?"

"Don't fucking move." I hold the gun out in front of me with two hands.

Michelangelo stops washing the dishes and gently sets the plates down in the sink.

"Move to the sofa," I say through gritted teeth as I follow him to the living room.

"For the record, I knew it was you the whole time. You took Nathan's money."

"Yeah. How did you know that?" With my free hand, I pat him down for more weapons. "Sit."

Casually, he sits down on the sofa. "I wasn't going to tell him because I needed Nathan dead, so I could take over the business. He was not giving me my full cut, and I do all the work. I track the girls. I arrange the private flights and the use of—how you say … indiscretion?"

I cock the gun, and with my finger on the trigger, I aim the gun at his head and fire.

34

Calder

The men take our weapons and our phones and zip-tie our wrists together.

"What the fuck are you doing here? What's your affiliation with Nathan Amben?" the leader of the group says. He's the tall one.

"None of your fucking business." There's no way in hell I'm going to tell them I'm here to rescue the woman I love. If she's in that house, I'm not leaving here without her.

A man leans over to the leader as he scrolls through my phone and whispers something in his ear.

The leader looks down at my phone. "How the fuck do you know Camilla Crane?"

I drop my head slightly and stare the man down. "How do you know Camilla Crane?"

Another man approaches the leader from the darkness and whispers something to the man for a bit.

The leader says, "Take off the zip ties."

The man motions to the team, and they take us by our arms and lead us into darkness.

After several minutes of walking, we finally reach a makeshift hut in the middle of a forest.

Casey leans over. "This is something out of a fucking movie."

The makeshift hut is big inside.

"Please, sit," the leader says in a nicer tone.

Two of the men stay outside, and two follow us in the hut.

The man lights a lantern that hangs from a log, which holds the middle of the hut up.

After a long pause, the man reaches his hand out to Casey and me. "My name is Landon Stone, and this is Steven Broker."

"What the hell is going on?" I ask.

Landon looks to Steven and back to Casey and me. "Camilla didn't tell you?"

"Tell me what? Who the hell are you guys?"

Landon presses his lips together in a tight line. "You're Calder Atwood. Born and bred in Dillon Creek, California. You were a damn good pitcher and almost played college ball until you hurt your arm. Casey Atwood, PBR champion with a baby on the way. You married Tess Morgan, your high school sweetheart."

"What? Do you think by knowing this shit, that will make us roll over? This shit is online," Casey spits out.

"And you, Cal, have been with Camilla since Joe died. About the same time we were hired," Landon says.

"Excuse me?" I say. "Hired? Who the hell hired you?"

Landon grins. "Camilla. And before you two yahoos showed up, we were about to make our move on the final three young women and free Camilla."

My breath leaves me. "You saw her?"

Landon drops his head and laughs. "She didn't tell you anything, did she?"

This comment makes me grow angry, as if I'm some sort of afterthought. "Enlighten me, asshole."

Landon laughs. "Do you know who Nathan is?"

"A drug lord. Possible Mafia ties."

"Sex trafficker," Steven finally says. "He brings women here from other countries along with American girls, only to sell them to American men for sex.

"Camilla hired us to help save sixty-two women who were taken from their families with the promise of a better life in America."

"Camilla is inside Nathan's house!" I yell.

"She's part of the plan, asshole!" Steven yells back.

"Wait. What?" I stand, placing my head in my hands, trying to wrap my head around what the hell is going on.

"She lured Nathan in, so we could free the final three women and get the hell out of here. Said something about her family being threatened and she needed to get out. That the money, too, had finally run out."

"Has anyone called the police?" Casey asks.

Landon and Steven chuckle.

"Once we do a final check to make sure all the women are out, we'll present the evidence to law enforcement, and they will make the appropriate arrests," Landon says.

Casey asks, "Who the hell are you guys?"

"We're retired Navy SEALs who do missions to help the world. All the money we make, we donate back to the Wounded Warrior Project."

"I knew it." Casey smiles.

"Knew what?" Landon asks.

"The way you guys came upon us and we didn't see a damn thing coming until your gun lasers appeared on our fucking chests—that had to be special ops." He laughs and runs his fingers along his jawline.

"Is she all right?" I ask Landon, my stare hard, my heart slamming against my chest.

"So far, she's all right. Unfortunately, we haven't had communication with her since she was carried inside."

"Carried?" My jaw tightens. "Christ."

"He used some sort of chemical warfare to knock her out. But we've got eyes on her."

Somehow, this doesn't relieve me.

Landon's eyes grow shifty. "Look, Calder, to be all in, she had to commit. Fully. She has to play the part, so we can make the rescue and so she can come out of this alive."

When he uses the phrase *come out of this alive,* bile gathers in my throat, and fear takes over. "Why would you let her go in there alone? What the fuck is wrong with you?"

"She didn't give us a choice. She's paying us."

"And how the fuck do you think she can take on a man like that by herself?"

Landon's eyes grow into slits.

"You don't know your girlfriend very well, Calder," Steven snarls. "We've been working on this for quite some time. And we won't let someone like you fuck it up because you can't deal with losing your girlfriend. If you trust us, we will get her out of there safely. But we could use your help. So, if you want in, you'd better drop in line with the plan or get the fuck out."

"You'll have to excuse my colleague. He's been a bit on edge," Landon says.

After a long silence that passes through the hut, I finally say, "We'll help—on two conditions."

Steven laughs. "Like we need your help. We're the fucking Navy SEALs."

Landon says, "I'm listening."

"One," I start, "Camilla comes out alive."

"And two?" Landon asks.

"Two, if push comes to shove, I get to go in there and get her."

"Deal."

And with that, Landon pours us a small drink, and we hash out the details of the plan.

35

Camilla

And nothing happens when I fire the gun.

Michelangelo laughs.

A cold chill fills my body.

I try to fire again, but the gun only clicks, creating a sinking feeling in my stomach.

"Give me the gun, Camilla," Michelangelo whispers, motioning to himself.

He slowly eases the gun from my grip, and I fall to the floor.

That was my last chance.

There's no one coming for me.

Fight! Camilla! You need to fight.

But before I can pull myself up, Michelangelo comes down to me on the floor and shoves a needle into my neck.

"Sleep, Camilla," he whispers into my ear.

And everything fades to black.

I can hear voices. Two of them. No, three. No, two.

I muster up the strength to open my eyes, and when I do, I realize I'm in a confined space. Small, dark. Wooden maybe.

Oh my God, I'm in a box.

Please, God, help me.

The voices grow closer and closer and closer, and though my vision is a bit hazy, I try to look and quickly realize there's something over my eyes. My hands are tied together in front of my body, my feet bound.

The voices drag redirect my attention.

They're speaking in a different language. Carefully, I maneuver my bound wrists to my face, bite my finger, draw a little blood, and rub my finger on the inside of the box. At least, if the police can get to this box, they'll see the blood and know I was in here if they test it for DNA.

The two voices stop, and I realize they're right above me when the box is lifted and begins to move.

I try to keep still, but when one side of the box is dropped at my feet end, I hear a long tongue-lashing between the voices and then feel some more movement. I feel the cooler air at my feet. Smell a tingle of ocean air.

I can try to scream as loud as I can.

Someone is bound to hear me, right?

But if I do, then they'll know I'm awake. They'll give me another injection.

Stay focused. I silently pray. *Stay focused, Camilla.*

But then I hear a plane engine.

We're flying somewhere.

A private plane? Not commercial. Cargo plane?

Going to the East Coast.

Wealthy men.

Leaders.

My entire body begins to vibrate as the plane engine grows louder and louder to where I can't hear voices or anything, except my own pulsating heart. My body is now at an angle, and we're moving up. A set of stairs maybe?

Breathe, Camilla.

The loud engine grows quiet aside from a low hum.

Two calm voices speak in whispers.

The box moves again, and then I'm set down.

"Put the other three boxes there." I hear a man's voice say in broken English.

Michelangelo.

Then, there's a shuffle of feet, and a door slams. The engine revs, like the plane is preparing for takeoff.

I try to think, but my brain is too hazy.

"Think!" I say, knowing no one can hear me over the plane engine.

With all my strength, I try like hell to pull my hands apart.

Try not to panic. Think. Think. Think.

With a jolt, we pick up speed fast and hard, and a piece of me wants the plane to explode midair because I'm not sure if I can face what's coming on the other end of this flight.

No, you need to fight. You have Malik to look after. Think, Camilla!

I remember an article I read somewhere.

In a case in the early 2000s, a plane crashed into the ocean. Years later, they discovered small boxes with women's skeletons on the ocean floor, where the plane had crashed. It was a private plane. The plane information given to authorities was fictitious, and they could never track the plane back to a rightful owner; therefore, no one was caught.

The article showed pictures of grieving mothers. Losing their daughters, who they thought had run away but they were just stolen. Taken. At fifteen, seventeen, and nineteen. Given unreasonable responsibilities and expectations. The flight was going from Italy to Washington, DC.

And now, I know that this operation has been in operation for far longer than I'd like to think. That there are more Nathan

Ambens and Michelangelos in the world, greedy and money-hungry.

I begin to rub the cloth that's tied around my wrists against the wood. I rub so hard that my knuckles begin to burn and bleed.

If I don't do this, I might not live.

I rub until my skin is raw. It burns so bad that I whimper. But I continue to push through the pain.

Finally—*finally*—the cloth begins to tear, and I free my hands.

I push my head as hard as I can against the wood to reach my feet and untie my feet

Pressing against the lid of the box, I feel the slow ooze of blood move down my head and onto the nightgown that Michelangelo left me in.

Malik's words trickle from the back of my mind. *"Mom, you're the toughest woman I know."*

Keep fighting.

I remember when the box was dropped. That there was a rush of cool air. Maybe there's a hole. I feel down by my feet, and I feel a gap in the wood. A fairly big gap. So, again, I push and flood my mind with thoughts of Malik and Calder. Desperately, I cling to them as I curve my fingertips around the wood, my wounds exposed, burning. I pull up, and a board finally breaks free.

More room.

I wedge my bare foot between the boards and feel a pinch on my calf.

I wedge deeper and deeper until another board breaks, and this time, it creates double the space. I keep feeding on the good memories as my body tries to twist and turn and break free from the wooden box my life was pushed into.

"Hello?" I hear a woman's voice.

I freeze and gently place my hands on the wood in front of my face, too afraid to breathe.

"Hello?" I hear again. "If someone is there … help me." Her voice breaks.

The plane shifts, and as it does, turbulence takes over, and my box falls from wherever it is, landing hard on metal. The whole back falls out, sending me crashing down to a metal floor.

With the air knocked out of me, I try to adjust my eyes to my surroundings.

It's not a jet at all. It's a cargo plane.

I try to stand, and when I push myself up with my hands, my knuckles burn so bad that I grit my teeth. I look down and see my raw, exposed skin under the blood that trails from the wounds.

I look from left to right and realize I'm alone.

But there are three more wooden boxes.

"Hello?" I hear the woman's voice again.

"He-hello?" I call out, broken, almost scared of my voice.

"Please." Her voice is muffled. "Please help me."

Pulling myself up from the hard steel, I run to the wooden boxes, and the woman's voice becomes stronger and clearer.

I search for anything to break the box, but it's nailed shut. I grab a board from my own, break it, wedge the sharp tip of the piece between the boards, and push with all my might.

"Try to keep your body away from the place I'm pushing," I say. "I don't want to hurt you."

Finally, a board pops free.

And then another board.

A third one pops free, and I'm able to take the woman's hand.

"It's going to be okay. Hold on," I whisper.

I push her box over the ledge of the shelf, and it breaks open.

The woman, bruised and broken, falls from the box, like a newborn baby into a mother's arms. She's no older than twenty-five. Sweat has created a sheen over her face. Her dark hair sticks to her face, and I crawl up by her side and help her to her feet. Her eyes are unclear and out of focus as she asks where we are, and I tell her I'm not sure.

And she begins to weep.

"He'll come for us." Her body shakes.

"What's your name?"

Her eyes dance from me to the box and back to me again. "Tia."

She isn't a woman I recognize from the pictures of the three left we have yet to rescue. She's new. And my stomach drops out again.

Does Nathan have another lair?

"Where are you from?" I try to comfort her.

"South Dakota."

"How long have you been gone?" I push her matted hair from her face, only to expose another bruise that runs down her jaw.

She shakes her head violently and begins to cry. "I don't— I don't know."

As she weeps, I pull her to me, as a mother would her child, and I whisper that she'll be okay. Somehow, someway, we will be okay.

"I need you to help me open the two other boxes, Tia, okay? Can you do that?"

Nervous, she swallows as she pulls away from me. "Yes."

We finally break through the other two boxes.

In one, a young girl, no older than fifteen, is unresponsive. *She has a pulse. Thank God.*

I suck back air when I pull up the last board on the other woman's box. It exposes her face, which is a bluish color. Her lips are the shade of a ripe blueberry. Another woman I don't recognize, no older than twenty, and she doesn't appear to be alive.

I instantly try to erase what I'm seeing. Replace it with something that makes sense.

I search for a pulse, praying for a miracle. Perhaps the shadows in the cargo plane give her this evil tint. But her eyes tell the story that she can't. She's staring up at the top of the cargo plane, and I cover my mouth, choking back tears. I use my other hand and slide it down her face to close her eyes.

We couldn't save her.

She didn't get away.
I've failed her.

"She's awake." Tia pulls the first young girl who was unresponsive up to a sitting position.

The young girl's eyes search nervously. Around the plane. To Tia, and me, and back to Tia, and then to the young woman's body. The young girl begins to sob.

She starts to sign.

I look from the young girl and back to Tia. "Do you understand sign language?"

Tia shakes her head, her arms still around the young girl. The young girl grabs a device and begins to type, and then she shows me the screen.

"Oh my God." I take the device from her hands and reread the message she typed.

I look back at the young girl in disbelief.

36

Calder

I heave anything that's left in my stomach when we exit Nathan's house.

Landon comes up behind me and doesn't say a word.

I heave over and over, but nothing comes out, except yellow bile, and my throat turns to fire.

"Here." He hands me a bottle of water and tells me to drink. "At least you'll have something to come up," he says. "Won't burn so bad."

I stand and chug the bottle of water and stare at the tree line that surrounds Nathan Amben's house.

Steven exits the house with papers in his hand. "A man fitting Michelangelo's description is flying a cargo plane from here to Washington, DC."

"How do you know all this?" Casey asks.

Steven smirks. "We're SEALS. We know everything. I just don't know how the fucker snuck past us."

Casey exits the house and gives me a look. "Don't worry, Cal; we'll find her."

Landon says, "It's time. Steven, call Derek at the FBI. Tell him it's time."

Steven walks away, and I can't help but wonder why the fucking FBI wasn't called sooner, so I say as much as I look to Landon. "Don't you think it would have been a better idea to fucking call the FBI sooner?"

Landon smirks. "Camilla said no police."

"And now, she's not here to call the shots!" I yell because I'm fucking pissed.

I throw the empty water bottle as far as I can. Worry and fear and grief burrow deep in my chest, and I try to figure out what to do next.

There's a long silence between Casey, Landon, and me.

"Listen, we saved the final three girls, and that's what Camilla wanted."

I drop my hands from my head and look back at Landon, staring long and hard at him, trying to figure out what the fuck he's saying to me. "Have you ever been in love before, Landon?"

"Depends on how you define love."

With everything I have, I run toward Landon with such force, but Casey, out of nowhere, tackles me to the ground.

"Get off of me, Casey. What the fuck?!" I call from underneath my brother.

"Did you ever think," he whispers breathlessly, "that he might know what the fuck he's doing? He's a fucking Navy SEAL, Cal, a fucking Navy SEAL. He knows top-secret shit that we will never know."

Landon says, "We have reason to believe that Camilla is on the cargo flight from here to DC." He pauses. "I also have reason to believe that she's still alive."

I try to pull my head up, but Casey pushes it back down with his palm. "You gonna fucking chill and listen and not go all Rambo again?"

"Yes. I'm chill. I'm calm."

Casey releases me and lets me get to my feet.

"If I've ever met a badass in my life, it's Camilla Crane." Then, Landon walks toward the driveway when police sirens are heard.

When the FBI arrives, there's a flurry of comings and goings. Unmarked police cars. Men in suits. And they move about the Amben property so strategically. Scientifically, methodically. This property is an experiment of interest and not a place where women were housed for sex trafficking. And I'm not sure how to look at this place either …

Landon approaches me again. "You're coming with me. Casey needs to stay behind, but I talked to Derek, and he's cleared you to come with us."

"Where? Where are we going?"

"To get your girlfriend."

Landon stares hard at me, and I stare back.

I slightly nod. "Thank you."

He motions me toward an unmarked car, and when I see Casey, he holds up his hand.

"I'll tell Mom and Dad, and we will keep Malik safe. Go get Camilla and bring her home safely."

I barely nod and stare back at my brother. I'd like to thank him for coming with me, for going into this without questions asked, and for just being here. But he knows by the nod that there are no words that can fill this moment. He just gets it.

"Don't get sappy and shit, all right?"

I smile.

The door opens to the black SUV, and with one last long look at Nathan Amben's house, I bid it farewell and hope to hell they light the house on fire with his dead body in it.

I know it was Camilla who killed Nathan.

I know it was her who fought like hell to kill a man who didn't deserve to live.

I've questioned that a lot, especially after Cannon Watson—if certain people deserve to die for the decisions they've made, the actions they've carried out. And while before I thought that dying shouldn't be a solution for people like that, now, I know with every fiber of my being that Nathan Amben deserved to die for the unmentionable crimes he committed. Especially after we found his souvenir room—of all the young women and young men he kidnapped and sold. Panties, bras, pictures of these women drugged and blindfolded. We might never find all of Nathan Amben's clients, those he sold innocent victims to, but if it's the last thing I do, I will die trying to find them.

We depart the property, and a layer of sadness leaves me. I can't explain it or question it, but as we pull out of the property, the evil stays put. I know I won't drag this experience with me, but I know I have changed because of it.

Landon's on the phone when we get on Highway 101 and head north.

"We're headed to Rohnerville Airport. Copy that." He hangs up. "Michelangelo won't know what hit him when he lands at Dulles International Airport."

My stomach grows nauseated. I try not to entertain ideas of finding Camilla's body.

God, please, watch over her. I'll do anything. I'll go back to church. I'll do whatever you ask. Just keep her alive.

"Would Michelangelo have reason to kill Camilla?" I hear myself ask.

Landon is quiet, then looks over. "If I don't give you the answer you want to hear, are you going to try to kick the shit out of me again?"

I smile. "No. Besides, I'd say that's a battle I wouldn't survive."

Landon nods. "My gut feeling is that he drugged her and took her. He'd get top dollar for her from prime clients on the East Coast."

Landon sees my face and grabs a plastic bag.

I throw up the water from earlier.

"See, it's better, right? At least you had something in your stomach." He chuckles and looks back out the window.

I push the thoughts out of my head. The ones where Camilla is forced to do things with her body that she doesn't want to do.

Then, I ask the question that I'm terrified to ask. No, it's the answer I'm terrified to know. "But you think she's still alive?"

Before he answers, he stares straight ahead, then slowly turns his head toward me, and I want to die because by the look on his face, I don't have to hear his answer. I see it all over his face.

"I'm cautiously optimistic she's still alive."

I try to swallow his words and tuck them away in my heart. *Cautiously optimistic.*

Then, Landon says something I don't expect. "Camilla is as smart as they come. And if she's got you and Malik to come home to, I know she will fight to the death."

"That's what I'm scared of," I whisper as we weave through the mammoth redwood trees that line the freeway. "That's what I'm afraid of."

It seems like forever until we arrive at a waiting jet at Rohnerville Airport.

The pilot stands as Derek, two other men in suits, Landon, and I board the jet.

Before Derek sits, he says, "Do you know what your girlfriend did?"

I prepare the answer I'm about to give him, to berate him for something he hasn't said yet, but before I can, Derek says, "She's saved the lives of thirty-seven women. Not many people can say that."

A lump in my throat forms, and my eyes begin to sting. I don't dare look at Derek, for fear he'll see the tiny glimpse of vulnerability. Shit, he probably knows everything about me.

"I know," I finally say, and then I pray again that we find the love of my life—alive.

37

Camilla

The young girl sits in front of me, wide-eyed, unsure, and terrified.

I hand her back her messaging device and play the words in my head. Her eyebrows furrow with uncertainty and pain, and I'm not sure I can ever make this right for her. If we live through this, her life will never be the same. And I'm reminded that I, too, am a survivor. A survivor of abuse, and maybe, just maybe, she and I were put in this life together, at this moment, in this situation, so we could march together—I'm not sure.

I play the words she typed in my head.

You're Camilla Crane.

I'm one of Sam's daughter's—Leah.

Why Leah? It can't be a coincidence, can it? And if it's not, then what the hell is going on?

"How do you know who I am?"

Leah types into her messaging device and types: *Facebook.*

I feel a need to watch over her, take care of her, keep her safe, and put her life before my own.

Leah ferociously types something else and hands me the phone.

Is she dead?

Leah shifts her focus to the lifeless body lying on the floor of the cargo plane.

I nod.

It's hard to see a young woman with a blue face, knowing the life left her. No more fight. Just stillness.

"How in the hell do we get out of this?" Tia's question is directed at me.

I look around. Shipping containers surround us, though it's more sparse than full.

Were we the last-minute add, an afterthought? *Throw the wooden boxes in here. No one will notice.*

I swallow hard and look at Leah and Tia, trying like hell not to show any fear. A poker face, my mother used to call it. Many years of holding a poker face in front of our church's pastor and school counselors when they noticed a bruise in a peculiar area.

"An odd place for a bruise," my teacher in the fourth grade said. She eyed me curiously.

"I got tangled up with my dog," I lied.

I became good at lying. Good at covering up the truth, for fear of what my father would do if we didn't do what he asked.

My mother said, "The better you hide it, the better off you'll be."

No one stood up to my father.

Except for Phillip—or Michelangelo. He stood up to my father once. He stood up for me. And now, I see why. Grooming, he called it.

I'd picked the wrong fruit that day, and my father hit me across the face with the back of his hand. Michelangelo didn't know what he was getting himself into that day. But he stood up for me anyway by stepping in and convincing my father that hitting me wouldn't change anything.

Little did I know that Michelangelo was trying to earn my trust. And he did. Because after that day, he asked how long the abuse had been going on. I didn't answer him at the moment, but later, I left a note for Michelangelo that said, *For as long as I can remember.*

Sometimes, it's easier to answer tough questions when you don't have to look someone in the eyes. Feel the weight of their empathy, their concern.

A day later, there was a note left for me in my picking basket. It said, *Left home because my father hit me.*

After that, I confided in Phillip—Michelangelo, whatever you want to call him—by the old oak trees. He told me that his mother told him at twelve years old to leave and never come back. He said he felt guilty for doing that.

And it's in this moment, when turbulence hits, that I realize I've found Michelangelo's weakness.

"Come on. I have a plan."

When the three of us feel the plane's descent, I jump awake and wake up the other two.

"It's go time."

I help Leah to her feet and reach for her device and type.

It's go time.

She nods and puts the device back in her pocket.

We fill the wooden boxes with anything we can find to make them feel as though an unconscious body is in them, waiting for the next client.

Diligently and quickly, we move like we've somehow done this before.

We use whatever we can to reattach the tops of the boxes. Though, if examined closely, they'll know the box has been tampered with, but by the time these boxes get into the hands of the waiting criminals, we'll be long gone.

We bury ourselves under the military tarp next to the back of the plane—our gate to freedom.

The plane makes a loud noise, and it changes speeds.

"We're getting closer to the ground," I whisper in the darkness, underneath the tarp.

"If we make it out alive, I will quit the drugs," Tia says.

Worn and tired is the face of Tia. I'm sure she was once beautiful in her early teens, but the drugs wore on her like a nagging truth.

"That is how I ended up in this place." She slowly nods. "I was tired of being a disappointment to my family. And now, I don't even know how long I've been gone." She smiles a sad smile and looks into my eyes. "They'll think I overdosed in a ditch somewhere. My mom and dad have probably already grieved their loss."

I pull the tarp from our heads because I need to see Tia's face. "Listen to me, Tia. You will make it out of here, and you will quit the drugs, and you will do great things with your life. Do you understand me?"

I think about Sam and what she must be going through right now. Her daughter is missing, and no one can find her. I imagine her heartache. Her wondering if Leah is suffering, scared, or dead. The thought of this makes my stomach lurch forward, and I pull Leah's head to me and kiss it. I silently will Sam to feel my warmth, to have faith that her daughter is in good hands.

The plane makes another loud noise as we make a slow and steady decline toward the ground.

A loud thud sounds, like an iron door shutting closed. Quickly, we cover our heads with the heavy-duty canvas tarp.

It becomes eerily silent in the plane, and I'm not sure how this is possible with a cargo plane, but it does. Desperation maybe.

I hold my breath and wait for something, anything.

The plane engine fills the cargo plane with roars of regret.

If we'd all just done things differently …

And then there's a prying noise. Like wood being pried apart with a crowbar. A loud creaking and then a pop, followed by a gasp.

The canvas we put in one box is being pulled out.

The next box is opened, then murmurs that grow louder and louder.

The last box is opened, then a loud, guttural yell.

And then the final box with the body.

We laid her to rest. A quiet funeral. Took a locket from her neck to give to her mother.

Young girls shouldn't die in that way …

A drug overdose is what I could conclude. They simply gave her too much, and her body couldn't handle it.

Feeling the locket between my fingers, I pray because we didn't expect for someone to come to the back of the cargo plane before landing. What we planned was for the plane to land, the door to open, and then we'd make our escape down the ramp and inside the terminal, anywhere other than this plane.

I hold my breath as the loud footsteps grow louder, angrier. Boxes crash, and all I can feel is my heart pulsating in my ears.

A bloodcurdling cry is let out.

One man, I tell myself.

It's one man.

Most likely with a gun.

But you have his weakness, Camilla.

I pull the canvas tarp from my head and cover up the other two. I see the back of Michelangelo looking down at the dead girl.

"You killed her, Michelangelo. As much as you didn't want to, you killed her," I croak over the plane engine.

Slowly, he turns to me, her head and limbs hanging like a rag doll.

"I did not kill her." His eyes fill with rage as he stares at me.

"But you did. You gave her too much. She was too little. Too young for what you did to her. Her organs failed. Her body shut down. And it was all too much for her."

"I am the good guy. I don't hurt people."

"But you do. Just like you did your mom. You left her, Michelangelo. You left her behind, and your father killed her. Don't you remember that part of the story?"

His face withers into an older man as he looks down at the young girl. "It wasn't my fault."

I take a step closer. "It was your fault. You didn't save her."

There's something to be said for men who take women and sell them to other men. What they must tell themselves to keep sane, the lies.

"Two dead women on your conscience can't be good, Michelangelo. Two."

His face grows red as he gently sets her body down, back in the box, folding her limbs inside. Quietly, he stands. "How did you all get out?"

"How can you sleep at night, knowing you're selling humans to men for profit? Do you know this young girl died because of your greed?"

"It is a business transaction!" he cries. He covers his eyes, unwilling to see the destruction he's caused.

"Open your eyes, Michelangelo!" I yell. "Look what you've done!"

He doesn't. He just weeps.

"That is someone's daughter, someone's sister, and you robbed her and her family of a life well lived. For what? Money? It surely wasn't to fix your soul."

"You don't understand." He rages and pulls the gun from his back and takes aim at me.

I step in front of the tarp and hold up my hands. My throat is rough like sandpaper, and I try to swallow, try to conjure up something that will connect us—to save the girls. "What's to understand?"

"I felt powerful!" he yells, wiping the sweat that began to form on his forehead. "Control. I could control the outcome.

I could control women." His chest heaves in and out. "For a long time, I didn't have control. Father hurt Mother, and I was just a boy. I couldn't control any of it! Then, he killed her!" Michelangelo laughs, the pitch ricocheting off the metal on the inside of the plane.

"And you killed her," I say, my eyes looking down at the young girl's body. "You can start to make it right, Michelangelo. It's never too late to start over."

"No. No. No! Things are out of control. Where are the other girls?" His eyes grow into slits as he meets my eyes. "Where did you put them?"

I don't have an answer for this.

He screams, "Where are they?"

He's losing control.

"What do I have to lose? I kill witnesses. Hide bodies. I leave."

The tarp starts to move.

Shit. Shit. Shit. Stay hidden, I scream in my head.

It's Tia.

Slowly, she steps next to me.

Michelangelo is enraged.

"Please," she says, "take me instead. Camilla has a young boy she needs to raise. Sell me. Do what you need. Just don't kill her."

"Michelangelo," I say, trying to leave the fear out of my tone, "you don't have to do any of this. Just give me the gun, and we won't say a word."

He begins to pace.

"Need to think. Need to think."

The plane descends, jolting us forward but we catch ourselves quickly.

"We're going to land soon, Michelangelo. What's it going to be?"

He stops. Takes aim and fires.

Tia falls backward.

"NOOOOOOOOOOOOOO!" I cry out.

The plane takes a nosedive, and we all fall ...

38

Calder

The Dulles International Airport is crawling with federal agents. Landon makes me wait at the goddamn gate.

My mom calls my cell phone, and my stomach fills with a familiar feeling—dread.

"Hey, Mom." I run my hand over my face. I'm tired and delirious from lack of sleep, running on pure adrenaline.

"It's all over the news, Calder," she whispers. "Camilla's picture. The missing girls. One of whom is one of Camilla's friend's daughters—Sam, I think her name is?"

"WHAT? How do they know who's on the flight?"

"She is deaf, and she has an Apple AirTag on her communication device she keeps with her. Sam went on national news to make a plea for help. It was heartbreaking, Cal." My mom's voice breaks. "No one's child should be taken."

"I know."

My mom and I make small talk for a minute. She doesn't ask if Camilla's okay because she knows I don't know—

Landon hasn't said—and there's nothing she can tell Malik. So, we let the topic go.

That's when I see the massive cargo plane coming for the runway.

"I'll call you back, Mom." I slide my phone into my pocket, mesmerized.

I make a run for the tarmac.

"Stay put," Landon said.

Forget what Landon said.

I take off in a full sprint. Outside the airport, I jump fence after fence before airport patrol and the Feds try to catch up with me. I watch as the massive plane thunders past me, wiggling, skirting, and shaking as the wheels touch down on the runway. Federal agents are waiting at the end of the runway.

And all I think is to run.

My legs move, and somehow, they feel detached from my body. I don't feel my shoes hit the pavement or the jolt in my legs every time my foot thrusts me forward. My arms move, and I think I should feel something, anything, but I don't.

The wall of sound from the plane comes to a screeching halt at the end of the runway. I feel its vibration in my chest. Smoke begins to pour from the landing gear, the friction between tire and concrete, and the scent of burning rubber infiltrates my nose, but I keep running.

I stop when the smoke almost makes the plane disappear into thin air. Then, the wheels shudder, there's a thunderous rumble, shaking the ground, and a crashing sound ensues, and the next thing all I see is smoke.

The federal agents are gone.

The unmarked vehicles are gone.

I'm surrounded by nothingness.

I pull my hands to my face to make sure I haven't disappeared.

Go get Camilla.

When I try to move, all I see is smoke.

That's when the explosion happens.

It blows my body back up into the air, and I land hard in the shrubbery that lines the runway.

I can't hear anything. My ears are ringing so loudly that I think my eardrums will burst. I can't move.

Another explosion makes me turn onto my stomach and crawl away.

Now, black smoke appears, and I can't bring myself to stand. I try to breathe, but when I do, I cough, and all I want to do is get to Camilla. I try to call out for help, but the words fall soundless from my mouth.

I close my eyes just for a moment, begging myself to get up.

Sirens bring me to light again, loud sirens that are moving closer and closer and closer.

I push myself up onto my hands. The smoke is still there, though not as dense. I struggle to my feet and stand.

A fire truck is already putting out the flames that dance from the plane.

"Oh my God. Camilla!"

I run toward the flames, and as I get closer, the smoke becomes clearer and clearer, and the cargo plane comes into view on its side, its belly showing.

Parts of the plane are strewn down the runway like lost garments.

The wall of federal agents, police, and firefighters are crawling in through an open door on the upper side of the plane. A ladder extends from a fire truck to the upper side while crews work diligently.

How long was I lying there in the weeds?

My eyes find Landon, and he stands there, watching the commotion. Then, he looks down at the ground, and the thought that hits me is that you don't have to know someone well for grief to be an outcome.

"Landon," I whisper and then begin to run toward him at full speed. "Landon!" I scream.

He picks up his head, and I see the sadness he wears.

No. No. No.

I reach him and pull him up by the collar of his shirt. "NO, Landon! Please. No. Don't tell me she's dead. You said you were cautiously optimistic!"

Landon doesn't take my hands from his shirt. He just stares at me. "I'm sorry, Calder. We couldn't get to anyone …"

"NO!" I push him with everything I have and run to the belly of the plane before anyone can stop me.

Someone does and pulls me back by my shoulders.

"My girlfriend is in there!" I scream.

Tears start to stream from my eyes uncontrollably. Landon drops to his knees next to me. Puts his hand on my back, unsure of what else to do.

I sit here for a long time and wait for my Camilla to come back to me.

"Come on." Landon takes me by the arm. "Let's go, Cal."

I shake my head. "I'm waiting right here. I need—I need to tell her son that I waited until I got to see her again."

"That might take days, Cal."

"I've got time." A tear slides down my cheek as I stare down at my hands.

Landon sighs and sits down next to me. "My wife died. Three years ago. Killed by a drunk driver. I had to identify the body." He's quiet for a moment. "No matter how hard we try to keep them safe, sometimes, it doesn't always work. You're not God, Cal."

I bury my chin into my chest. "I have to tell her son."

"Telling my daughter wasn't easy."

I listen. "What did you say to her?"

"The truth." He shrugs. "It was the only thing I could tell her."

Yelling ensues from the top of the ladder. Federal agents point and run toward the other end of the runway.

Two women emerge.

A young woman.

And Camilla.

I choke out a sob and scramble to my feet, following the agents.

I cry out and try my best to keep my vision of them.

They're real, right?

This is real?

Doubt fills the pockets of hope.

I'm not just seeing this.

No. No. No.

I look at the men and women ahead of me.

The young woman, no older than twelve, is leaning on Camilla, crying.

Camilla is barely covered by what looks to be remnants of a nightgown.

"CAMILLA!" I run at full force until I reach her.

I take both women in my arms and will my head to believe this is real and not just what I want it to be.

"Are—are you all right?" I look at both of them. They're dirty, broken, tired, but alive.

Camilla tells the EMT to take the girl and examine her. "Her name is Leah. She's deaf and lost her communication device when we landed with the parachutes." Camilla's voice is weak.

She turns to me, and I kiss her face and her neck and her chest and pull her to me and cry.

Camilla begins to cry too. Pulling me to her so hard that her fingernails dig into me.

"You're okay, baby. You're okay. Oh my God," I whisper into her hair.

"Sir, we need to make sure she's all right. You can come with us, but we need to get her to the hospital to be checked out."

"Not without Leah," Camilla says.

"No, ma'am. She will be going too."

"Hey." I peek my head into Camilla's room.

"Hey," she says and smiles the way she does when she's lost in her thoughts. "What happened to you?"

I reach her bed, set the crutches against the wall, and sit at her bedside. "Sprained ankle and three broken ribs—but no broken heart." I kiss her on the top of her head.

Camilla beams.

"Media frenzy out there." I motion down the hallway. "They all want your story."

My phone rings, and I know who it is. I take my phone from my pocket and hand it to Camilla.

"Answer it," I whisper.

And when she does, our son's beautiful face appears, and Camilla begins to sob. Not from sadness, but out of gratitude.

They both cry, and when they stop, Malik says, "Mom, you look beat up."

Camilla laughs and traces her finger along the edges of Malik's face. "Yeah, it's been a few rough couple of days."

"Mom, everyone is talking about how you're an American hero! It's all over the news!"

Camilla doesn't like recognition. She never has. "I miss you so much, baby. I can't wait to hold you in my arms."

Malik rolls his eyes. "I'm not a baby anymore." We laugh. "Can I talk to Cal in private, please?"

I reach for the phone and grab my crutches and walk to the corner of Camilla's room. "Hey, bud. You okay?"

Malik's eyes fill with tears. "Thank you for saving my mom." He nods, biting his lip, trying his best not to cry.

A single tear rolls down my face. "Your mother saved herself. All I did was love her."

39

Camilla
Three Weeks Later

I *t feels good to be home.*
It feels good to have my family.
I'm sitting in a chair in the backyard. Red is chasing Malik, and Malik is chasing Calder.

Sam said that I saved Leah.

I said Sam saved my mom.

"That's what friends do for each other." I smiled and hugged her when she came to headquarters in Quantico, Virginia, where an FBI agent—Simone—asked me to tell my story twice. Asked Leah to do the same.

We did.

Tia didn't make it, and I know today that she died with her head held high. Something tells me it was one of the first admirable things she'd done in a long time. So, I made sure to tell Simone her story too.

Tia, in a small way, reminded me of my father. She was an addict. She'd been addicted to drugs, and that was what Nathan had seen in her. In some small South Dakota club. He picked the girls who were overlooked. He picked the girls who were addicted. He picked the girls whose families could blame it on addiction or girls who were naive to the dark underworld that is alive and well and thriving because of men like him, like Michelangelo, all for the clients they served. But they're nothing like clients. They're men, typically, who do awful things to women. Sick men who have expendable incomes and careers in high places, and they pull the wool over others' eyes.

But I know better.

Leah now knows better.

Why did Michelangelo nab Leah? I'm not sure. Maybe because of her disability; maybe because of me. I don't know. Coincidence? Who knows? However, I truly think God made sure we were together, knowing we'd fight to the death to save each other.

It was Leah who found the parachutes.

It was Leah who snuck out from under the canvas to search for something, anything, to save our lives.

And after she found the parachutes, she came up behind Michelangelo and gouged out his eyes with her fingernails.

Leah is the true hero.

And Leah and I gave the locket of Melissa Ray, the young woman dead in the box on the plane, to the FBI to give to her grieving mother. I wasn't brave enough to give it to her myself. I guess we're always a work in progress.

It also made me think about my son, Malik. He's far more capable than what I allow him to do. For now, I'm not going to worry so much about school. I'm not going to worry so much about the future.

Malik starts to laugh, and it brings me to the present moment. My heart fills with joy.

Cal limps over to me with one crutch and reaches for my hand. "Come on. Malik and I have something to show you."

With one hand, he helps me from my sitting position.

Once I'm standing, Malik takes my other hand, and we take a short walk to the field. In the tall grass sits a picnic for three.

I smile up at Calder. "What's this?"

He leans down and gently kisses me on the lips. "You'll see."

Malik opens the gate, and we take a seat on the blanket. Malik is beaming.

"What's this all about, kiddo?"

He shrugs.

Calder pulls food out of the basket. Red and Williams scamper over, and Malik gives them a bowl of food to share.

The sun begins to set.

But the next thing that happens takes my breath away.

Calder carefully gets down on one knee. "Camilla, when I first met you, I knew my heart was meant to love you for the rest of my life, and I didn't care what that meant because I knew your heart belonged to Joe. I'd always settle to be second, take the back burner if it meant I just got to be in your presence now and then. But what we didn't anticipate was Joe passing. And I know that day, your heart broke in half. Mine did too— for you and Malik. I didn't want to be the man to fix it. I just wanted to be there for you both. I just wanted to help. What I hadn't anticipated was the need I'd feel for the both of you. What I hadn't anticipated was the protection I wanted to give you. What I do realize now is that I want you both forever."

Malik starts to giggle when Cal removes the small box from his pocket.

Cal looks over at Malik and grins and then looks back at me.

"You would make me the happiest man on earth if you married me, Camilla. And I hope that you'll allow me to adopt Malik as my own."

Gently, I press my fingers to my lips, and tears fill my eyes as I stare up at Cal and Malik.

"And I've cleared it with your mother. She gave me her blessing."

Tears roll down my cheeks. *That's why he went down south to meet with my mom.*

"Oh, Calder. I'm so sorry I got ma—"

But before I can finish, he shakes his head. "No. You had no idea, Mil. And that's what I love about you most. You love your family fiercely."

"MOM!" Malik says. "Are you going to say yes or not?"

I laugh and pull Cal to me so that I can feel his heart thumping against my chest. "Yes! A million times over, YES!"

Cal grabs for Malik, and Red and Williams tumble into our hug.

At this moment, I realize that life might not pan out the way we want it to, the way we expect it to, but it does work out the way it's supposed to. I have faith in that because my whole world sits with me right now, and there's nowhere else I'd rather be.

"What about next week?" I ask Cal and Malik.

"For the wedding?" Cal asks.

"Yes. Here. At the ranch. I'm sure your mom will help me get everything done."

"Okay. Let's do it."

My—*our*—twelve-year-old son falls into Cal's arms. Malik has been doing this since he was little—falling into Calder's arms—and I'm so grateful God delivered Calder to us. It isn't what we anticipated, but it's what we needed so badly.

"Dad, I love you."

Cal kisses his forehead. "Love you too, Malik."

It's late into the evening, and Malik and Red are fast asleep in his bedroom.

Calder and I are on the couch, our hands entangled together. The light of the candle dances off the walls.

"What are you thinking about?" Cal asks.

I smile and look up at him. "About how happy I am."

He pulls me to him and puts his lips on mine.

"We can't. You're still healing."

"So are you." I pull myself from the couch and stand. "Come to our bedroom, Calder. I need to make love to you."

Cal looks up at me. His eyes are full of wonder and curiosity. He stands and takes me by the hand and leads me to our bedroom. Quietly, he shuts the door, and I remove my blouse and my bra and my jeans as he watches.

I walk to him and slide his shirt over his head and put my mouth on his.

Kissing Calder is like finding home.

I feel his length between my legs, against my panties, as he gently lifts me, holding me to his chest, his heart slamming against its walls. He lays me down on the bed.

"Camilla, you are the most beautiful woman I've ever seen in my life."

He places his knees below my thighs, so I'm angled upward. Cal leans down and kisses me, and I sigh against his mouth, needing more. I take his hands and place them over my breasts, and this makes him groan. He pulls away and stares down at me, and then he puts his mouth over a nipple and toys with it with his tongue.

Cal traces his fingers down my stomach and reaches my panty line. He smiles when his finger gently moves inside my panties.

"You're a tease, you know that?" I whisper and close my eyes as his finger pushes into my folds and reaches the center of my body.

He pushes, and I moan, taking my breasts in my hands, my body rocking against his finger.

He leans down and whispers in my ear, "Let go. Because the second I put myself inside you, I'm going to lose it."

His tongue moves down my neck as his finger presses on my center, and then he applies just enough pressure and movement that I whimper against his ear as he removes my panties. "I need you inside me, Calder Atwood."

Slowly, he laughs against my neck and removes his finger. He takes off his pants as I pull the covers back. He climbs back on top of me and slowly thrusts inside me a few times. I reach for him and put his mouth on mine.

We rock together. Our naked bodies tangle in the night like sheets on a warm summer breeze. Cal pushes inside me again, and I watch his face, illuminated by the moonlight. His eyes open, and he stares back.

I reach up and trace the lines around his mouth, to his chest, and then to his ass, where I pull him further inside me. He moves, and I move, and we both explode together.

We fall asleep, naked, nestled by the moon's light.

We wake up and make love again, and then we let our tired bodies take us into a deep slumber until the sun calls up another day.

40

Calder

Malik walks Camilla down the aisle.

I try like hell to hide the emotion she evokes in me in her white dress. It's a simple dress that dips below her shoulders and fits her in all the right places.

All of my brothers are here. My parents.

I arranged for Camilla's mother, sister, and Sam and her family to be in Dillon Creek.

My dad says, "Who gives this bride to marry this man?"

Malik says, "My father, Joe, and I do."

Malik and I agreed that Joe needed to be here, represented somehow.

Malik said that Joe had come to him in a dream. That he said he was proud of Malik. That he was happy for Camilla and that she needed to marry me. That he was everything good left in this world, a true cowboy. And he would be an even better father and husband.

I know that Malik speaks only the truth. I'm not sure about all the afterlife stuff, but there are times on this ranch when I've felt Joe, making sure I'm doing right by his wife, his son.

When I take Camilla's hand, Malik stands beside us as my father asks us to say the wedding vows we prepared.

We invited all of Dillon Creek to the wedding.

Stores shut down on Main Street so that everyone could attend.

We dance well into the evening.

The next week, our wedding picture is on the cover of the *Dillon Creek Echo* with a written apology from Michael. I'm not sure what Camilla said to him after the stories he ran, but he hasn't run a shitty half-truth story again.

Just cold, hard facts.

And the cold, hard fact in this installment is that Camilla and Malik Crane became Camilla and Malik Atwood, and I feel like the luckiest guy in the world.

I have everything I want and everything I need.

I hold Camilla in the moonlight when everyone leaves.

"I feel like I won the lottery, Mil." And I press my mouth to hers.

"You and Malik will always be all I need."

We stand here for a moment and kiss, smile, and laugh, and then we kiss more.

We make our way inside, and that's when the phone rings.

Old feelings die hard.

My jaw goes rigid. I pick up the phone. "Atwood residence."

"Yes, is … Camilla Crane available, please?"

"Can I ask who's calling, please?"

"This is Tracy Langley from Universal Pictures."

"Oh, just one moment."

I hand the phone to Camilla.

She covers the receiver and says, "Who is it?"

I smile. "You're going to want to take this."

She uncovers the phone. "This is Camilla."

Camilla has a story to tell. A story of bravery, courage, and whether she wants to tell it, well, that's up to her. But I have a feeling that if she tells her story, she's going to encourage many others by telling her story.

She's not her mother at all. She's not her father.

She did what most would have walked away from.

She went back to save women even if it meant risking her life. She's never one to take the easy road, and she never will be.

She's turned down interviews from NPR, *Dateline*, 20/20 because she doesn't feel like a hero. It was her calling, as she puts it. It was the right thing to do, she says.

But I will say one thing. I know I'm married to a badass, and there's no other place I'd rather be.

I hear her hang up the phone, and then it's quiet.

I hear her footsteps come into the living room, and she plops down next to me in her dress. Mil is staring straight ahead, her mouth half-open.

I take her hand. "What did Tracy have to say?"

Camilla closes her mouth and looks at me. "She just offered me an ungodly amount of money for my story."

"And? What did you say?"

"I said—I said that I needed to talk to my husband and my son first."

I laugh. "Your husband. My wife. Our son."

We both start to laugh, and when it comes to a slow stop, taking both her hands in mine and say, "I think you should do it—not for the money, but to raise awareness that human sex trafficking is real."

Camilla nods and slowly looks at me. "You think I should?"

"I think you should. But let's check with Malik?"

We both walk to his bedroom.

"Buddy, we need to talk," Camilla says. All the details we'll work out. The travel. The trips to Los Angeles. The time it will take.

Because all we can do is take it one step at a time. One day at a time. All we have is today, and we've learned this from experience. Tomorrow is not promised, and we'll take advantage of the time we have together, as a family.

There's no one left to tell the whole story, except Camilla.

Nathan Amben died, and when Camilla was asked, she told the truth. Self defense. And that was good enough.

Michelangelo went down with the cargo plane.

So, that leaves Camilla to tell the right story. The story will encourage young women to always be aware of their surroundings, to always be on the lookout, and it will expose the sick individuals who participate in such evil.

From a small town in South Dakota to a small town in Northern California, evil exists everywhere. Even in our backyards.

Somehow, Camilla survived.

41

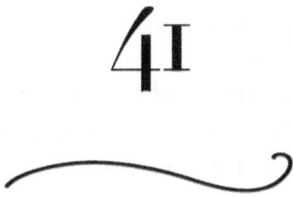

Camilla

Somehow, I lived to tell the stories of strong women who just wanted a fair shake at life, a second chance to make better choices.

I survived my father, but I couldn't kill him. I didn't have it in me. But somehow, my mother freed us. For years, she cowered down to him and told us to roll with the punches, so we wouldn't get hurt—or worse, killed. But it was that final act that my mother did that freed the broken little girl inside me. It allowed me to see courage and bravery.

Sam got my mother off. Nobody believed her confession. She's in a home now off the coast of California, near Grover Beach. She has a window and an ocean view, and she has everything she needs.

I wonder if that was liberation for my mother—to finally get the death of my father off her chest. We haven't talked about it yet, and I'm not sure we ever will. But I will say, her eyes are brighter, and her shoulders are lighter.

I took Malik down to Grover Beach to meet his grandmother for the first time last week. It was a good visit.

My mother, Granny, as Malik likes to call her, asked if Malik wanted something to drink and that's when Calder stepped in and said, "He's good. Thanks, Mildred." My mother and Cal exchanged smiles, an inside joke, I suppose.

Anyway, I've had examples my entire life of what to be and what not to be. I've always had good examples of what life can be.

I get to be the person I am today because of how I was raised.

I'm painting again, too, and I'm extremely grateful for that.

I don't know what the future holds; however, I do know that Calder, Malik, and I will remain in Dillon Creek to finally live our happily ever after.

Epilogue

Up on top of the Dillon Creek Cemetery, Joe Crane, Tripp Morgan, Conroy Atwood, Don and Erla Brockmeyer, Clyda and Borges Atwood, Ike Isner, John and Francine Muldoon stand and look down upon the Crane ranch.

Joe looks to Ike. "Cal got the message."

Ike laughs. "It wasn't subtle, that's for sure." He pauses and then says, "You're a good man."

"Calder is too," Joe says. "He'll take good care of them."

Clyda says, "He's just like his father."

Borges agrees.

Conroy says, "Never a more loyal guy than that guy down there. Well, aside from Dad."

Clyda turns to Conroy and reaches around his middle. "He misses you something fierce, Conroy."

"I know." He hugs his grandmother.

Borges clears his throat and leans against the tree. "Wish they knew we were still with them."

Clyda and Borges exchange loving glances.

"I suppose if I had known you'd still be with me, I'm almost certain it wouldn't have hurt so bad when you died," Clyda says to her husband.

Erla leans into Don. "I'm just glad some of us are back together. When we all get together again, it's going to be one grand party."

"But for now," Don starts, "we'll wait."

John says to the group, "It won't be long before Mabe joins us. I can feel it."

Clyda puts an arm around her old friend. "Same here, John. Can't put my finger on it, but it's soon."

Mabe Muldoon is laid to rest in the Dillon Creek Cemetery. She died peacefully in her sleep. She died sober, and she died with a smile on her face.

John and Francine are there to help Mabe cross over to heaven—a family of three once again after all the years—and after a few long moments, the rest of the gang on top of the cemetery welcomes Mabe.

"Erla and Clyda! I have a bone to pick with you two!" Mabe says through her smile as she hugs her cousin and longtime friend. "Up and leaving me like that!"

The truth is, we can't control how long we have on earth.

We can't control how we go.

But we do have the ability to live each moment to its fullest.

Through the sad times.

Through the uncertain times.

Through the happy times.

We get to go through ups and downs and twists and turns. Life is a get-to.

So, live it.

The End

A Note to the Reader

THANK YOU FOR READING *LOVING CAMILLA*.

If you enjoyed the book, please consider leaving an honest review on the website you purchased the book from. By leaving a review, it makes the book more visible to more readers. The more reviews, the better promotional opportunities for the author.

Get the latest information on book releases, sales, and more.

Sign up for J. Lynn Bailey's newsletter at http://bit.ly/2VVmqna to get sneak peeks, early excerpts, and free books.

Have you joined my reading group *The Bailey Bunch*? Join below for behind-the-scenes book information, giveaways, and top-secret book information. Learn about the inter-workings of my writing process, and my crazy ideas.

The Bailey Bunch: http://bit.ly/2EscfjT

Connect with J. Lynn online

www.facebook.com/AuthorJLynnBailey

www.instagram.com/jlynnbaileybooks/

https://twitter.com/authorJLynn

www.jlynnbaileybooks.com

Acknowledgements

First and foremost, a huge thank you to my editor, Jovana Shirley, who always goes above and beyond for my books and can shine and polish my words like no other. What started as a professional relationship has turned into a friendship, and I'm extremely grateful for you.

Julie Deaton, my proofreader, a huge thank you for her eagle eyes and attention to detail. You are a treasure. It should also be noted that I only send you voice messages so that I can get yours in return. Your Southern accent gets me every time.

Ashley Bolton at Ashley Bolton Photography, for the incredible book-cover photography and your ease and patience behind the camera. You, my friend, have a very special talent.

Hang Le, my cover designer, thank you for taking my thoughts and input and creating the masterpieces you have with the entire Dillon Creek series. It is an absolute joy to work with you.

Thank you to Holly Roberts, the cover model.

A huge thank you to my readers and the book bloggers that work so hard to support my work.

Thank you to an incredibly group of humans, The Bailey Bunch, my favorite group of readers, for all your love.

Brandon, Teyler, and Kate, you are my world, my soft place to land. Thank you for your patience and your grace with each book that I write.

And last but certainly not least, thank you to God. Without you, I'm nothing. Thank you for this life, for filling me with stories and the courage to tell them.

About the Author

J. Lynn Bailey is an award-winning author who has loved to write since she learned to read, around the second grade. She's earned a bachelor's degree and master's degree from Humboldt State University.

When she isn't running her children to their next sporting event, watching *North Woods Law*, or on the hunt for her next Laffy Taffy joke, you can probably find her holed up in her writing room, feverishly working on her next book. She lives in Northern California with her family.

If you enjoyed the book, please consider leaving an honest review on the website you purchased the book from. By leaving a review, it makes the book more visible to more readers. The more reviews, the better promotional opportunities for the author.

Don't miss out on J. Lynn's latest book news and more.

Subscribe to her newsletter!

www.jlynnbaileybooks.com

OTHER BOOKS BY J. LYNN BAILEY

THE GRANITE HARBOR SERIES

Peony Red
Violet Ugly
Magnolia Road
Lilies On Main

THE DILLON CREEK SERIES

Taking Anna
Little White Christmas
Saving Tess
Leaving Scarlet
Loving Camilla

STAND-ALONES

Standing Sideways
The Light We See
Black Five